THE LAKE CHING
MURDERS

A MYSTERY OF FIRE AND ICE

THE LAKE CHING MURDERS

DAVID ROTENBERG

McArthur & Company
Toronto

First Canadian paperback edition published
by McArthur & Company in 2002.

First published in Canada in 2001 by
McArthur & Company
322 King Street West, Suite 402
Toronto, ON M5V 1J2

National Library of Canada Cataloguing in Publication Data

Rotenberg, David (David Charles)
The Lake Ching murders

ISBN 1-55278-260-3

I.Title.

PS8585.O84344L24 2002   C813'.54   C2002-900449-7
PR9199.3.R618L24 2002

Design & Composition: *Mad Dog Design Connection Inc.*
Jacket Design: *David Baldeosingh Rotstein*
Printed in Canada by *Transcontinental Printing Inc.*

The publisher would like to acknowledge the financial support of
the Government of Canada through the Book Publishing Industry
Development Program (BPIDP) and the Canada Council for our
publishing activities. The publisher further wishes to acknowledge
the financial support of the Ontario Arts Council for our
publishing program.

10 9 8 7 6 5 4 3 2 1

For my mother, Gertrude Rotenberg,
who never had a chance to read this one

Acknowledgements

Writing a novel can't be done without a great deal of support and encouragement. First and foremost from my wife, Susan Santiago, and my two kids, Joey and Beth. Then my father and brothers — then my friends who mean more to me than they often understand.

A special thanks to Bruce, Michael (aka The Papal Envoy), David and Scott — and to the many many gifted actors who have allowed me into their hearts and minds.

Then there is Ruth Cavin, my incredibly talented editor. How do you adequately thank someone for her tireless effort to keep me on track?

And finally, to my translator, friend and the original Zhong Fong — Ms. Zhang Fang.

CONTENTS

Author's Note

In *The Lake Ching Murders* I have been — at
times — light-handed with Chinese geography, flora
and fauna. Unlike in *The Shanghai Murders* where
you can actually walk the routes that Zhong Fong
walked and see the things he saw, in this novel if
you attempted to retrace Fong's steps you would
find yourself quite lost. This was done only for the
purpose of helping the fiction and is in no way
intended to be disrespectful.

CHAPTER ONE

A TELEGRAM FROM ANOTHER LIFE

Lily's English was, at the best of times, difficult to understand unless you knew a lot of English and a whole lot of Lily. Zhong Fong possessed the requisite knowledge in both instances. So when he retreated to the crumbling cinder-block structure that passed as the village's police station, he was reasonably sure he could decipher what Lily was trying to tell him.

Just fifty-four months ago Fong had been the head of Special Investigations, Shanghai District. Lily had been his inside source and confidante in forensics. But that was fifty-four months ago. A past life — or so it had seemed until the arrival of Lily's missive. Fong slowly tilted the telegram forward to catch the rays of the setting sun through the sheet of cracked plastic that took the place of a windowpane. He needed as much light as possible to read these days.

Lily's voice spoke in his head as he read her words: *HEY HO SHORT STUFF* [stop] *HOW FAR NORTH IS EATING YOU?* [stop] *CAR FULL LET YOUR RICHARD FREEZE NOT* [stop] *WATCH OUT* [stop] *TONS OVER HEAD GOING DOWN ON YOU SOON* [stop] *REAL SUCKING TONS, YOU NEED A HAT*

[stop] *YOURS WHENEVER, WHYEVER* [stop] *WHATEVER – LILY.*

Lily loved to speak, but only sort of spoke, English. She had an ear for the idioms and a nose for the slang, but no sense of how the language really worked. Unlike Fong, who had studied it seriously, Lily had picked up her English from TV and tourist hotels. The combination of Jerry Springer-speak and pimp lobby-hustle produced an extremely unique form of the language.

The telegram's surface darkened. Fong looked up. A cloud had drifted in front of the sun. He rubbed his eyes with his calloused fingers and returned to Lily's words. Communication of any sort was a rarity for him since he'd been banished to internal exile west of the Wall. There were no telephones in the village. There were no fax machines or computers. He was allowed into the telegraph office, but was not permitted to send messages, just to receive them – and this had been the only one since he'd arrived. He had no access to a vehicle and, as a convicted political felon, he wasn't allowed beyond a two-mile perimeter of the town. His only contact with what he had taken to thinking of as "the great over there" was the weekly Communist Party newspaper. It gave him just enough information to let him know that he was completely cut off from anything that really mattered. And that was exactly as Beijing intended.

In theory he was still a police officer, but that was just some bureaucrat's idea of a joke. In fact, all he was allowed to do was wait – indefinitely if Beijing wanted it so – to plant his feet deep in the dusty soil of this far distant edge of civilization, wither and then to rot in obscurity. A just reward for a traitor.

The cloud passed and an oblique ray of sunlight hit the paper. HEY HO SHORT STUFF, the first line, he knew was nothing more than a jab at his stature. The second line he assumed was the result of a common Mandarin mistake. Because there is no "ree" sound in Mandarin, the "tree" sound in English often went missing. So Lily wasn't asking how the Far North was *eating* him, but rather how the Far North was *treating* him.

"Just great," he said aloud.

CAR FULL LET YOUR RICHARD FREEZE NOT puzzled him. *CAR FULL* was no doubt *careful*, but he couldn't figure out *RICHARD. LET YOUR RICHARD FREEZE NOT? Richard freeze not?*

Then he remembered the night he and Lily had begun their unusual relationship. It was in Fong's fifth year on the Shanghai police force. He'd already established himself as a comer, the force's new black-haired boy. Until that evening he had known Lily only as an attractive, if gangly, techie who worked in the forensic labs.

The head of the crime site unit, Wang Jun, had sent him to forensics with a vial of unidentified pills found in the hotel room of a dead Tibetan. When Fong arrived at the lab, he was surprised to find the door unguarded. After a moment's hesitation he entered the large dimly lit room. This place had always struck him as other-worldly. But that night its emptiness and silence made it even more surreal. Then, beyond the aisles and aisles of bottle-covered desks, he saw a large figure moving in the shadows at the far end. He was about to call out, but something warned him to hold his tongue. He crouched down and moved silently closer.

It was not one figure as he had first thought, but two. The one with his back to him was the young cadet who should have been guarding the door. The one pressed against the table was Lily. Her skirt had been thrown aside, her panties were in shreds at her feet, her eyes were closed tight. Hurt and fear etched cruel patterns across her face.

Fong leapt forward. As he did, Lily's eyes snapped open. They locked on him. But there was no plea for help there.

She signalled him to go away, to creep away.

He did.

Later — much later — he returned to the lab and found her sitting on the floor in a darkened corner, a mug of steaming tea in her hands. He crossed the room to her and, not knowing what to do, stood over her. She looked up. Her face was pale. There was a welting sadness in her eyes.

"You saw." It was a statement of fact. Her voice was harsh and carried accusation in its depths.

"Yes. I'm sorry." He took a breath and asked, hopefully, "He is your boyfriend?"

The laugh that came from Lily hurt both of them. It was a Chinese laugh — one that understands that the world is a complex place. He turned away, but she reached out and grabbed him by the leg, "Don't leave."

He looked down at her, unsure whether he ought to

kneel. "He's not your boyfriend," he said slowly.

"You're not too bright, are you?"

"I'm not . . ."

Then in English she added, "Or too tall." She put down her tea, pressed her back against the wall and rose to her full height.

"Too tall for what exactly?" he responded in his textbook English.

A flicker of a smile danced across her face. She went on in English, "To buy friend me."

"To *boy* friend you?" he asked, confused.

"No! Or what stupid you? To *buy* friend me," she shouted at him, her long arms whipping about like the strands of a canvas windmill after a heavy storm.

"Oh, you mean to *be* my friend . . . I think."

She snapped back in staccato Shanghanese, "I said that. You deaf *and* short, or what?"

In Shanghanese he replied, "Maybe it would be better if we spoke in the Common Speech."

Angrily, she shot back, "My Engrish enough good not you for?" Her chin was stuck out so far that Fong almost laughed. But he was glad he didn't because that chin soon began to quiver and tears fell quickly from her deep, dark eyes. She moved past him and leaned against one of the long lab tables. A sharp cry escaped her lips before her hand could seal her mouth shut. Then she rolled forward, curling her spine.

He watched her and, as he often did, marvelled at the beauty of the female form. Its simple rhythm and flow. Its planes and contours. He stood in the darkened room for a long time until her crying cooled to tiny whimpers and then finally stopped.

"If he assaulted you, I'll arrest him."

She turned back to him, a twist of anger on her strong features. In her beautiful Shanghanese she hissed, "Yes, he assaulted me."

Fong took out his notebook and pen and began to write. "What's his name? I'll find where he lives and . . ."

"And nothing. You won't do anything." She grabbed his book and pulled out the page. In response to Fong's stunned look, she continued, "He's named Tong Tzu. He lives off Nanjing Road near Xian. But you're to do nothing with this information. He's a party boss's son." Fong took back his book and headed toward the door. "Don't be a jerk," she said. "I'll have justice in my own way."

Fong turned back and took a long look at Lily. He didn't know why, but he believed her. Six months later, when Tong Tzu was found blind and raving in a K-TV room at a tourist hotel, his body fluids almost 0.7 percent rubbing alcohol, Fong's admiration for this wiry woman increased. It was Fong's second major lesson in Shanghanese justice: bosses who overstep their bounds must be dealt with — but in an appropriately surreptitious manner.

Fong pocketed his notebook and asked in Shanghanese, "Do you want anything?"

"Yeah."

"What?"

"A promise you'll not talk about this even to that gorgeous actress wife of yours."

He was surprised that she knew about his marriage. "I promise."

"Good, and one more thing."

"What?" he asked totally at a loss as to what he could do to help Lily.

"A hug." She opened her arms. He moved to her. The pain was still in her body — he could feel it. He held her close. Tremors began to take her then subsided. When they stopped, she hugged him harder then pushed him away, saying in English, "One of you Richards is enough for one night."

He looked at her — lost again.

"Richards! Don't talk Engrish yous?" she shrieked. The glass beakers on the desk behind him rattled in their stands.

"Richards?"

She shouted in Mandarin, "Cock, prick, pecker, member, thing."

"Ah, Richard — you mean *dick*," he said.

"Yes, Richard, like President Nixon. Richard."

"*Dick* is the word you're looking for," Fong said, more than a little confused to be supplying this sort of linguistic information.

She didn't answer him so much as dismiss him with a running commentary of "*Richard, dick, stick, shick*, who fuck give?"

When he left she was still muttering to herself in half-English, half-Mandarin. Fong thought of it as "Manglish."

So RICHARD was *Dick*. Lily was telling him not to get

his organ frozen off out here. Solid advice, but easier said than done. He looked at the next line. *WATCH OUT*. "Will do, Lily," he said aloud. *TONS OVER HEAD GOING DOWN ON YOU SOON*. Fong understood Lily's attempt to underline her warning. And her emphatic addition of *REAL SUCKING TONS, YOU NEED A HAT* was just her way of underlining the underline.

Fong stepped out the door and looked at the snow-dusted fields. "Tons overhead going down on you soon, real sucking tons," he said to the cold air. Then he sighed. He didn't know if he was up to the challenge. To any challenge. He'd been out of commission, in every conceivable sense, for over four years. Four years — forever. The most serious problem he'd investigated during that time was a dispute between two village farmers over a misbegotten calf. The farmer with the cow blamed the bull; the farmer with the bull of course blamed the cow. The calf was beyond blame. Actually almost beyond recognition. Two legs and a stump. A bloated head. Ulcerous belly. A preternaturally ancient thing. A natural-born monster ready for the grave. Fong beat the poor thing to death with a tire iron and then ordered the owner of the bull to return half the stud fee to the owner of the cow.

This solution was greeted with toothless disapproval by Fen Tzu Hong, the only "officer" assigned to Fong's command. "City nonsense. Both farmers hate you now. Make one pay and at least you have made one ally. Must have allies to live in China, dumb city man." He wagged his old head in disbelief, "You will never learn." He'd thrown up his liver-spotted hands and muttered, "A Shanghanese moron will always be a Shanghanese moron — a Shanghanese moron traitor."

"Maybe you're right, you old thief," said Fong out loud. "Maybe you're right." His breath misted before him. He looked up at the cold night sky where the clusters of stars maintained their silent vigil.

Two days after Lily's telegram arrived, just past midnight, Fong dreamt of the mongoose again. On his very first day in the village he'd seen a young mongoose kill a large snake. The lithe creature had leapt above the lunging serpent and come down, teeth first, just behind the reptile's head. As it shook the lengthy snake to death, the mongoose stared unblinking at Fong. Then the rodent dumped the snake in the dust and ran between Fong's legs into his hut. The thing was just a baby. Fong fed it and it kept him company through several long nights. Then one night Fong dreamt the mongoose. Dreamt his life. Dreamt honouring him. Dreamt him whole. The next morning, the animal was gone. But from then on Fong thought of the animal as sleeping inside him. At the base of his spine.

The crunch of a heavy vehicle coming to a stop in front of his mud hut awoke the mongoose. Before the second door of the vehicle slammed shut Fong had pulled on his pants and his padded Mao jacket, which had his one remaining valuable possession sewn into its lining. If he'd owned a hat, he would have put it on as Lily instructed — but he had no hat.

Fong knew that whatever was coming down on him was just outside his hut.

He went to open the makeshift door, but was a step too late. The rotted wooden planking splintered under the sharp blow of the butt of an automatic weapon. Two more blows and the thing fell off its ancient hinges. Fong was going to say, "I could have opened it for you and saved you the trouble," but kept his mouth shut when he saw the size of the man with the AK-47 and the tall, thin, cruel-eyed northerner standing behind him.

Fong recognized the technique. It's always best to display unassailable physical superiority in making a night arrest. That and the darkness are often enough to intimidate a suspect into saying whatever you want. Fong had found this approach useful when he needed information from pimps. But he was not a pimp and these were not policemen. The big one was a water buffalo parading as a man. A thug. The tall one who lit a cigarette and leaned against the door frame was a politico. Fong swore softly under his breath.

The politico coughed out a laugh and spat on the mud floor of the hut. He took a long drag then tossed the barely smoked thing onto the wet floor. Fong felt the impulse to reach for the cigarette. He'd been without his beloved Kents for over five years. The butt hissed out. "A traitor doesn't get to smoke, Zhong Fong." The man extended the vowels of the word *traitor* just to ensure that Fong understood their relative positions. He was master. Fong was serf. Fong dropped his chin to his chest, a posture he'd learned in Ti Lan Chou, the political prison. The man smiled. "Good, Traitor Zhong. It is good to remember who one is and what place one holds in China. Don't you agree?" The man's voice was high. He lisped. The accent was northern. The question was no question.

The man lit a second cigarette and began to talk — something about the swift and sure nature of justice in the New China. Fong smiled inwardly. This man liked the sound of his own voice. Such men talked too much and often said more than they ought to. The man laughed again. Fong didn't care. The politico could laugh all he liked. Fong knew it was an act.

They had come for him because they needed him. There could be no other reason to bother with him. To awaken him. To dig him up. They needed him to do something for them. He didn't need them; they needed him, so he was in the position of power.

The man's chatter stopped. A darkness crossed his face. Fong panicked. Had he spoken his thoughts aloud? Then he saw something else in the tall man's cold eyes. A real hatred. Beyond politics. Personal. Fong wondered where that came from.

The northerner signalled to the big man. The water buffalo, after a slight hesitation, rushed at Fong and threw him against the wall. Before Fong could get his balance, the thug cuffed his wrists in front of him then shackled his legs. The politico sidled up to Fong and leaned down so that he was no more than an inch from Fong's face.

"You're a prisoner, Zhong Fong. You will always be a

prisoner, Zhong Fong. As I said, it is important to remember one's place in China. And you, Zhong Fong, are not only a traitor, but you are also a homeless vagrant. You stink like a street person. Decent people can smell you coming. They catch the whiff of Shanghanese shit stuck to your ass."

"So that was it," Fong thought. This man hated him because he was from Shanghai. Because he understood the special reality of growing up in the largest city in Asia. A city that knew and was influenced by the best of foreign cultures. A city that never slept. That gloried in being alive. Fong had met bureaucrats like this back in Shanghai. They were often from the north. They never bothered to learn Shanghanese despite the fact they'd lived in the city for twenty years. They were good party stock. That was all. Like this one. This guy was all dressed up but he was nothing more than a hick with power. A hick who hated Fong because he came from a great city. Because Fong understood it. Loved it.

The leg irons bit into Fong's ankles. The water buffalo half-carried, half-dragged him out of the hut. The politico ran ahead and climbed into the driver's seat of the large, black, Russian-built Chaika. He turned on the high beams. They were badly aimed. One lit the roof of a row of huts across the way while the other pooled on the dirt road inches in front of the fender. The northerner pressed hard on the car's horn. The thing spluttered into sound and soon awoke the villagers. As he intended.

The politico took a bullhorn and, standing on the Chaika's fender, shouted, "Come out, honest comrades, and see the traitor, Zhong Fong." Bleary-eyed peasants emerged from their huts. Mothers clutched children. Old men attempted to stand straight.

"Now is the time, comrades, to lodge your complaints against the traitor. Your government is here to help you. This man is a disgrace to China. Tell us how he has harmed you and he will be punished accordingly."

Something hit Fong in the chest. It was a rotten turnip. Then more things followed. And screams. These people whom he hardly knew seemed to hate him. Then he reminded himself that they were only acting their part in this little morality play.

The big man stepped in front of Fong, lifted him off his feet and carried him to the back of the Chaika. He unlocked the huge trunk.

"The traitor will ride in the trunk like common baggage," the northerner announced.

The thug threw Fong in.

Fong twisted his body just in time to avoid the large metal latch on the car's frame and he landed with a thump on his back. He turned to look out into the night. As he did, the two farmers he'd tried to help both began screaming complaints at the politico. Behind them stood his old assistant, Mr. Fen. He was shrugging his shoulders and looking at Fong. He mouthed the words, "I told you."

Then the trunk lid slammed shut, blotting out the stars.

Fong felt the car's ignition engage and the wide heavy vehicle, more tank than car, start to move.

Sound boomed off the surfaces of the confined space as it picked up speed. "Well, I'm finally out of the village. That's positive," he thought. But where were they taking him? And what was the shit coming down on him so hard that he needed a hat?

He consoled himself with one thought: "They wouldn't have come to get me unless they needed me. They need me for something — to do something for them. And if they need me to do something for them I might be able to broker a trade. My services for a way back to Shanghai — a way home."

CHAPTER TWO

IN THE TRUNK

The darkness in the trunk of the Chaika was almost complete. It was getting colder. Fong slowed his breathing and ordered himself to think. As the head of Special Investigations, Shanghai Division, he'd come across more than one body that had suffocated in the trunk of a car. His eyes slowly adjusted. Murky shadows took on shapes. He reached upward and felt the rusting inside of the Russian-made car's trunk lid. He had some room above him. He propped himself up on his elbows and his head touched metal. Flakes of corrosion fell into his hair and down his neck.

Then the Chaika hit a bump. The rocklike shock absorbers did little to cushion the blow inside the car and nothing for Fong in the trunk. His head smashed against the lid then his elbows slammed to the floor. Blood quickly matted his hair and dribbled down his forehead. One elbow was skinned almost to the bone. He curled into a ball on the floor of the trunk, ignored the bleeding and tried to think.

Another bump.

His whole body went straight up, hit the lid and then thumped back down.

The car accelerated and took a hard right. He shoved his hands straight out over his head as he slid along the floor of the trunk. He hit hard. As he did, his hands scraped across a cavity in the metal sidewall. He reached in and touched rubber. A small spare tire. He yanked it free of its strappings and skittered back to the centre of the trunk. The tire could protect his head like a cushion.

The air in the confined space was already rank and Fong knew that carbon monoxide was probably coming up from the tailpipe. Chaikas were not famous for their fine workmanship. He turned over and using his finger-nails scraped at the edge of the trunk's shredded carpet. He tore a large patch of skin from the back of his right hand but ignored it as he wedged his hand beneath a corner of the coarse material. Then he leaned back and pulled with all his might. Several square feet of the mouldy stuff came up. He reversed himself so he could work on the section where he'd been lying. It took him time — and two substantial bumps — to make the shift. This side of the carpet came up quickly. Fong gathered it together and pushed it as far forward as he could.

He was breathing hard and his sweat was already mixing with the blood from his head, elbow and hand. He stank of fear.

Another bump. Fong's head snapped back and he took the blow on his forehead. When he landed, his hand caught on the corner of something on the floor. He yanked it open. He reached in and found a partially inflated inner tube.

He looked into the tire well. The metal was so rusted

that it was almost translucent. He searched desperately for something to poke a hole in the metal. Finding nothing, he got himself into a half-sitting position, leaned back on his elbows and stuck his foot into the well. Several kicks later he had a hole — and enough air to stay alive. He repositioned himself beside the air hole and drew his knees up. He put the small tire beneath his head and the inner tube on top of him. Then he covered the mound of himself with the shredded carpet.

Through the hole he watched the road whiz by — China whiz by. He'd been confined to that village west of the Wall for over two years. Before that he'd been in Ti Lan Chou prison for . . . it felt like a very long time. But now he was travelling. Moving. He watched China through the hole. Pebbles and dirt, then moments of pavement, then pebbles and dirt, slush, pavement, dirt, pavement — and finally sleep.

And dreams.

He was on a palette on the ground, his mother standing over him. She was crying. He tried to speak but blood came from his mouth and a deep rattle sounded in his tortured lungs. Fong knew where he was. He was in their home in Shanghai's Old City. He was a boy. It was before the liberation. He'd gotten typhoid from handling the night soil. He wanted to reach up and tell his mother that it was okay, that she mustn't cry. But he couldn't speak.

His grandmother came in and shrieked at his mother who bowed quickly then put on her "brave face" and hurried back to work in the dark streets. Fong looked at his grandmother's lined, stern face. It betrayed nothing. She barked out, "You're not going to die. Night soil has been the business of this family for twelve generations. We've all had what you have. Don't be a coward and it will go away — or it won't then it won't matter if you are a coward or not."

He went to call for his beloved father but found himself running.

Running. Wang Jun, his older friend and colleague at his side. It was fifty-four months ago on Shanghai's waterfront. No, in the Pudong industrial area. Federal troops firing at them. Ting of bullets off brick. Thunk against a car door. Sliding skip of metal jackets against blacktop. A windshield shattering. Then thud. Wang Jun hit and crashing to the ground. Then thwap, thwap, thwap — Fong's feet on the pavement. Running. Running. Not looking back. Never seeing Wang Jun's body. Never looking. Just running.

Running — into Fu Tsong's outstretched arms.

"Be still, Fong, and we'll get through this.

"This is a dream," he said.

"Hardly. A nightmare more likely."

Fong looked up. He was in a theatre, his deceased wife, the famous actress Fu Tsong, at his side.

"But be good Fong and as I've said, we'll get through this."

The bounce of the stage lights came out into the house just enough to illuminate her beautiful features. Fong held his breath. He didn't want the illusion to return to drops of mist. He hadn't been able to dream her for years.

Then she laughed.

Tendrils of joy, the very heart of her life force, spread out through the fetid air of the place. And he gloried in her presence.

Then she reached over and took his hand. Her elegant tapered fingers interlocked with his calloused ones. He caught a hint of her perfume.

He coughed.

For a moment Fong couldn't figure out what a tire was doing beneath his head.

Then he remembered.

Dust was pouring in through the hole in the wheel well. He rolled away and covered his mouth.

And curled up once more with his memories. A wave of loneliness the likes of which he hadn't experienced since he entered Ti Lan Chou prison swept over him. For the first time since he had killed the assassin Loa Wei Fen in the construction site in the Pudong, he felt tears coming to his eyes. He blinked them back. He was too old to cry.

The car bounced. Fong's body rose; the inner tube protected him from the trunk's ceiling and when he fell the tire protected him from the floor. He wondered where they were taking him. Then he stopped wondering and accepted. The mongoose stopped its pacing and sat at the base of his spine. Where they were going was out of his control. No point wasting energy on that. They'd no doubt get wherever they were going soon enough.

CHAPTER THREE

ANOTHER NIGHT IN JAIL

A bright light pierced Fong's sleep. He shook his head, trying to stop the glare inside his skull. Then he realized that the light wasn't coming from within, that it wasn't part of a dream, but rather it was the beam of a high-powered flashlight. He shrugged off the inner tube and held up his manacled hands to blinker the glare.

Through his fingers he saw the silhouettes of the thug and the politico then they bent over the opened trunk. The light bouncing off his hands lit their faces. The thug scowled. That didn't bother Fong. But the politico's knowing nod sent a shiver down his spine. That all-understanding nod, that I-told-you-so smile, let Fong know that the inner tube and the tire had been provided intentionally. That they had been planted. Prepared. That much forethought had been put into this little excursion.

Fong kicked aside the shredded carpet and struggled to a sitting position. A thought sprouted in his head. This asshole thought putting the tire and inner tube there for him to find proved how powerful he was. Fong knew that it proved the opposite. They put the stuff in the trunk because they didn't want him too badly hurt. Roughed up, yes — but hurt, no. Because they needed him to do something for them. Lily's telegram said *TONS OVER HEAD GOING DOWN ON YOU SOON. REAL SUCKING TONS, YOU NEED A HAT.* Maybe, Lily, maybe. Fong was careful not to smile. But inside he was gleeful. They wanted him scared but basically unharmed. They were concerned that he survive the ride. They must really need him to work on something big.

It was dark. He could smell the deep intensity of manure in the air. They must be in a small village. No doubt still a commune-dominated place that turned out the street lights, perhaps all electricity in the town, at 9 p.m. There was a time when all power went off in Shanghai at 10 p.m. Big daddy government saying, Enough kids — you've got a lot of work to do tomorrow, go to bed. In Shanghai, all that did was spawn a new business in illicit generators. The Shanghanese loved their pleasures and were not about to be denied them by some Beijing government edict!

The thug lifted Fong from the trunk with shockingly little effort. Fong's knees gave out when he hit the ground. It was muddy. The politico laughed. "You've allowed your physical skills to deteriorate badly, Traitor Zhong. Even a disgusting traitor ought to take care of the vessel of life."

Fong struggled to his feet and took a good look at this flower-eater. "Vessel of life?" he thought. Has the world changed that much? Or is this guy just too . . . too . . . Fong couldn't find the right word.

The thug grabbed his upper arm and walked him forward. The smell of the politico's cigarette caught in Fong's nostrils. The acrid smoke stung his eyes but he longed for a drag. Just one.

They crossed the deserted street and opened the door of a single-storey concrete-block building. They were met by two young men in federal uniforms. Quickly, papers were signed and Fong was hustled down a corridor of empty cells.

"This evening's accommodations," Fong thought. But he was careful to keep his eyes down. No point fighting now. "Fight when there is the possibility of winning. Attack when they assume you are going to defend. Never show the enemy your formation because the outside betrays the inner self. Attack only when you know the enemy." That advice from Sun Tzu's book *The Art of War* popped into Fong's head. It was the only thing, besides Mao's little red book, he'd been allowed to read in Ti Lan Chou prison.

The jailer pressed the coded cell lock and the door swung open. Fong sensed more than saw the young man huddled in the back reaches of the cell. "We thought you'd enjoy some company after your lonely trip." Fong hadn't noticed that the politico had followed them down the corridor. "Prisoner Tao, this is traitor Zhong. Traitor Zhong, this is prisoner Tao." He allowed a slight pause then hissed, "Tao's to be executed for crimes against the state — at sunrise."

Fong was shoved forward. He tripped as the ankle chain snagged. To his surprise his fall was cushioned by prisoner Tao.

The laugh from the corridor behind him was totally humourless. The door clanged shut and the electronic locking mechanism slammed the bolts into place. Fong nodded his thanks to Tao as they both listened to the retreating footsteps. The footfalls silenced. Prisoner Tao moved to the far corner of the cell. When he turned back, he held out a bowl of half-eaten rice and a set of chopsticks.

Fong nodded and took the food. He positioned the bowl between his raised knees. Chinese handcuffs are joined by a longer chain than their sisters in the West to allow for the use of chopsticks. Fong looked at the rice. He wasn't sure how long it had been since he'd last eaten. It was one of the many things that had changed in his life. Food was just a matter of refuelling now. So unlike his time in Shanghai.

Fong shook the thought from his head. That was past. Now was right before him. A bowl of rice. A prisoner about to be executed. The need for clarity was obvious.

He tilted the container and scraped a few grains into his mouth. Although the food in the western village had been simple, it had been pure. Here Fong tasted the edges of saltpeter and dust that were so familiar from Ti Lan Chou prison. His gorge rose, rejecting the food, but he stopped it. Saltpeter and dust or piss or shit — it didn't matter. He needed the sustenance of the rice to keep up his strength or he'd never make it to the end of this. Whatever this was.

"You are hungry." Prisoner Tao's voice was gentle. His accent was from the south. He spoke the Mandarin words as if they were part of his second language.

In the dim light Fong looked at the young man's face. The smooth skin. The clear eyes.

Fong's time in prison had taught him to mind his own business, to deal with his own problems — to be alone. That proffered friendship and a warden's snitch were often one and the same. But something else said talk to this boy. Comfort him. He is important to you.

"You are not from here."

"No, from Sichuan province."

Fong had never been to that part of the country. "How did you get here?"

"They brought me."

"Why?"

The young man looked sharply at Fong. "Have you been sent here to torment me at the end? Is this the final insult?"

"No." A long silence ensued.

At last Fong spoke. "I have no way of proving that to you." Fong gave him back the remainder of the rice. "Thank you for your food."

A silence grew like a dark cloud between them. Finally the young man pointed to Fong's shackles. "Do they hurt?"

Fong snapped back. "Yes. Of course they hurt. They were made to hurt. They are intended to hurt. They put them on me to hurt." Why was he being hard on this boy? He was about to apologize when the young man turned away and, stretching his long arms along the wall, tilted his head so it rested against the cool stone.

"It's all *intended* isn't it, Traitor Zhong?" He turned to Fong and there were tears in his eyes.

"Yes, it's all planned," Fong answered slowly.

"So I'm just part of their plan?"

For the first time it occurred to Fong that this young man's death may have been specifically designed for him to witness — to learn from. To remind him who was in charge in China. He wanted to get up and yell through the bars that it wasn't necessary. That he acknowledged that they owned him. That there was no reason for this object lesson. That it was sinful to execute a boy to prove a point to him.

But he didn't. He sank to the floor and hung his head.

Later that night, Fong awoke to the boy's gentle crying. No words were spoken, but the two came together. The boy's head rested in Fong's lap and Fong ran his fingers through the young man's greasy hair until finally the youth's breathing deepened and sleep took him.

Fong sat in the darkness and allowed himself, just for a moment, the grace of thinking of himself as the boy's father.

Then lines — favourite lines of his dead wife, Fu Tsong — came to him:

Ay, but to die, and go we know not where;
To lie in cold obstruction and to rot;
This sensible warm motion to become
A kneaded clod; and the delighted spirit
To bathe in fiery floods, or to reside
In thrilling region of thick-ribbed ice;

To be imprison'd in the viewless winds
And blown with restless violence round about
The pendant world.

Fong shivered as he remembered the final lines of the speech:

The weariest and most loathed worldly life
That age, ache, penury and imprisonment
Can lay on nature is a paradise
To what we fear of death.

Fong traced the beauty of the young man's face with his fingers — and remembered. On his release from Ti Lan Chou political prison and his banishment to internal exile beyond the Wall, the authorities had allowed Fong three hours in Shanghai to collect his things. They knew he'd return to the two rooms at the Shanghai Theatre Academy where he and his wife had lived.

When he opened the door he was shocked to find the rooms empty. Unoccupied rooms in Shanghai were rarer than shrimp in shrimp dumplings. At first he was unable to enter. All the furniture was gone. The walls were bare. Everything that was "them" was gone. How small rooms appeared when emptied of their lives.

In the bathroom he found the only vestige of Fu Tsong — her *Complete Works of Shakespeare*. It was open on the cracked tile. The ammonia smell of urine rose from the still damp pages.

He had clutched the book to his chest for the entire seven-day, hard-seat train journey to the west.

When he finally arrived on the edges of the Chinese

known world, the party man who met his train assigned him the "job" of head constable, gave him a ration card and pointed to a mud-floored hut. Then he gave Fong papers to sign and departed, all with a bare minimum of talk. Eyes watched Fong as he moved in the small village. They all knew who he was — the traitor from the hated city of Shanghai.

Silence was his constant companion. When work ended, the real punishment began — boredom. He had nothing to do. Nothing to read. Nothing to see. He wasn't permitted beyond the village's outer perimeter and he, of course, had no means of leaving. The nights seemed to grow longer and longer.

In those tedious hours, he'd taken to devising ways of hiding Fu Tsong's *Complete Works of Shakespeare*. She'd treasured the collection with its Mandarin translation. Now it was his. Now he treasured it. It was his last link to their life together. He understood that the authorities had allowed him to keep the book only so there was still one more thing they could take from him. It was a potent weapon.

He initially thought of hiding the book in the village. Quickly he gave up that idea. They'd find it even if he buried it deep in the ground. It was only when he was mending his torn Mao jacket with the needle and thread he'd been given as part of his twice-yearly household rations that he landed on a solution.

Every night by candlelight in the cold of his hut, he'd carefully cut single pages from the text. Then he sewed them together, the bottom of the first page to the top of the second. He found he could manage between fifteen and twenty pages before the rationed candle began to splutter. Once he saw the light start to give out, he'd pick open the stitches of his padded Mao jacket's lining and insert the pages into the pockets that he had sewn there.

Chinese characters are much more compact than English sentences. A hundred-page play in English could be as few as twenty pages in Mandarin. So coping with Shakespeare's works in the Common Speech was not too time-consuming and more important, when carefully smoothed and inserted into the pouches beneath his coat's lining, the pages were not noticeable beneath the jacket's padding. But Fong's English was very good and he was loath to give up any of the original versions of the plays. He understood, though, that trying to keep all the plays could endanger the entire enterprise. So he'd have to choose. Which plays? The answer came to him one night. It was simple. He'd keep the English language versions of the plays in which his wife had performed. *Twelfth Night, Measure for Measure, Cymbeline, Othello, Hamlet* and *Pericles*. The rest, the ones she hadn't brought to life for him, he'd leave behind. *Measure for Measure* had been one of her favourites and she had insisted that he memorize many of the speeches from the play.

Fu Tsong often sought his help with new roles. She found his didactic approach to the plays helpful. Over and over again he looked at plot twists and specific lines as a detective would the layout of a crime scene. Why would someone say that at that exact moment? Doesn't her saying that imply that she knows this? Why would he go there rather than here? His most crucial insights were about what was missing from a scene or a character. What wasn't said or done told him more than what was. His interpretations were occasionally difficult for Fu Tsong to incorporate, but from time to time they were invaluable. In the case of her Isabella in *Measure for Measure*, they formed the basis for one of her most famous performances.

Fu Tsong loved Shakespeare.

"Because of his deep humanity and his belief in love," she said coming into the bedroom, a cup of steaming *cha* in her hands. Her favourite silk robe, sashed at her waist, clung to her slender frame. A bath towel swathed her hair. He stared openly at her beauty. She smiled then shook her head slowly.

"What?" he asked, feigning innocence.

"Later, Fong. Later. The play first. 'That' later." Her laugh tickled the walls and lit up their modest rooms. "So tell me what you've found for me in this play. You have done your homework, I hope."

He had been examining the text on his lunch breaks. "I've read this *Measure for Measure*, Fu Tsong."

"That's a beginning. So?"

"It loses me. All the time, I'm off-balance with this one. Are there sections missing from it or something?"

"No, I don't think so."

"But what the characters do doesn't make sense."

She took that in and nodded, "An example, please."

"Well, Angelo's the villain, right?"

"So it would seem," she said sitting beside him on the bed.

Turning to her, he went on. "Then what kind of punishment is it for the villain to have to marry Marianne at the end? For that matter, how do the rewards in this play work anyway? I mean 'Measure for Measure,' the title, refers to equal for equal, doesn't it? Rice bowl for rice bowl."

"It's a reference to the long nose's Bible. Biblical justice."

"Justice." The word came from Fong's mouth like something spat to the ground.

She was surprised. "Fong?"

Fong was on his feet, his angular body tense. "Justice! Justice! Who knows anything about justice? How does justice work?"

"This from a police officer, sir?" she said, twinkling, but was careful not to mock.

He turned to her. His face a mask of anger. "I've been a cop for twelve years and I don't know if I've been involved in a single case in which justice was the issue. Retribution. Setting an example. Simple frustration. Putting an end to something. Prevention. Yes. But justice? I don't know. When foreign delegations come to the city, we sweep the beggars off the Bund promenade. Is there any justice in that? When a peasant, freshly arrived at the North Train Station, looks at the wealth of the thieving Taiwanese and helps himself to some of it, is it justice that we throw him in prison? Why shouldn't the whoreson Taiwanese be thrown in prison for the theft his father must have committed to allow him that much money?" Fu Tsong knew better than to try and stop him. "I spend whole months as a police officer where justice isn't even mentioned. Not even thought about." He turned from her and stared out the window. A group of untalented student actors lounged on the grass as if they had somehow earned the right to green space in the concrete jungle that was Shanghai.

Fu Tsong stared at him. She had come from a comfortable background. A loving mother and doting father. A whole family that had contributed to her education as an actress. Fong's life had been much different. He pretended his life had begun when he met her. Only on occasion did she get glimpses into her husband's past — most often when they went to Shanghai's Old City. There he'd change before her eyes. People seemed to know him there. He'd stop standing erect and hunch over, crowd into himself, become a thing of that dank and dark place.

It always amazed her. He became so unlike the proud man that she knew and loved. This was an urban peasant. A spitter.

What she didn't know was that in fact this was a night-soil collector. A person who makes his living from others' waste products has a very different view of life than those who deposit their filled honey buckets on the street at night, and then retrieve them magically emptied in the morning.

"Are the first lines in scenes in Shakespeare the first lines of the conversation?"

"Fong?"

He turned toward her. "Is the first thing said in a scene the first thing said between the characters?" he repeated.

Fu Tsong thought about this for a moment. "Not always. Often it's the first important thing said. Why, Fong? Have you found something in *Measure for Measure* that . . ."

"This Isabella. This nun person?"

"My role."

"Yes," he threw up his hands and began to pace. "Yes, this unlikely casting of my lascivious wife as a nun." She took the towel from her head and snapped it at him. "Fine. This aggressive, lascivious wife of mine who's supposed to be a nun . . ."

"Yes, dear — and your question would be?"

"Isabella, this woman who wants to be a nun, who you're about to play?"

"Yes, Fong?" She tapped her foot in mock impatience.

"What's the first thing she says in the play?"

Fu Tsong looked at him. He repeated his question. "What's the first thing she says in the play?"

Fu Tsong reached for her *Complete Works of Shakespeare*, but Fong pulled it away.

"The first thing that this nun person says in *Measure for Measure* is 'And have you nuns no further privileges?' And what more privileges does she want? A second rice bowl, a new dress — a new lover — what? And isn't it odd that that's the first thing out of her mouth? This supposed virgin. And what about this Duke who walks away from his responsibilities? Hands over his kingdom to this villain Angelo. Is he not guilty of some offence? And what is he doing at the friar's place when he leaves the court? He wants a disguise. Fine. But what does his opening line in that scene mean? 'No, holy father; throw away that thought.' What thought? That he is here for some lecherous rendezvous? And obviously from the way he's speaking to the man, he has been there before. So is this Duke, this lecher, the man who will mete out justice? And going back to Isabella. Why is she anxious to join a nunnery? She doesn't seem religious. Why is she going there? Is she spurned?"

"I love it when you talk like that, *spurned*." She patted the bed beside her. He sat. "Say it again Fong. Spurned." Her voice was suddenly hoarse.

"Spurned."

She touched his lips with a hand soft as velvet. Then her fingers parted his lips and entered his mouth. Her eyes never left his. His tongue tasted the perfume on her fingertips.

She got to her feet. The sash whispered to the floor. "You going to spurn me, Fong?"

"I believe not," he tried to say, but no sound came from his lips.

She smiled and let her robe fall away.

He managed to say her name, but his voice was pulled so far back in his throat that the words sounded as if they came from someone else. Someone far, far away.

After, entwined, she talked through her ideas of the

character — of seeking piety, of celibacy and purity. He countered with Isabella's refusal to face her own carnal desires. Her selfishness in the face of her brother's death. Finally she threw aside the bedcovers and walked, lithe and naked, to the closet. He got up and sat on the side of the bed, waiting.

She returned with her Peking Opera stage paints and brushes. She straddled his leg and held out two large combs. He felt her wetness — their wetness — on his thigh. He reached up and put her long hair behind her shoulders. Then he pinned back her long bangs.

She stared into his eyes and began to talk. Just ideas of Isabella. Images. Flows of self. Currents of character. As she spoke he took the paints and brushes and began. Long ago she'd taught him the art of Peking Opera makeup. He'd been a swift and avid learner. Applying a beautiful artifice to the true beauty of her face sent razor shards of erotic shocks through his system. It was so close, as close as they could get.

Over his shoulder she looked at her reflection in the full-length mirror. And slowly the naturalistic Isabella grew beneath the artificial surface of the makeup. When he finished, she allowed her hands to trace his naked torso.

"Who's touching you, Fong?"

He always marvelled how her entire persona shifted beneath the paint.

"Who's touching you?" she asked again.

"Isabella." His breath was tight in his chest. Raspy as it hit the air.

Then a smile appeared through the miracle of the classical makeup, a smile he'd never seen before on the wife he adored — the smile of a lascivious nun. Her eyes held his as she guided him into her — into Isabella — the complex leading lady of a white man's play about justice.

The crack of the rifle report was so loud that Fong smacked his head hard against the wall of the cell. It came from outside. From the courtyard. He looked around him. The boy from Sichuan province was gone.

Fong sprang to his feet and tried to hoist himself up to the barred window. He was desperate to see out. "They couldn't have," he told himself. "They couldn't have executed him."

Then they were in the cell, checking his hand and foot manacles. He started to resist then stopped himself and bowed his head. A long fingernail scraped beneath his chin and tilted his head upward. The politico's face was smooth; his eyes had a renewed cruelty. The man canted his head slightly and looked into Fong's eyes. Without a word the two communicated perfectly. The politico's silence said, "Do you see, Traitor Zhong, that we completely control you and your life and your hopes?" And Fong's silent response said, "I see." But in his heart he said, "Those with real power do not need to use it. A real warrior wins without fighting. And you — you are a running dog who needs my help." Then the real question rose in Fong. "Needs my help for what?"

CHAPTER FOUR

AN ENVELOPE IN A CAR

That day the thug drove. The politico sat beside him. Fong was in the Chaika's back seat. His leg shackles were tightened, but only one wrist was cuffed. The other manacle was clamped to the handle of the door. It didn't bother Fong. After a day in the trunk, this was like moving from hard seat to soft sleeper on a train.

The village of his exile was in the flat emptiness beyond the Great Wall. Few animals. Fewer people. Lots of land. More dust than soil. Loess. Fine granules that were always in the wind. Always sifting beneath the door, worming through the cracks in the mud walls and adhering to every orifice of the body. It was hard for Fong to adjust to waking with the taste of sand in his mouth. Even the cup of hot water he drank every night before sleep managed to collect a layer of sand from the time he cleaned it to the time he tilted the warm liquid into his mouth.

But here, out the car window, was a different China. A land of rounded hills. An abundant, verdant China. Fully occupied. Every inch of every hill covered with sculpted mud terrace upon sculpted mud terrace. Each supported by hewn stonewalls. Each with hand-carved stone steps leading up to it and away from it. Wooden sluice gates permitted water from higher terraces to lower ones. Long narrow metal screws, some several yards long, moved water in the other direction. Layer upon layer, paddy upon paddy of green ripening rice shoots. All densely packed, until finally, on the valley floor, flat-bottom land. At last, a field that would support rice cultivation without the back-breaking work of building and maintaining terraces.

"The hills look like giant peach pits," Fong thought. It struck him as quintessentially Chinese that the peasants in the country turned hills into giant peach pits while artists in the city turned dried peach pits into incredibly detailed carvings of country life.

Fong did not come from farmers, but he appreciated the labour and ingenuity involved in the terraces. The Chineseness of it all.

A nature harnessed although never really subdued, still somehow wild.

The car was thick with the politico's cigarette smoke. Usually this wouldn't bother Fong. He'd been smoking since he was ten. But now he wanted to smell the land. The deep, manure-laden land that gave birth to them all. To the black-haired people.

He turned the handle and cracked open the window.

Immediately the thug turned to face him. "Drive," the politico barked. The thug's shoulders tightened as if he didn't take orders from the likes of the politico.

"Odd response," Fong thought.

The thug turned back to the road. As he did, the

politico pivoted in his seat, his left arm draped almost to Fong's knees, "Close the window, Traitor Zhong."

Fong looked out the window and turned the handle. The pane squeaked its complaint. He sat back in his seat. The politico was looking out the front window again. But on the seat beside Fong was a stuffed manilla envelope that had not been there before. Fong looked up into the rear-view mirror. The politico kept his eyes on the road as he lit another cigarette. A smirk crossed the man's lips as he exhaled a line of white smoke.

Fong took his eyes from the mirror and looked at the envelope. It was a standard issue postal item.

He looked from the thug's still tense shoulders to the politico's forced casualness. "There's some division here," Fong thought. Another quote from *The Art of War* came to him: "Cause disruption among the enemy ranks and victory is more likely." He smiled inwardly and said, "You dropped something back here."

"I didn't drop anything, Traitor Zhong," snapped the politico, his casual posture immediately a thing of the past.

The thug's eyes bored holes in the politico. "This was good," thought Fong.

"But you did," he said. "This." He tossed the envelope onto the front seat. The thug hadn't taken his eyes from the politico.

"Watch the road, you idiot." Again the thug didn't take the order like a man used to obeying commands. And only after a display of pique did he return his eyes to the road. "You'll get us all killed before we even get to the lake."

"So we're going to a lake," thought Fong. "To take the waters or what?" But he ignored his own question and watched the tension grow between the thug and the politico.

The last four years had taught him to enjoy the small pleasures life has to offer. Enemies at odds with one another was a small pleasure to be savoured.

CHAPTER FIVE

THE SPECIALIST

More than three months earlier, a plane without markings prepared to land on a deserted runway on the military side of the Xian airport. The aged specialist on board was accompanied by a small contingent of federal troops, several crime scene officers and a high-ranking party member, although if you looked into the old man's eyes you would see that he was utterly alone — as all specialists are.

The specialist hadn't been on a plane for quite some time. During the flight he'd marvelled at the ground passing beneath him, the intense, almost terrifying, beauty of China from the air, the densely packed landscape, the sudden shifts of colour — then, the crystalline ice-coated terrain around Lake Ching.

It was the early morning of January 1.

Captain Chen, all five-foot-four intensely ugly inches of him, stood at the front of the welcoming party of Xian police. He shifted his weight from foot to foot, trying in vain to keep the frigid cold of dawn out of his bones. Chen had responded to the initial, hysterical call from the lake just over three days ago. Since then the case had "become his." He might have been nothing much to look at, but he wasn't stupid. He was aware that the case had fallen to him because everyone above him knew the implicit danger to any officer investigating the murder of seventeen foreigners.

So did he.

The night of the murders had begun with freezing rain that was quickly followed by bitter cold. The icy roads had made the two-hour drive from Xian to Lake Ching take the better part of five. Just outside Ching's city limits, Chen passed a broken-down Russian-made bus being pushed by the driver and several young, overtly attractive women. Whores. They flagged him down but the best he could do for them was radio for assistance. The night was tough on everyone.

When he finally got to the docks of the small city, the man who'd called in the report was disappointed that he had come alone. Chen ignored the snide man's protests and ordered him to arrange transport out to the boat that was now stuck far out on the lake.

Temperatures continued dropping. The ice pelted down unmercifully. The ride out froze first his skin then his bones. But when they got close enough to see the large flat-bottomed boat, Captain Chen forgot his personal discomfort and stared in amazement.

The ship had run aground on a shoal of rocks. Its running lights were refracting through the two-inch-thick coat of ice that was continuing to build on its surface. The whole thing was like a bizarre beacon in the midst of the dark, frigid lake. It was an eerie sight the likes of which the young captain had never seen.

Chen noted the painted 14K Triad markings on the outside of the hull just above the waterline and swore, "Damn Triads — things are getting out of hand. Now not only do they do the deed, they claim it."

He went aboard.

The harsh emergency lights cast the multiple murders in livid contrast to the intended luxury and pleasure of the place. So much death in a small space.

He did a body count and headed back to shore.

Because the victims were foreigners, he immediately got in touch with the police commissioner of Xian, who told him not to go back to the boat but to stay put at the local police station in Ching. He did what he was told. Seven and a half hours later, as the ice storm abated and the milky sun rose on the morning of December 29, the commissioner's office ordered him to secure the crime site then get back to Xian.

Exactly how to secure a boat, now totally encased in ice almost three miles offshore, proved challenging. He began by ordering the Ching police to close the city's docks and all access roads to the lake. Then he had all activities on the water banned until further notice.

It was past noon before he ventured out to the boat a second time. It seemed bigger in the daylight and it glistened beneath its icy skin. On board, the obscenity of seventeen murders had not changed.

Chen and the two local cops he brought with him festooned the boat's exterior with yellow crime scene tape. It was while taping the vessel that Chen first saw the large black scorch marks underneath the thick coating of ice on the exterior of the starboard side of the ship.

He looked at the markings closely. Fire? Had he noticed indications of fire the first time he'd been on board the ship? He didn't think so. True, he'd never been anywhere with seventeen corpses so it was possible he'd overlooked things. But still. Fire?

He reached down to the waterline of the pleasure boat. He took off his glove and ran his hand over the largest of the scorch marks. It sat in an indentation of the ice. Not a hole, just a gentle dip in the thick layer of ice. A second large burn stain had punctured the hull but was plugged by the ice. He noted its exact location and headed toward shore.

The locals naturally grumbled about the inconvenience of not being able to use the lake but were, in fact, more curious than annoyed. The fringes of the lake were beginning to freeze. Who could work in this kind of weather except those damned cormorant fishermen anyway?

Death was an accepted part of a rural community like this, but murder — murder of foreigners — murder of many foreigners made for wonderful hours of gossip, speculation and inevitably both colourful and hateful accusations against "those half-wit islanders."

Because it was Chen's case he would be the big city specialist's guide to the crime site. He stamped his feet on the tarmac and swore under his breath at the cold. Then the specialist emerged from the plane.

The old guy looked frail leaning heavily on the arm of

a young uniformed soldier as he made his way slowly down the steps from the plane. He hadn't dyed his hair. It was snowy white — an oddity in China where hair-dying was one of the few accepted vanities. As the specialist stepped onto the ice-slick pavement, Chen stepped forward. Before he could speak, the specialist held up a hand and nodded.

For the first hour of the drive the old guy didn't say a word — it was spooky. Finally, Chen asked, "Are you hungry, sir?"

The man shook his head. Then he reached into his coat and took out a small pad and pencil. He quickly slashed the characters for, "How far to the lake?"

Chen tried not to show his surprise and answered, "It depends on the roads after the ice storm, sir."

A scowl crossed the old man's face.

Chen realized that he'd spoken slowly and loudly as if to a hard-of-hearing or slow-witted child. He opened his mouth to apologize, but the older man wasn't paying any attention. He was staring at the passing fields. Later he breathed on the window to produce a mist on the surface within which he'd etch figures with the long nail of his right baby finger.

The affectation of long fingernails surprised Chen. This old guy was street cop incarnate. It was etched all over his features. Even the distance in his eyes was clear to see. Classic.

"It's very cold here," the specialist wrote.

"Yes, sir." Chen made sure that he was speaking normally.

"How long?" the characters on the pad demanded.

"Two days now. Very cold. It began with a sudden ice storm. Odd for these parts."

"And the murders were two days ago?"

"Two days and three nights, sir."

The older man didn't reply. He just pulled his coat more tightly around himself, folded his arms across his chest and stared out the window.

When they finally got to the lake the wind was howling and the blown snow stung like needles when it hit exposed skin. Pockets of ice were already forming on several sections of open water near the shore. The older man took his pad from his pocket and wrote: "Will the lake freeze?"

"It hasn't frozen for decades. There are strong currents in the lake and it's fed from underground hot springs. Only the very old recall it ever being even ice covered. But there's no telling with this freak cold snap."

"The boat is still out there?" the specialist wrote.

Chen nodded as he put his gloved hands to his ears trying to shield them from the rising wind. Two Jeeps pulled in behind them. The second had the specialist's crime site team. The first, the covered one, had the party man. Somewhere farther back would be a truck with the soldiers. The party man was on a cell phone.

On the other end of the phone a silence greeted the party man's report. Machines whirred, collecting the data from the ether while a tall Han Chinese male stood beside a speaker phone staring out at the beauty of

Beijing. At what he and his had built. At what was now foolishly endangered by the doings on a boat in the midst of far-off Lake Ching. He had a long distance look in his eyes and a copy of Sun Tzu's *The Art of War* in his hands. He reread it every three months. He had done that since he had first begun his rise to power. He had read the book many, many, many times.

He depressed the speak button on the phone. "So the boat didn't sink? That's not good. Is it?"

"No, sir," said the party man as he drew a locked metal case from beneath his seat.

"I assume you came prepared for such an eventuality?"

"I did, sir." The party man in the Jeep opened the case and set the timer.

"Good."

The party man's voice began to bleat about bad luck, freak cold spells and ice storms. The man in Beijing walked away from the speaker phone on his desk. He'd review the tapes later.

After that damned boat was sunk — and the danger to China's future passed.

Chen pointed toward the small motorboats he had arranged for them. "Shall we go, sir?"

The specialist looked at the boat then at the young officer. He hadn't noticed before but Chen was one of the squattest, ugliest men he'd ever seen. "It inspires confidence," the specialist thought. "Odd, but ugliness in a man inspires more than that. It inspires faith."

Two hours later, Chen sat behind the specialist by the

motor of the rocking boat. Before them the partially burnt boat's skin of ice sparkled in the hazy light. An oddly fascinating beauty.

The ice that seemed to grow up the side of the large flat-bottomed ship had secured its purchase on the shoal.

The irony of a burnt boat encased in ice wasn't lost on either Chen or the specialist. It seemed to escape the crime site team and the federal troops who hunched down in their open boat and the party man who followed in a covered cabin cruiser. The party man was still talking on his cell phone — as if he were narrating a sporting event or something.

The wind howled.

"I'm too old for this crap," the specialist thought. But he wrote nothing, just signalled that he wanted to go on board.

The specialist had investigated many crime scenes, but nothing like this. Seventeen corpses. Gunshots. Knife wounds. Violent rippings. Mutilations. And a body swinging.

Only the virulent colours of the whorehouse decor of the boat stopped the victim's blood from standing out like insults to heaven. As it was, the partially frozen dark blood had seeped into the bright red carpets, making them crunch under the specialist's feet as he moved from the large bar to the ornate bedroom to the private video room to the peculiar room with the makeshift runway.

The death rooms.

Seventeen men. Two Caucasians. Five Japanese. Three Koreans — no doubt South Koreans — and seven Chinese who, by the labels on their clothing must have been Taiwanese.

The specialist had an awful taste in his mouth. He spat.

The boat groaned and rolled to one side. The specialist looked to Chen. "It's not solidly held by the shoal, sir. The fires onboard weakened the hull. It could very well sink. Only the ice seems to be keeping it together and afloat." The specialist nodded but his face showed neither concern nor comprehension. "We have all the victims' documents at the Ching station, sir. But we were told to leave the bodies for you . . . to see." The specialist nodded again then scrawled on his pad and turned it to Chen. "How many people have been on board since this happened?"

"Just me and the two officers who helped me collect the documents, on my second trip to the boat."

A sour look crossed the specialist's face. Chen was about to speak but the old man walked away from him. He slashed a single character on his pad. Since he didn't turn the pad to Chen, there was no way of knowing if the man thought him a liar or thought that two officers to help him was too many — or for that matter — too few.

The specialist knew it was a lie. It couldn't be just Chen and two officers. There were indications everywhere that more men had been on the boat. What he didn't know was whether Captain Chen knew that or not.

The specialist filed it away under: politics. And he was old enough to know better than to get involved in that.

The slashed word on the pad had nothing to do with politics though. The specialist had written: "Carnage." It was the first thing that came to him. These men weren't just killed. They'd been annihilated. As if someone was trying to wipe them off the face of the Earth.

The specialist flipped the page and wrote again. This time he turned the pad to Chen. "I need to go back out-side."

Chen followed the specialist as he walked carefully along the icy deck. He helped the old man down to the motorboat where the crime scene photographer was waiting.

The specialist directed the shooting of the exterior of the boat starting with the 14K Triad markings on the hull. He was extremely specific about what he wanted in each shot. After over three-quarters of an hour in the brutal wind and bounding waves, during which time he'd had shots taken from all the cardinal directions, close-ups of the ice formations at the base of the boat, context shots taken of the portals and many, many dif-ferent shots of the scorch marks on the starboard side, he ordered the photographer to follow him back onto the boat.

He started in the bar — with the Chinese. Seven bod-ies. All male. Each more rotund than most mainland

Chinese. From the texture of the skin on their arms and their cuticles he guessed that they were all between fifty and seventy-five years old. From their personal effects that Chen had collected, he knew they were Chinese. He couldn't use their faces to discern their ethnicity because none of the men had faces.

Their features had been carved off with some sort of wide-bladed sharp tool. Wide-bladed because the damage seemed to have been inflicted with one stroke. The specialist couldn't even venture a guess at the implement's name or normal use. A face remover. "I'd like two AK-47s, five banana clips and a face remover for good luck." He didn't laugh at the thought. It could happen in the New China.

He scanned the room. Where the facial skin and cartilage were now, he had no idea.

Three of the Chinese men had been shot from behind while they stood against the mirrored wall. The splatter lines were consistent with the pattern of a small weapon's discharge.

The specialist took out a handkerchief and rubbed it across his face. He was freezing cold but the sweat on his face was hot and stank of dark places. "Have them start up the boat's generator. I want the electricity on in here," he wrote on the pad. Chen immediately relayed the orders.

The specialist took a deep breath. He began showing the photographer the pictures he wanted of these three faceless men. Straight on close-ups. Full body shots. Profile body shots. Wide-angle shots of each body taken from the cardinal points of the compass. Lastly, he ordered shots showing where the bodies were in relationship to each of the glass portals.

The overhead lights flickered on.

He had the bodies turned over and repeated the process. It took more than an hour to finish photographing these three. The position of the fourth dead figure drew his attention. This man had been stabbed with a knife while he was on his knees. The depressions on the carpet and the collection of blood around the depressions suggested that the man had been killed and then held in that kneeling position while . . . while what had been done to his face?

He instructed the photographer to repeat the process with the kneeling man and the two dead men on the barstools.

As the photographer did his methodical work, the specialist prepared himself then moved to what he believed was the oldest of the faceless figures. A knife had been used on him too but this time just to sever the tendons behind the ankles and knees. The man had been tied like a hog then lifted by a foot to dangle from the chandelier. Thickness in the rug beneath the dead man once again told the tale. The man had bled to death, but not from the knife wounds. There were no slashes or gunshot holes in his torso. Just the attempt to obscure, no, erase the face. He must have screamed through the curtain of blood or maybe he was lucky and fainted. The specialist stopped himself. He'd been away too long. Thoughts like that were senseless — worse — they were useless.

The specialist looked at the photographer who nodded that he had completed his task. The specialist indicated that he wanted to be left alone. Once by himself he slowly memorized the room from east to west. Seven dead faceless Chinese men now frozen in their horror. "Or was it my horror?" the specialist asked himself.

He slipped his hand out of his glove and leaned in close to one of the desecrated faces at the bar. He touched the edges of the wound. No raggedness on the forehead cut but a slight flap of skin where the chin ought to be. The upper edge of the cut was bevelled downward. Putting that together with the flap at the bottom seemed to imply that the cut came from top to bottom.

He checked a second faceless man. This one had the same markings. Then he looked up at the figure that dangled from the chandelier. "To die is one thing. To be mutilated after death another. But to be carved up before you die — that's a third," he mouthed silently.

He allowed himself to walk the space. In his inner self he heard their cries. Then he didn't. These were Chinese men — from their suits, wealthy Chinese men. They wouldn't have grovelled. An eerie silence would have greeted the presence of death in their midst.

He heard the boards of the ship creak beneath his feet. Then he stepped in a partially frozen blood patch in the carpet. It crackled under his weight.

How many men were needed to kill and rip the faces off seven Chinese men? He made a note for himself, "Check toxicology for sedatives." How many men? At least three, no more than three hundred, he couldn't even venture a guess. Men and implements . . . guns, knives and face removers.

Then he stepped on something hard buried in the carpet. He leaned down and ran his hand over the rug. There. He pulled back the nap of the rug to reveal the object. It was a jade character on a medallion strung from a broken chain. No doubt the man who wore this would have a duplicate tattooed on his left breast. Triads were seldom subtle. He took a pencil from his pocket and prodded the piece. It shifted in the nap of the carpet. Using the pencil, he picked up the chain. He brought the broken link close to his face, frowned and signalled for the cameraman to shoot the piece. Then he got the man to carefully photograph the broken link on the chain. Four times.

He put the medallion and chain into an evidence bag then took a closer look at the gunshot wounds on the two men at the bar. Clean holes. Old-style wounds with none of the lethal tearing of modern bullets. Before he could come to any conclusion about the wounds he spotted something else in the carpet — dead centre in the room. Two very old spent cartridges. Old-style wounds. Old-style cartridges. He bagged them then stuck his head out the door. Captain Chen hustled over to him. "Tag and take their clothes," he wrote. He passed by Chen and stopped.

Something had caught his eye. A brown splotch on the carpet. Near the door. He knelt down and pressed his palm against the stain. It wasn't frozen as solid as t' blood puddles. He had the photographer shoot the spot and record its location in the room. "Got it, sir," said the cameraman.

The man looked a little green. He was young. He'd get over it. The specialist nodded and motioned the man to follow him into the next room.

The small room with the video monitor.

The Koreans' faces had been left alone but they were nonetheless dead. All three had been shot twice through the right armpit and thrown to the floor. Some marksman! Or else the men were being held still — very still — and then shot from a few feet away. The specialist got to his knees again and leaned in close to the wounds. His knowledge of forensics was encyclopedic but he'd been away from this for a while. As he poked at the dried lacerations, he recalled the telltale signs of a wound caused by a close-range gunshot — burnt hair from the gun-barrel gasses and burnt striations on the skin. Both were clear to see on all three bodies. There was no marksman here — just an executioner. Then he saw the ligature marks on the wrists. He picked up one stiff arm and looked more closely at the markings. Wire? He pushed at the man's shoulder. The arm was loose in the socket. As if it had been pulled out while hanging by the arms. He looked up and there were the cut marks in the overhead beam. Wire-hung from the beam then shot through the armpits. It struck a chord. He looked about him for the wire the killers had used but found none. "Probably in the same place as the seven Chinese faces," thought.

He returned his attention to the cut marks on the beam. The men had been yanked up by wire; that was clear from the depth of the cuts in the beam. Then shot? But not hung. The cut marks were single lines. No enlarged gouges that would have been evident if the men had been hung and struggled. So they had been shot through the armpits then let down. Maybe the murderers were interrupted? By what?

As the photographer took shots of the dead Koreans, the specialist looked at the room. It was lavishly furnished. All the chairs pointed toward the monitor. A VCR sat beside the large screen. He looked at the machine. He had used one of these in the past, but this model was much newer. He punched the power button and watched the digital icons flicker into life. He didn't know what most of them meant.

He pulled the knob on the television. Light came from the screen. Then he hit the play button on the VCR. It must have been on fast forward and he couldn't stop it, but the specialist recognized the images. Hong Kong porno films. Blond European women servicing bespectacled Asian men. He punched another button. The image froze. The man's member on the cheek of the blond girl. A glazed smile on her face.

An old twinge — more an ache — went through his groin.

He looked around. He didn't want anyone seeing him looking at this stuff but he couldn't figure out how to turn the machine off, so he unplugged it from the wall. When he looked up, Chen was there. Pointing at t

VCR and monitor, he scratched on the pad, "Tag and take these too."

He left the room and headed below decks. He was sweating again. This wasn't a crime site, it was an abattoir. He wondered if these men had children. If they would be missed by their wives.

Below deck, he found the five Japanese bodies in a room that had curtains at one end of a small raised runway. All were tied to their chairs — two on one side, three on the other and an empty chair at the foot of the runway. Two had expensive cameras at their feet. All had been cut from just beneath their chins to their navels. Their entrails had been dumped in their laps and then cut so a single strand of intestine dangled down their fronts like a raw purple tail. One man had an expensive pair of Parisian glasses still perched on his face.

On closer examination, it became clear that the spectacles had fallen off and been replaced. No one wore one eyeglass arm behind the ear and one in front. "After the photographer is finished, dust these glasses for prints," he wrote. Chen nodded and scratched a note for himself. "Why would they bother with the glasses?" he wondered.

The photographer began his documenting as the specialist walked around the room. He parted the curtain and found a sound system. He powered it up and hit the play button on the CD player. An American rock band. The music was loud. He turned it off and ejected the disc. He wondered who the group was.

He signalled to Chen. On his pad he wrote, "Take ese back too." As Chen began to dismantle the CD player, the specialist stepped through the curtain out onto the stage.

There was dirt or mud or some kind of thick earth on the runway in patches all the way from backstage to the centre of the platform. He knelt, touched it and brought his finger to his nose. There was no smell. The cold. Thank heavens for the cold or the whole place would have reeked. He signalled Chen for an evidence bag into which he scraped the material. He sealed the bag and handed it back to Chen who took it with him to add to the rest of the collection.

When the specialist stood up, he found himself alone on the runway. The disembowelled men strapped to their chairs seemed to be staring up at him. Ghastly purple penises hanging in front of them. And an empty chair at the end of the runway.

From the small stage, the meaning of the tableau was clear even if the reasoning behind it was not. A thought occurred to him. He carefully stepped off the runway and approached one of the Japanese men. With a pencil he pushed aside the frozen purple grizzle then took out a knife and cut open the man's pants.

Where a penis should have been only a frozen black blotch remained. He stepped back. Chen noticed. "Sir?" All he did was point at the rip in the man's pants. Chen crossed to the dead man as the specialist made his way to the door.

The soldier entered the party man's boat.

"Done, soldier?" he asked holding the cell phone against his chest.

"I put your suitcase where you told me to, sir."

"Good," he said and raised the cell phone to his lips. The soldier stayed for a moment hoping for more than a job-well-done smile. But that was all he got for putting the party man's metal case in the bowels of the boat.

The last room held the Americans. Two men. Both elderly, although he found it hard to be sure of Caucasians' ages. These men looked as if they were lying on their backs on the large, plush bed so they could admire their reflection in the ornate mirror that hung from the ceiling. But on closer examination the specialist saw the cut line on their necks between the Adam's apple and the clavicle. He reached over one of the bodies and put his hands into the man's hair.

The frozen blood resisted him. So he pulled harder.

The head came free of the torso with a sickening plop. He felt his gorge rise and he stumbled back against the far wall. He sank to his knees, his head in his hands. He concentrated and tried to slow his breathing. To collect himself. Then he felt the hair in his hand and looked through his fingers. The dead man's eyes were open and looking right into his.

He dropped the head and looked up. There, on the mirror over the dead Americans' bed in bold red paint, were slashed the characters of the feared 14K Triad. Beneath the name was their motto which had first appeared in the Opium Wars: *Foreign Devils and Traitors Die.*

Up on deck, the specialist leaned over the ice-coated rail. The shoreline wasn't that far away. The sun was setting over the city of Ching. A large cultivated island was far off to one side. It all seemed so peaceful. So . . . so romantic. Yeah, sure. Seventeen dead men — romantic.

A single bird dropped from the sky and plunged through a hole in the ice. Moments later it appeared with a fish in its beak. It stretched its long neck and tilted backward. The fish must have been positioned badly because the bird tossed the wriggling thing into the air. The fish arched as it glinted in the sun. Then the bird grabbed it again — this time by the head. The bird's dinner, still squirming, was pulled in by the bird's throat muscles, then down into the stillness of its belly.

So alive. Then suddenly so dead.

The specialist turned back to the boat. No doubt there had been a lot of activity on board before the murderers arrived. A celebration perhaps. A party. For what? A celebration then sudden swooping death.

Chen's men were busily tagging garments and evidence bags as the specialist carefully descended the ladder and left the ship. Moments later a muffled sound came from the belly of the boat — no more than a cough in the blowing wind — and the boat began to list. Chen and his men got off the vessel quickly. Shortly afterward, it began to sink beneath the lake's icy surface.

The specialist watched the boat enter the nothingness. And he shivered. Then he stopped and began to plan. He knew what Beijing wanted. He also knew what he wanted, no, needed. Slowly, as he watched the las parts of the boat disappear beneath the dark waters of the lake, a plan came into focus.

In Beijing the speaker phone announced the sinking of the boat. The tallish Han Chinese man smiled. But only briefly. This was far from over and he knew it.

Three hours later, at the Ching police station, Chen showed the specialist the documents that had been taken from the men.

One of the Taiwanese had a ship pilot's licence. "Well, that settled one question. Only five thousand left," he thought.

Another document showed a receipt for the boat rental. The specialist circled the name of the boat operator. In another wallet the specialist found a receipt for a large amount of prepared food. The specialist circled the name and address of the restaurant in Ching.

Much of the rest of the material was in languages the specialist didn't understand. He pushed them aside and looked at Chen.

"Yes, sir?"

"Tell me about the local 14K Triad activity," he scratched on his pad.

Chen did.

"So they're big enough and strong enough to do this sort of thing?" the specialist inquired.

"I guess, sir. Shall I arrange to bring in their leaders?"

The specialist put down his pen and stared at his ncient hands. He closed his eyes and forced himself to mentally retrace his steps through the death rooms on the boat, ending with the 14K Triad insignia on the mirror. He sighed and opened his eyes.

Chen awaited his orders.

The specialist snatched up his pen and slashed at the pages, "Make sure the Triad leaders don't go anywhere. Tell them they are to stay put until we find out who murdered the seventeen foreigners on the boat. You can do that tomorrow. Right now bring me some suspects, Captain Chen. I have a plane to catch and I need to make an arrest."

At Chen's shocked look, the specialist turned to the window. How very different this small city was from his home. He sighed silently. How very different his life had become since the night he was shot in the Pudong industrial area, across the Huangpo River from Shanghai.

Chen held out an arrest warrant.

The specialist took it and signed the bottom — Inspector Wang.

CHAPTER SIX

PHOTOS, PEASANTS, ANKLETS

ong drank in China's heartland as it sped past. He wished he could open the window but wasn't about to give the thug and the politico the joy of hearing him ask.

He was slowly piecing together where they were going. They'd been travelling southeast for two days. This area of China, either in Shanxi or Shaanxi province — he couldn't tell which yet — was far from his stomping grounds in Shanghai, but he was a lot closer to home than he had been a mere three days ago. At least he was on the right side of the wall and blessedly far from the windswept loess plateau on which "his" village in the west stood.

Then he saw the first of the road signs. Five hundred kilometres to Xian — the ancient imperial capital of the Qin Dynasty. Fong stared at the sign with its shadowed image of the terra-cotta warriors. For a second he couldn't figure out what was bothering him about it. Then he got it. It was in English. Of course, Xian was a major tourist destination.

Good.

He sat back in his seat and allowed his eyes to shut.

The growing heat and the rumble of the car engine lulled sleep out of his bones. And in this sleep there were visions. Visions so sweet he dreaded that on his waking they would make him cry out to sleep again.

That night they parked him in another jail cell. This one was older than the previous night's and gratefully, as far as Fong was concerned, empty.

Fong caught an image of himself in the polished steel mirror that was set deep in the cell's brickwork. For the first time in a very long while he allowed himself to examine his appearance closely. The hardness of his features surprised him. His skin, as if somehow rougher, no longer accented the delicate bones of his face. He removed his Mao jacket and dropped it to the floor. The rustle of the Shakespeare texts he'd hidden there was reassuring. He pulled his shirt and undershirt over his head. The assassin's wound stood out in high relief on his side, an ugly reminder of a near ending. He turned sideways. His body was undeniably thickening. "I'm no longer young," he thought, "no longer able to . . ." He didn't bother completing the thought. He turned from the mirror and put on his clothes. He'd already had two great loves in his life, Fu Tsong and the American, Amanda Pitman. He expected no more. Two loves were unusual largess from the Great God Irony, who rules unopposed in the hearts of the Chinese. Fong knew that to be true.

He looked down at his hands. On the night of his exile from Shanghai, a train porter had slammed the carriage door on his left hand. It had snapped a small bone and broken a blood vessel under the nail of the ring finger. The snapped bone he had ignored, but the broken blood vessel had forced a small pool of blood to form at the very base of the cuticle between the nail and the skin. The pain caused by the pressure took four days to pass, three days before the hard-seat journey to the west ended.

The purple stain rose as the nail grew. It was now, more than two years later, all but gone. "Like much of my life," he thought as he walked around the cell consciously avoiding looking into the polished steel mirror a second time.

Late that night he awoke. The cell's mesh-covered overhead bulb flooded the cell with a garish green light. Fong had no idea of the time, but he knew it was late because of the silence in the place. Jails are noisy, except in the dead of the night. Then he saw three large manilla packets on the floor of the cell.

They were the same as the one he'd seen in the car. He knelt down and opened one. There were over a hundred 3 1/2" X 3 1/2" photographs. The second contained a few less. The third a few more. The top of each photo had a hole punched in it.

He tossed the packets aside — but not through the bars.

He knew they wanted him to look at the pictures — to be lured into analyzing them. Despite that. Despite knowing that, he picked up a packet. Once he looked at the first photo he was hooked. Suddenly he was back in Shanghai. A real police officer again. The head of Special

Investigations. For, if ever there was a case for special investigations — a crime against foreigners — this was it.

A boat. Naturally — they were going to a lake!

He sorted the pictures. Exterior shots, shots of a bedroom, shots of a room with a small runway, shots of a video room and shots of a bar. Shots of Triad markings and a 14K medallion.

He went back to the exterior shots of the flat-bottomed boat. He examined the Triad markings just above the waterline. They glistened. At first it was hard for him to discern that the boat was covered in ice. Then he saw the scorch marks through the ice and a shiver shot down his spine — the mongoose rolled over and blinked into waking.

Fong got up and paced. He went to look out the window, as if he were still in his office on Shanghai's Bund. As if he could see the rising figures of the great new buildings of the Pudong industrial area just across the Huangpo River. Of course, all he saw was brick and bars. This was hardly the splendour of his office on the Bund. This was a provincial jail and he was being used, but he didn't care. He felt alive. On the trail of something. Then he stopped himself. No. Not on the trail of anything — except a way home.

He flipped through the pictures of the boat's exterior, separating out the photos of the Triad insignias and the scorch markings. Then he took four that had close-ups of the portals. He went to lean the pictures against the base of the wall then noticed the surface was covered with small nails placed at four-inch intervals, perfect for hanging photos like the ones in his hands.

"Fuck them," he thought, but he couldn't resist hanging the four pictures he'd selected. Then he chose photos of the rooms that showed exterior windows. It took him some time, but eventually he figured out the positioning of the four rooms in the boat. All were in the bow. The video room on deck level to port, the room with the raised stage beside it to starboard, the two other rooms directly beneath them.

He couldn't guess what was midship or aft. He'd never been on a boat. He hated the water almost as much as he hated the countryside.

Then he sorted the photos of the victims. Using the wide shots of the spaces, he was able to divide the victims into their respective rooms. Quickly he realized that the five gutted men were Japanese, the two decapitated men were Caucasian (from their clothes he guessed American but he'd noticed in his last years working in Shanghai that most Westerners dressed like Americans — he couldn't for the life of him imagine why). The three in the video room were Korean. He guessed that the seven faceless men were Chinese.

Fong hung the full-body shots beneath the photos of the rooms in which they'd been found. Then he hung the many detail photographs of each victim below the full-body shot.

He paused for a moment and approached the pictures of the bar room. Something was missing. He checked the wide-angle shots. What was missing? What? Then he figured it out — and smiled.

By the time he had all the pictures arranged it was midmorning and there was hardly any empty space on the cell walls. It had taken him at least six hours. Maybe more. It was as if he'd fallen into the photographs and time had slipped away. Now, surrounded by the gruesome gallery, he examined the panorama of his handiwork, the order he had brought to this stupendous chaos. Another shiver up his spine. He couldn't tell whether it was from excitement or fear.

Fong turned slowly in the midst of the images. He was an intruder here, a voyeur of the dead. Then he stopped. He understood why he'd shivered. All this death made him feel alive. Gave him a reason to be. "No," he told himself. "A way home," he insisted. Yet he wasn't sure.

"Nicely done, Zhong Fong."

Fong turned to see a uniformed officer standing outside his cell door. He immediately tucked his chin to his chest and bowed his head. But even in his brief look at the man, Fong was struck by his blunt, stocky, pimply ugliness.

"No need for that. My name is Captain Chen. I am in charge of the investigation. We are honoured to have a man of your reputation working on the case."

Fong looked up. Captain Chen was younger than Fong. Probably in his late twenties, definitively ugly. His square hairless face bore just the slightest wisp of foreign markings. Tibetan? No, Korean. They were the only things of delicacy in his entire being. Fong pulled his eyes away from the younger man's face. He noted the army bars on his uniform. Only Shanghai, Beijing and Ghuongdzu had their own police forces. The rest of the country was policed by the army.

Chen repeated himself. "We are honoured to have a man of your reputation working on the case."

"I bet you are," Fong thought. But when he lifted his chin, the smile on his lips was completely noncommittal. A Chinese smile.

Chen pulled on the door and entered. It wasn't locked.

"If I may, Zhong Fong," he said as he took a close-up of one of the Americans and put it under the other American's full-body shot. "The heads had been switched."

Fong found himself raising his eyebrows. Interested. He immediately covered by coughing into his hand.

"A specialist from the North supervised the taking of these pictures. I hope you find them adequate."

"This 'specialist' knew what he was doing."

"He was very efficient."

Fong looked at the photos again. Each was one of a set. A shot of a body then the same from a higher elevation. Perhaps standing on the shoulders of another man. Perhaps not. But meticulous. A professional. Someone who knew his way around a crime scene. Fong took in the pictorial display again. "A lot of dead people on a boat," he said.

"A boat covered in ice, stuck on a shoal, out in a lake. Ironically, it was also burnt."

"Burnt in the ice?" Fong was surprised by the intensity of his own interest.

"We had a freezing rain followed by a frigid snap. The three coldest days in living memory."

"So can I assume these were taken in March?"

"If you did, you'd be wrong. January. Very early January."

"January? That's over three months ago!" Fong almost shouted.

Captain Chen nodded. "It's a sensitive case. Beijing wanted all due care taken."

"Now why would that be?" Fong thought, but he put a false smile on his face and asked, "What is it you want from me, Captain Chen?"

"Nothing, Traitor Zhong." The politico stepped out of the shadows across the way. "Captain Chen wants nothing from you. This kind of personal thinking got you into trouble to begin with, Traitor Zhong. Captain Chen wants nothing from you. Your country wants something from you. Is that understood, Traitor Zhong?"

Fong tilted his head, but only after a pause that was clearly noted by all three men. The politico was about to rise to the bait, but then he backed off and lit a cigarette. The sweet fumes tugged at Fong's nose. "You were the head of Special Investigations, Traitor Zhong. You have dealt with crimes against foreigners before. We want to know who did this to the foreigners. What else would we want?"

Fong chose to dodge that question but noted that the "we" the politico used sounded strangely like a first person pronoun. "Why the delay? Three months is a long time." Fong thought he knew the answer to his question, but he couldn't resist hearing the man admit that they couldn't solve this one on their own.

The politico smiled. "Even you, Traitor Zhong, can understand that this has become a matter of international concern." Then, as if it were an afterthought, he added, "Foreign governments want to see justice done."

Fong stared at the man. Finally he spat out, "Just pick out some dumb peasants and claim they did it. Execute them in public if the West wants blood for blood." He almost said "measure for measure."

"The specialist did that — picked out some dumb peasants, Traitor Zhong."

Fong again stared at the man in front of him. This was all the more baffling for his admission. "So?" he asked, completely at a loss.

"Would you like to interview them, Traitor Zhong?" The politico was smiling.

"They haven't been executed?"

"Obviously not, unless, Traitor Zhong, you're capable of interrogating the dead."

It was hard to argue with that. But it bothered Fong that the politico's final statement was the only thing out of the man's mouth that made much sense.

Fong had seen both sides of a jail's bars. He preferred the side he was standing on now. The side that had a corridor leading to an unlocked exit door.

The three men in the cell on the other side of the bars

were nondescript men of the land. More like stones than men. They looked a lot like each other. They were brothers. The guards prodded them to taciturn awakening. Three flat resigned sets of eyes focused on Fong as he entered the cell. Fong looked down at the files Captain Chen had given him.

Fong knew that interrogations were best done in private. But he decided against causing a scene by asking the thug, the politico and Chen to leave. There was Fong's vanity too. He was always a gifted interrogator and he couldn't resist showing these men that he had lost none of his talent.

He did his best not to wince when the door slammed shut behind him.

Fong looked at the three brothers who stood accused of masterminding and then carrying out the murder of the seventeen foreigners on the luxury boat on Lake Ching. According to Chen's files, all three were from a local island community. All looked to be in their early-to mid-twenties. One of them had the unlikely given name of Hesheng, meaning "in this year of peace."

Fong started with that.

The year of peace was 1949. It would make the man fifty years old. He was clearly less than half that. "Your parents played a joke with your name, Hesheng."

The men didn't laugh. The men didn't do anything. "How old are you, Hesheng?" Fong asked casually.

Something passed over the man's face. Was it anger, rage, fear — what? Then it was gone. No, not gone — stopped behind the hard mask of the man's hatred. Fong did his best to calm his Shanghanese accent and tried again with his best country speech. "So are you twenty or thirty, Hesheng? Just give me a hint."

Again that cloud crossed the man's face. This time it also crossed the faces of the other two. "Well, I'm enjoying this, how about you?"

Fong turned from them and then whirled back on Hesheng. "They're going to execute you for a crime that you're too stupid to have committed and too fucking frightened to deny. Do you understand that, you ox? Or is that beyond your limited capabilities? Ever see what happens to a man when he's dangled from a rope? His face turns purple, he shits his pants, he fights for breath. He claws at the noose. He kicks his feet . . . and the crowd cheers. Trust me on this, Hesheng, they cheer, and loudly. Is that what you want? Is it?" For a moment, it looked as if the man was going to speak then he turned away. "Open your fat mouth and tell me if that's what you want?" Fong shouted.

"Go away," another of the young men said. His voice was surprisingly low. The timbre like aged liquor. Fong whirled around. When Fong stepped toward him, the man repeated his command. "Go away." Again that low voice. A sense of having been places. Seen things.

The third man came to the speaker's defence and repeated his command. Another deep, aged voice in a young face. Fong found it incomprehensible. "I know you three didn't do this. I know it. Now help me prove it."

"Why?"

That low voice again. Fong looked at them almost

unable to answer. "Because . . . it's your life."

"That's what we told him," said Hesheng.

A moment passed before Fong demanded, "Who?" The other two drew Hesheng behind them. Fong had missed his chance. He cursed himself. He was out of practice. Back in Shanghai he'd never have missed the opening that Hesheng had offered. But that was almost five years ago. "Who did you tell, Hesheng?" shouted Fong, knowing full well that there would be no answer.

The men turned away from him and returned to that dark, still place from which they'd momentarily surfaced. Fong thought of them as three large rocks. Only marginally alive.

Emerging from the line of cells, he found the politico smoking in the front room. The man at first hid the smile on his lips, then gave up the effort and did everything but laugh in Fong's face. "So did you get a confession, Traitor Zhong?"

"From the look on their faces you managed to bludgeon that out of them a long time ago." Fong stepped in close to the politico. "So what is it you really want from me here?"

"Are you threatening me, Traitor Zhong?" Fong hadn't realized that he had grabbed the man by his lapels. He pulled his hands back and turned away. "Find out who did this, Zhong Fong. That's all that is wanted. Do your duty. Use your talent."

The anger and sarcasm lathered on the word *talent* was so deep, so fulsome that it took Fong's breath away.

man snapped his fingers and two uniformed came into the room. One knelt quickly and ped a metal ankle cuff on Fong.

Fong looked down at the thing. "It's electronic, Traitor Zhong. A little something that happened in the world while you were on vacation. It can tell us exactly where you are whenever we want to know."

Fong stared at it. The single red eye blinked up at him. He had to use his considerable will power to stop from reaching down and tearing at the thing.

"No, Traitor Zhong, it can't be taken off without the proper code. And I assure you I will not supply the code until you find out what we want." The "we" that sounded like "I" again. "Welcome back to the police force — Fong. Second chances are rare in this life. Don't waste this one."

The man rose and moved past Fong, close enough to touch. A challenge. Hit me! But Fong didn't. The confusion in Fong was whether he didn't slug this guy because he knew better than to hit a ranking party official or whether he was no longer capable of fighting back.

He didn't know.

He hung his head for a second.

The hideous anklet blinked its red eye up at him.

CHAPTER SEVEN

IT BEGINS

{ quat Captain Chen drove up in an army issue Jeep. The thug and the Chaika were nowhere to be seen. The politico hopped in beside him. Fong climbed in the back. "At least I'm not handcuffed," he thought. Then he looked down at his ankle and knew that wasn't really true.

They drove into downtown Ching — downtown nowhere as far as Fong could tell. Not because it was a small city on the edge of a large lake but because little of what, at one time, must have made this place distinct from any other place remained. Like so much of the country, it had been made over in the Soviet-dominated period. The place reeked of a false practical-ity. Straight lines that people didn't want to walk, square buildings that housed people but not souls — and worst of all, no old town. What little withstood the Sovietization of the place had probably been demol-ished by the Red Guards.

The air tasted of some sort of industrial pollutant. Fong couldn't tell which one. The streets were grime-coated. This was no resort town. Xian was far away. Ching didn't have to be kept nice for tourists.

They whizzed by the docks. Little activity to do with the lake was in evidence. It was as if the water didn't really exist, or that it was seen as nothing more than a momentary impediment to the growth of this non-place. In fact it was eerie quiet.

The politico pointed to a street corner and a coyly marked party hotel. Captain Chen pulled the vehicle over and the politico hopped out. He pulled open the back door and Fong stepped out onto the cracked pavement. Then, like a hotel doorman, the politico opened the front passenger door.

Fong looked at him.

The man smiled. His sharp pointy teeth looked rusty and his breath smelt heavy on the snap of the spring air. "Do your duty for China, Traitor Zhong," he hissed.

"I have always done my duty for China, comrade." Fong's voice cracked. The politico's smile widened. "Am I to be supplied with the equipment needed to launch a major investigation?"

"You will be supplied with the necessities, Traitor Zhong. These are hard times. We all must do our duty with as little as possible . . . and as quickly as possible. In this new age, time is money."

The man turned and walked into the hotel. Fong caught a glimpse of the interior as the door swung open. The opulence reminded him of the photos of the rugs and draperies on the burnt, sunken boat — the one with seventeen dead foreigners.

He got back into the front seat of the car. "Where to, Captain Chen?"

The politico's phone call travelled on totally secure lines. It was answered on the second ring. "Yes." The voice was distorted by the speaker phone.

The politico took a breath. "He's in place, sir."

"Good." The speaker phone crackled for a moment, then the line went dead.

The politico lit a cigarette and let out a rope of smoke. But it didn't relieve his tension. He'd never get used to speaking to one of the three most powerful men in the Middle Kingdom.

Twenty minutes later, Fong stood on the filthy floor of a single-storey abandoned factory. The west side of the high ceiling had a bank of grimy slanted windows that at one time could have been louvered open. But that was clearly long ago. Rows of the kind of struts used to mount machine lathes stuck out of the floor. The lathes were long gone. Rusting metal barrels were stacked all the way to the ceiling in three of four corners. The place was dark and dank. "As they intended it to be," Fong reminded himself.

Against the south wall was a square, raised concrete slab that had at one time been tiled. A few chipped tiles still remained. Fong assumed there had once been walls to demarcate an office. On the slab were two desks, two chairs, two phones and a typewriter. A large topographic map was spread out on the floor. The crime scene photos were tacked to the wall.

Fong looked closely at the wall. There would be listening devices. He didn't look for them. What would he do if he found them? Better to accept them as part of the working conditions of the job.

After a few minutes of questioning, it became clear to Fong that Chen was the only officer assigned to assist him. "Great. We each solve eight and a half murders and we're done," he thought.

Fong turned to the map and with a sigh asked, "How big's the lake, Chen?" Fong consciously left the Captain part out of the ugly fellow's name.

Chen noted the impoliteness, then responded. "Over ten kilometres at its longest. Just over two at its widest . . . Fong."

Fong looked at the younger man. "Toady," he thought. "What do I care what a toady calls me?" Fong smiled. "Is Ching the only town on the lake?" This time Fong left his name off altogether.

Again Chen noted the rudeness but answered, "There's a smaller town to the north and a village on the western shore."

"And this?" Fong pointed at the only large island in the lake.

"The Island of the Half-wits, the locals call it. If it has a real name I've never heard it. The people in the city have little to do with the residents there. It's a farming community. No one remembers when those families got there. Very likely centuries ago. The locals won't inter-marry with them because the families on the island have intermarried with each other for . . . for however long they've been there."

"Hence the Island of the Half-wits?"

"That would be my guess."

"And the three brothers that were arrested . . ."

"Were from the island, sir."

Fong hadn't heard anyone call him "sir" in a very long time. He tried not to be influenced by it. But he was.

"The specialist needed to make an arrest. That's what he said. He left it up to the local officers. They brought in thirty or so suspects. I think it was only local prejudice that those sorry men you saw were included."

"Any indication why the specialist chose those three?"

"None, sir. He interrogated them in private. It took a long time before he made up his mind and charged those three with the murders."

"If he just needed to make an arrest, he could have charged the first ones that he saw."

"I don't deny that."

"I want to see the transcripts of the interrogations."

"That's not possible." Before Fong could question him further he added, "None were made."

"What?"

"It wasn't in our hands. The whole thing was run by the specialist. He had his own political adviser and a small army of soldiers and technicians. It was his show, sir, not ours."

"Were local Triad members interviewed?"

"They were contacted."

"Who exactly?"

"Pak Tsz Sin."

"The White Paper Fan?"

"Yes, sir."

The White Paper Fan was the ritual name for a Triad's financial officer. Like all Triad members, he was also identified by a code number drawn from Buddhist and Taoist numerology traditions. Fong was amazed that he could recall that 415 was the Pak Tsz Sin's numerical assignation.

"Who else was put on warning?"

"Cho Hai . . ." The Grass Slipper was a Triad's liaison officer. Sort of a gangster PR guy. His number was 432 . . . "and Hung Kwan . . ." also called Red Pole. He was the Triad's field commander. He was often well versed in martial arts but was considered expendable by the upper echelons. His number was 426.

"No one big was contacted? No Shan Chu or Fu Shan Chu?" These were the boss and the sub-boss. "Not even the Heung Chu or the Sing Fung?" The former was in charge of rituals and was traditionally third in command. The latter was fourth in command and looked after franchising the Triad.

"No, sir. The specialist didn't think it necessary."

Fong thought back to the Triad mark on the exterior of the boat and the slashed markings and message on the mirror. Then he thought of the four close-up photos of the broken chainlink on the Triad medallion.

Why four of the same thing?

Fong had dealt with the Triads in Shanghai. They were a sultry mix of ritual and fear-mongering. Women, gambling and extortion were their stock-in-trade.

Not mass murder.

Triads had been active in China since 1674 when the Manchu invaders ended the Ming Dynasty. Myth had it that five monks established the initial five Triads to try and reinstate the Mings. Because the Ming family name was Hung and their royal colour was red, the Triads took both upon themselves.

The Triads played major roles in the Szechuan, Hupeh and Shansi rebellions in the 1790s, the Cudgels uprising in the 1850s, and in the Boxer Rebellion in Beijing in the 1890s. Dr. Sun Yat Sen, the founder of the Republic of China, allied himself with the Hsing Chung Triad in 1906 to begin the revolution that eventually led to the fall of the Manchu Dynasty in 1911. Sun Yat Sen's successor, Yuan Shih Kai, openly worked with the Triads. When he gave way to Chiang Kai Shek, the doors of power opened to the Triads because the generalissimo was a high-ranking member of the Shang Hai Green Tang. From his capital in Nanking, Chiang led his Triad in battles against the Communists under Mao Tse Tung. During the Japanese occupation, the Triads collaborated with the enemy. Later they aided Chiang Kai Shek's retreat to Taiwan.

However, by that time several of the "franchises" of the major Triads had thought better of their alliance with Chiang Kai Shek. The old generalissimo was obviously losing. The Triads from the interior, especially around Xian, cut a deal with the Communists. In return for their support against the nationalists, the renegade Triads were to be left to their own devices. As long as they were discreet.

Seventeen dead foreigners didn't strike Fong as very discreet.

Fong looked at Captain Chen again. "How'd you get stuck with this duty?"

"I was first there. I took the call."

Yes, but . . . the man was hiding something. Fong only took a moment to figure out what. Chen was young — and not unlike himself at that age — ambitious. Fong smiled.

"What, sir?"

"Nothing, Captain. I was young once, too." Before Chen could question him on that, Fong continued, "What was this specialist like?"

"Old."

The word came out angry. Chen had obviously not intended that and he quickly apologized for his disrespectful statement.

"It's all right, Captain. The alternative to getting old is even more complicated to think about. What else about him?"

"He had white hair that he didn't bother dying. His legs seemed unsteady. His face was broad. No wedding ring."

"Accent?"

"He didn't speak."

"Huh?"

"He didn't speak. He was a mute. He did nothing but write on his notepad what he wanted done."

The mongoose stood on its hind legs beside Fong's spine, tasting the air.

Fong turned away and looked around the deserted factory. What had they built here? Why was it closed? How many people no longer had work? What terror lurked in those corroding metal barrels? He walked past Chen to the array of photographs on the wall. Again he admired their precision. The ordered detail of the workmanship. Somehow familiar. "How tall was he?"

"Tall for a Han Chinese. Maybe five foot eight. Why? Do you know him?"

Fong shook his head, "How could I? China's a big country. There are many crime scene detectives. Many experts." Though something about this specialist did seem familiar. But a mute CSU guy? Whoever heard of that? "Did he have any visible scars?"

Chen nodded.

"On his neck," he pointed to his throat just below his Adam's apple. "It looked like a surgical scar. He signed the arrest warrant *Inspector Wang*."

Fong told himself it wasn't possible. Gunshots in the Pudong industrial area had ended Wang Jun. Besides, Wang was a common name. Shit, all Chinese names were common. Call out "Chan" in a crowded market and a hundred heads would turn. Fong considered it for a moment more then changed the topic. "Let's get started. I want the photographs duplicated, the second set labelled then hung on the far wall."

"I have access to photographic equipment, I could get full transparencies made, sir."

Fong had no idea what transparencies were but said, "Fine. But first get all the dead men's documents translated, catalogued and laid out beneath their pictures. All the evidence bags opened and associated with the correct victim. Locate the man who owns the boat. And the owner of the restaurant who supplied the food. And any dock worker who touched that boat that night. And everyone who might have been on the lake that night. And . . ." Fong looked up.

Chen was writing furiously. The Captain finally caught up with Fong and looked to him for further orders. "Something else, sir?"

"Yes, Captain Chen." Fong held his breath and told himself that there was no other way. That he had to keep his eye on the goal — getting home. And there was no way to get back to Shanghai without finding who murdered those men on that boat. And there was no way to find that out without his people. Fine. He sighed. Just one problem. He wasn't sure if he'd survive the beating that would no doubt follow his demand. But he saw no other choice available to him.

"What, sir?" asked Chen.

Fong took another deep breath and let fly, "Tell whoever runs you, Captain Chen or whoever the fuck you are, that I need my people from Shanghai to work on this or else they haven't got a chance of finding out what really happened out on that lake. Get me Lily from forensics and the coroner from the Hua Shan hospital. Tell whoever it is that owns you that if these people aren't here, I'm not working on this case."

Chen's mouth flopped open.

"While you're at it, tell them that I need some chalk

and a wide-topped desk, a model of that boat and, oh
yeah, where's the can in this place?"

Far to the east and north, the events in the deserted factory in Ching were being monitored closely. "Why
would they resurrect the murderer Zhong Fong?" Her
assistant's question hung in the air as Madame Wu
looked out her office window. She put her hands up to
the cool glass and pressed. She had old peasant hands.
Like her mother's. But not scalded and blistered like her
mother's from picking the cocoons of silkworms out of
vats of boiling water. She remembered the agony on her
mother's face as winter approached. She remembered
the humbling poverty.

Then the Japanese and the resistance. And change.

She tapped the glass of her office window. "So many
changes," she thought.

Her assistant repeated his question. "Why would
they resurrect Zhong Fong, Madame Minister?"

She didn't answer although she knew the answer to his
question. She was thinking about the principles of leverage. She had been trained as a civil engineer, after all. If I
could stand on a platform far enough away from the
Earth, I could move the planet by simply pressing down
on a stick. Leverage and distance did that. The principle
was sound. Positioning, not strength, determined victory.

"Could he be made to work for us, Madame
Minister?"

She felt herself on the platform. All she need do is
press — and with luck the entire world would change.

The whole history of China would be redirected. Back. Back to where this all began. Back to a time before money was everything. "We will soon regain Hong Kong. Our window on the world is secure. Now all we need do is shut the door," she thought.

Madame Wu turned to her assistant and said, "Yes, he could be made to work for us." But what she thought was: "He had better be made to work for us or all my years of planning and all the risks I've taken will be for nothing."

Madame Wu smiled.

"Madame Minister?" asked her assistant.

"Nothing — nothing that you'd understand." She turned from him and looked out the window. It was beginning to rain on Tiananmen Square.

CHAPTER EIGHT

GETTING BACK TO THE TEAM

"They're not going to be pleased about this," Captain Chen said, then turned on his heel and left. Fong looked up at the slanted bank of filthy windows in the ceiling of the place, then stepped into the fading squares of light on the floor.

He just nodded. "No shit," he said to the air.

His two years west of the Wall had taught him the value of simple pleasures — like watching day's end. He removed his padded jacket, then his shirt. The milky rays of dusk felt cool on his skin. He sat and enjoyed the movement of the sun's dying light on him, around him.

When it was finally dark, he took a deep breath and flipped the wall switch on. The light from the naked bulbs had no warmth or movement to it. Fong turned to the wall of photos. So much death. So many passings at once. And such brutality. He focused on the pictures of the Chinese men with the scraped-off faces. Obliterated faces. Why do this? Fong got up and went to the pictures. He ran his fingers across the first photograph. He had seen violence in his time but nothing like this.

Fong glanced at the photos of the Japanese men with

the lengths of intestine down their fronts, and nothing in their pants.

Erased faces — removed genitals.

He glanced at the Triad markings, but his eyes quickly moved to the Americans whose heads had been switched. This message Fong recognized. Many Chinese couldn't tell one Caucasian from the next. Switch the heads — what's the difference.

But so much death. Hardly discreet. Un-Triad-like.

The ancient word *chi* welled up inside him like something long buried coming up in the spring rains.

Chi was a word that evoked both awe and fear. Chinese mania, the foreigners called it. There had been famous outbreaks before. Reports of those infamous eruptions of *chi* were whispered about at the dark end of alleys in Shanghai's Old City when a white person made the mistake of thinking it a cute San Francisco Chinatown.

Fong took one more look at the pictures then turned off the light. He walked in the gloom. Only the steady blinking of the red light on his ankle cuff broke the darkness.

He lay on his back and tucked his rolled shirt beneath his neck. He pulled the Mao jacket up to his chin and listened to the silence of the place for a moment; then sleep took him.

Fong never felt the plastic mask slide over his mouth and nose. The clang of a cymbal woke him. Somewhere, deep in the recesses of the deserted factory, he thought he heard an arhu's mournful notes added to the cymbal's insistence. He struggled to a sitting position, disoriented, unable to tell if this was a dream or actually happening.

The mongoose lulled in a drugged sleep.

Then a single light cut through the darkness. A spotlight. Into the light stepped Fu Tsong in full Peking Opera makeup and costume — ready for her role in *Journey to the West*. A drum sounded and she pulled a four-foot-long feather from her headdress down into her mouth and struck a pose.

"I'm asleep," Fong shouted then leapt to his feet. The light snapped out. Silence. Then the drum sounded just once. Another light snapped on. This time it was right in front of him. Fu Tsong stepped into the light. She was so close that Fong could smell the greasepaint. She raised her elegant arms and the costume's long sleeves furled down to her shoulders. Her hand reached out and touched his throat — and he knew. He closed his eyes — and accepted.

Her hands. No, its hands. Cold. Male. Then the hypodermic pierced his neck.

Fong's eyes fluttered open. He maintained consciousness long enough to look into the eyes behind the greasepaint. They were unblinking. Hard.

"The hallucinogen should wear off soon." It was a voice Fong didn't recognize. He felt a cold hand on his face. Then strong fingers pried open his eyelids. A shard of pain shot through his skull as a bright penlight snapped his irises shut.

He spat in the direction of the light.

A curse. A kick to his head. A shouting match. "Break his teeth. He has too much pride." The sound of far-off cracking. Hard chips on his tongue.

"Typhoid and toothless sounds good. Shoot him up again."

A pinprick breaking the continuity of his skin. Then delirium. Gentle delirium.

Fong laughed in his sleep. Then he felt a strong hand on his throat and saw those hard eyes again. He found himself falling. As if down a well. As if backward. At night.

"His fever's breaking." A soft voice.

"That's quick." A hard male voice.

"He might have been infected before."

"Is that likely?"

"No, but it's possible I guess. Damn!"

"I want him under longer!" The politico.

Fong gasped for air. There was something covering his mouth. He wanted to scream, but found himself awash in a place between wake and sleep where everything slid and changed and lashed out.

Snippets of voices.

"Well, what did he say?" The politico. "What was his plan?" The politico again.

"Well, he asked me to do a stack of things for him." Chen's voice.

Then a laugh. Not Chen's. It could have been the thug's laugh but Fong wasn't sure.

"Open his mouth."

A gasp. "What happened here?

"He fell." The politico. General laughter.

"Very funny. This could take days to fix."

"It can't." The politico.

"Well, there's a faster way."

"Do it." The politico.

"Hold him still. This'll hurt."

A whirring sound. Something prying open his mouth. Then something hot. Molten on his teeth. Spikes of pain. Then on his upper teeth. More spikes.

Then his nose was covered and he floated — tasting oblivion.

He was in a bed. He could feel the crisp coolness of hospital sheets. He sensed it was morning. Which morning he couldn't guess. He allowed the light to filter through his eyelashes and he slowly turned his head from side to side. The window was to his right.

He opened his eyes.

Sunlight streamed through a large glass pane. A slender silhouette interrupted the square of light.

"Hey ho, short stuff," the silhouette said in English. "You more looking than usual rotten." Sort of English.

Lily.

The hawking sound of an old throat being cleared announced the presence of the coroner from Shanghai's Hua Shan hospital. Fong couldn't see him, but he could hear him move the phlegm up and down his turkey neck.

A squat, blunt silhouette entered the light. Captain Chen.

Fong tried to say, "What brings you brigands to this part of the Middle Kingdom?" but it came out as, "W'ings u'ds'to s'art o'd Mi'l K'dom?"

Lily turned toward the window. The light caught her features. Fong saw a look of horror there.

"They must have hurt me badly. But they didn't annihilate me like the killers did to those people on the boat. No. They need me. They even brought my team together," he thought.

He reached up and Chen helped him gain a sitting position. "Time to get back to work, sir?"

The sound of a stick match breaking fire and the whiff of sulphur drew his attention. "Looks fine to me. Not ready for my autopsy table yet," the coroner spat out the phlegm. "Soon though."

Fong smiled at the old man. "Why aren't you dead?" he articulated carefully.

"Bad luck, I guess."

Fong nodded and slowly swung his legs out of the bed. Neither of his Shanghanese colleagues missed the blinking of the ankle bracelet.

Fong ran his tongue over his teeth — they felt odd. He signalled to Chen to lean in. The ugly young man did. Fong spoke slowly, enunciating clearly, "Tell Lily I'm starting a new fashion." He lifted up his cuffed leg.

Chen relayed the message. Lily stepped forward. The light picked up her sharp facial features — lit her beautiful, pained eyes. She pointed at the ankle bracelet. "Do those come in green?"

Fong tried to laugh. But it hurt. "Help me stand."

Chen helped him to his feet. "How long have I been out?"

"Two and a half weeks," said the coroner flipping through the chart he'd taken from the foot of the bed. "A fast recovery, I'd say."

"From what?"

"Typhoid, it says here. You've been on heavy sedatives for the past three days."

"Waiting for you two to arrive," Fong thought, but didn't speak. Just nodded. That hurt too. What hurt most was Lily's refusal to look at him. She kept glancing out the window as if there was something to see.

"Ready, sir?" asked Chen as he held up Fong's Mao jacket.

For a moment Fong panicked, but then he heard the reassuring rustle of the Shakespeare texts he'd sewn into the lining. He tried to take a step but nausea overwhelmed him. He fell to the floor and quickly released the contents of his stomach.

Chen helped him to his feet.

"The nausea should pass soon, Fong. It's from the sedatives," said the coroner.

He nodded. They headed out.

Lily's eyes never met his.

CHAPTER NINE

THE 14K TRIAD, THE RECREATION, THE MEETING

The building in which the meeting was taking place was new but the ideas were as old as the organization itself. The youngest of the men in the room claimed direct ancestry with one of the five original monks who were supposed to have begun the Triad societies back in the days of the first Manchu incursions. No one questioned his claim since this young man was now at the pinnacle of his power. It was a new time indeed that one so young could climb so high. All the way to Shan Chu.

The eldest man in the room had been a small boy when the group took the bold step of separating from the coastal head office. That move and the subsequent deal with Mao's men had secured the group's present power. And its present power was substantial, as evidenced by the brisk sales of franchises throughout the Xian region.

"This Detective Zhong?" the young leader ordered a response.

A heavy-set man rose, bowed, then laid out Zhong Fong's history in full. Quick rise through the ranks to head of Special Investigations in Shanghai, his fall from grace, his years in Ti Lan Chou prison, his internal exile then his recent resurrection.

The young leader, the Shan Chu, turned away from the others at the table and stared out the window. He didn't fear the present circumstances — the matter of the deaths on that boat — the mess. But he knew that at times of turmoil gain can be realized. He was trying to figure out what benefit could be wrought from the murders of seventeen foreigners. What new foothold of commerce could be purchased from this interesting situation.

"Did we supply the girls?" he asked.

"Naturally, from Xian," came back the simple reply.

"And their transportation to the ship?"

"We pulled in a favour from a bus driver. But he broke down along the way. The girls never got to the boat."

That surprised him. "None of the girls got to the boat?"

"Not unless they got there on their own."

"Is that possible?"

"I guess. Whores can be quite resourceful." The man laughed. The young leader didn't, so the rest of the room decided that the jest was in bad taste.

After allowing the man to sit for a moment of embarrassment, the young Shan Chu said, "Get me the calling cards of the girls — of all the girls." He turned to the rest of the table and smiled. "It is a rare opportunity for a Triad to help the police in their investigations, don't you think, gentlemen? We must grasp such opportunities to be good citizens of the New China." He laughed and the rest of the table followed suit. Evidently this gibe was not in bad taste.

Fong set tasks for Lily and the coroner that brought them into town. He returned with Chen to the warehouse.

Chen had secured an oval meeting table, chairs and Japanese-style futons for them. He'd also found the large, flat-topped desk and chalk that Fong had requested.

Fong nodded.

"The transparencies will be ready shortly, sir."

Fong nodded again, still unsure what a transparency was. "What about the model of the boat?"

It's been ready for some time. We just have to pick it up."

Chen drove him to an old-style workshop just outside the city limits. From the twin front doors it might well have been a stable at one time. When Fong knocked at the door, the sound echoed.

After a few moments the door was opened by a tall, elegant, aesthetic-looking man who was about ten years older than Fong. The man wore army-issue wire-rimmed glasses. His eyes were oddly pale; his fingers long. His nails were buffed, yet his palms were deeply calloused. His handshake was firm.

"Welcome, Detective Zhong." His voice was light, breathy. His clothing appeared to be standard issue but made of extremely fine fabrics. He took off his clunky metal-rimmed glasses and cleaned them with an expensive linen handkerchief. "I've been expecting you."

Fong glanced up into the man's face. He found no trace there of anything but a carefully kept mask. The man stepped aside. Fong entered the surprisingly generous space. Before he took two steps, the man quickly crossed behind him and closed the door, leaving Captain Chen outside in the cold. Fong turned. As explanation, the man said, "At a recreation, the recreationist is king. Besides, talent has its privileges — even in our China." His eyes twinkled.

Fong nodded slowly, unsure that he wanted to agree with anything someone who called himself a recreationist said.

The man walked past Fong to one of the two large tables that occupied the centre of the space. On the first table a partially completed terra-cotta figure of an archer lay on its side. Scattered around it were hundreds of terra-cotta shards, few larger than an inch across. On the other large table sat an object some four feet by three feet covered in a grey canvas shroud. Pinned on boards on three sides of the object were duplicates of the crime scene photos.

The man walked past Fong, knelt and plucked a stone from a pile on the floor. He allowed the rock to roll in his palm for a moment, then placed it on top of a slender column of free-standing stones. It was like a stalagmite growing from the hard earthen floor. There were two other columns of stones nearer the wall, each a miracle of balance; each rock fitted perfectly to the one above and below. Before Fong could ask, the man spoke. "The stones are a way of marking time, Detective Zhong. Time. One stone for each . . ." His voice trailed off before he completed the thought. He got to his feet, pulling down his jacket over a shiny black vest bearing an English tag — "100% Thinsulate" — thinsu-what? Fong had been on the other side of the Wall for a long time.

Fong's eyes returned to the terra-cotta figure on the table.

"Have you seen the terra-cotta warriors at Xian?" the man asked as a thin smile creased his lips.

"The Qin Dynasty soldiers?" Fong blurted out, stunned to think that the thing on the table was one of the famous statues.

"Yes," the man widened his grey eyes, "the very ones."

"No. I've never been to this part of the Middle Kingdom before."

"That's a shame." The man turned from Fong and, without further explanation, walked to the canvas-covered object on the other table.

Fong didn't follow him and snapped, "Why?"

"Why what, Detective Zhong?" the man replied.

"Why is it a shame?" he asked feeling silly — no — totally off-balance with this man. Shit, he didn't even know the man's name.

The man's smile was surprisingly sad this time. He was about to say something then stopped himself. When he spoke, his smile was gleeful again. "Because I have been in charge of that excavation from its onset in 1976 just after the silly old farmer stumbled into the first tomb. The heavy roof beams had fallen. Perhaps they had been burned by the rebels or perhaps the wrath of the gods brought them down." He paused. Fong waited. "At any rate, the beams had crashed down on the figures shattering them to bits. I often think that leading the reconstruction of those thousands of clay warriors in the first pit was my greatest accomplishment. I think of it as a recreation of what was."

"That strikes me as a reasonable thought," Fong said, carefully keeping any trace of awe out of his voice.

The man's pale eyes twinkled again.

Fong didn't quite know what to make of that.

"Have you ever seen a recreation, Detective Zhong?"

"I've been to Grandview Gardens . . ." Fong was stopped by the man's high-pitched giggle. He laughed like an old woman. It hurt. "I guess you've never been to . . ."

"To the slut fest by the sea? Oh, I've been. It just goes to prove the depth of humour inherent in the Chinese character, wouldn't you agree, Detective Zhong?"

"I guess," Fong said slowly. Although he agreed with the man's assessment both of the place and the Chinese character, he felt that he'd been bludgeoned into the accord.

"Don't guess, Detective Zhong. There's nothing to guess about. Grandview Gardens is a mockery of life. What I do makes time stand still. I enhance life." He indicated the canvas-shrouded structure on the table. He put his hand on the canvas. "The real is not always more terrifying than the artificial. Your wife was an

actress, wasn't she?" Fong nodded slowly, uncomfortable that this man knew anything of his past. "Surely the
husband of the great Fu Tsong knows that artifice in the
hands of a true artist enriches the experience of life. It
doesn't imitate it."

Fong nodded. With this he was willing to agree, without being pushed.

"Fine," the man said then pulled the canvas aside.

There sitting on the table was a beautifully constructed
wood reproduction of the boat. Fong looked at the man.

"You are impressed, Detective Zhong?"

Fong nodded, "I am . . . I don't know your name."

"Forgive my impoliteness. Dr. Roung," he said, "I am
an archeologist by training, hence my title: Doctor."

Fong put a hand on the model. "The recreation is
even more impressive when you open it up, Detective."
He reached forward and removed an upper section of
the wall to reveal the death room of the two Americans.

Fong peered in. "Where are the photographs of this
room?" The man pointed to the board on one side. Fong
quickly spotted the ones of the dead Americans. He
allowed his eyes to travel from the photo to the model.
Even the looks on the dead men's faces matched. He
leaned down and looked up into the tiny mirror. The
Triad warning was there. Fong looked to his right.

The man was smiling.

Fong removed the opposite wall section to reveal the
bar room with the swinging man. Dr. Roung offered the
pictures, but Fong ignored him. He lifted out the room
itself to reveal the video room beneath. Even the cut

lines on the beams were present. He replaced the upper room.

"There are no nails or screws," Fong said.

"There is no need when everything fits one piece into the next."

Fong ran his fingers along the edges. Smooth, perfect. Then he lifted off the room with the Americans to reveal the room with the runway. It too was perfect down to the curtains and mudstains on the runway. The five miniature Japanese men sat in their brutal death positions, cameras and glasses in place. Fong assumed that should he open their pants that reality would have been reproduced as well. His eyes scanned the room. So much detail. So much accuracy. So terrifying. He looked at the man. His eyes twinkled. "I hope you find it adequate for your purposes, Detective."

"It's more than adequate."

"It's a piece of art," Dr. Roung said.

Fong nodded.

The older man smiled, clearly pleased.

Fong crossed to the door and called for Chen. They carried the model back to the Jeep and then Fong returned to the workshop. The archeologist was at the table with the terra-cotta warrior. He turned. "Something else, Detective?"

"No, nothing." Then he added for no particular reason, "For now."

The man's smile vanished.

Fong was surprised yet again.

Back at the factory Fong stood staring at the model. He once more marvelled at its construction, its precision, its ability to freeze a moment in time.

His thoughts were interrupted by the return of the coroner who announced to the world, "The food in this place stinks."

Lily followed him into the space. "The forensic facilities aren't much better than the food."

Fong covered the model with the canvas and moved toward the table. "Now that we've established those two important facts, perhaps we're ready to have our first meeting."

"What did he make of the model?"

The politico weighed his words carefully, "I wasn't inside, sir, but I'm sure he was impressed, although he kept his mouth shut when he left."

The head of internal security for the People's Republic of China allowed himself ten seconds of silence then said, "Good," and snapped off the speaker phone on his desk.

Each investigator had become familiar with the photographs and the physical evidence. Each had prepared a first report. Now they gathered around the oval table.

Fong caught Lily staring at him. He wasn't surprised. He'd taken a good look at himself. The skin of his face was worn and greying and the veins on his chin and left cheek had shattered into thousands of spiky red lines. His smile was a little crooked. Then there were his new teeth. Well, two teeth actually. The politico's dentist hadn't bothered to build up individual teeth, but rather had just put an enamel layer over both his upper and lower sets so that it looked like he had only two very wide teeth. "Government toothes very p'actic'l, short stuff, but hide you us," Lily had commented.

He'd filed down the enamel layers so that he could talk more like himself. He'd even considered trying to etch in individual tooth lines, but had given up when he poked a hole in the bottom set.

He'd just have to get used to being "but hide you us." He'd also have to try and figure out what "but hide you us" meant. Lily's English came from so many different media sources that the exact meaning of the phrase could be hard to determine. He could have just asked her, of course, but he was worried about her response. He wasn't prepared to be old in her eyes.

Fong called their meeting to order. He stood at the head of the table. Lily and Chen had large jelly jars filled with steaming tea in front of them. The coroner sat to one side, dyspeptic and farting loudly.

It didn't feel like any meeting Fong had ever attended. Why should it? Fong was now a convicted felon. He hadn't even seen these people for five years. Then, of course, there was Chen. Who was he? Whom did he report to?

For his part, Chen felt out of place. The two new people totally ignored him and when they did take note of him they always spoke Shanghanese. On occasion they referred to him as "Shrug and Knock the Second." They never explained the reference. Although he could understand their Shanghanese dialect, he was often lost with the complex slang. But he didn't need to understand every word they said to know that they thought him nothing more than a local party hack. It angered him. It was wrong and it was stupid. If nothing else, he knew his way around this part of the Shanxi and he could be of real use to the investigation.

Fong turned to the coroner. He looked ancient — more ancient. Even five years ago he'd looked like he'd been recently exhumed. Now he smelled like it too.

Lily looked older too. She must be thirty-four by now, Fong thought. She still dressed exquisitely and entirely Western. She'd have to be accompanied out on the streets here. It wasn't Huai Hai Road out the door. He watched her sip her tea. Her slender lips poised to accept the heat. Her deep, liquid eyes, eternally sad, now seemed at least a little bit at rest. His eyes drank her in — the arch of her hand, the curve of her fingers, the length of her neck. Then she smiled. "Talk time, short stuff."

"No fair. I don't understand English," barked the old coroner. "You drag me all the way out to the very centre of nowhere and then talk that jibberish. It hurts the ears. Besides I don't believe it's really a language at all. When none of the black-haired people are around I'm sure that they speak Mandarin like everyone else. This English is just a big scam. It's their version of a joke. Not funny. Stupid."

"I'm sure you're right," said Fong in the Common

Speech. "Let's get started. I hope that by the end of the meeting we'll know where to begin with this . . . thing."

"Show us the model," said Lily.

"Later. Last," Fong replied.

"Why not now?" asked the coroner.

"Because I said so," replied Fong. Reasserting his authority wasn't going to be simple. Then he caught Lily's eye. She approved. "Let's start with the victims. That would be you, Captain Chen." Fong was careful to use his full title.

Chen was anxious to make a good impression on these Shanghanese. He opened his book and readied his notes. "I was assigned to updating and collating material on the victims. I'm going to do this by country." He looked up for confirmation. None was forthcoming so he put his head back down and read from his notes. "The Americans were both lawyers for a big firm in California. They were corporate litigators. Both specialized in something called patent law. I've got calls in to try to explain that to me."

"Well done, fire plug, solid investigative work that," snarked the coroner.

"It's all I could find on short notice," Chen snapped back. The air momentarily crackled with anger. Then Chen backed off. "I'll find more in the morning, Grandpa."

The coroner stared hard at Chen for what he considered an uncalled-for familiarity. Then he reminded himself that this was the country. "Grandpa?" he grunted.

Chen was about to apologize when Fong broke in.

"Better than old fart! Any guesses what brought them over here?"

Shoulders were raised, heads shook, the usual blank looks that a Chinese person gives when asked about a foreigner's behaviour or motives. They were baffling — beyond rational comprehension — completely inscrutable.

"Let's move on. What about the Japanese?" asked Fong.

"Scientists," said Chen, happy to get back to his notes. "I've just begun to piece together what kind of scientists they are — were. One was the head of the biology department at a major university in Tokyo. Another worked as a researcher for an industrial conglomerate."

"What did he research, Chen?" Lily asked in her beautiful Shanghanese.

Chen had trouble with the Shanghanese idiom for a second then got it. "Genealogy. He researches genealogy."

"Genealogy needs researching?" asked the coroner, hawking to get some unruly phlegm up his throat.

"Evidently, Grandpa."

"I'm not your grandpa, Captain Chen," the coroner said simply.

"There's always something to be thankful for, huh?" said Fong. "What about the other Japanese?"

"Microbiologist, geneticist and computer analyst," Chen said, flipping through his notes.

"Anything else on the Japanese?"

"Yeah, like where were they during the rape of Nanjing?" asked the coroner.

"They're old enough to have been there. All of them," said Chen.

"Then maybe they got what they deserved," said the coroner bluntly. Fong looked at the old man. He'd known him for years, but really didn't know much about him. Was it possible that he had lost people in the slaughters at Nanjing? Possible. Fong looked back at Chen. "The Koreans?"

"Industrialists. All three. They own scientific laboratories all over the stupid peninsula." Chen looked up quickly to see if anyone was offended by his comment. No one was. "Government-backed corporations of some sort," he added.

Fong noted the flare of anger when Chen spoke of Koreans. Interesting. He filed it away and asked, "And what about the dead Taiwanese?" This time it was he who was careful to hide the edge in his voice.

"A little of each. Some in banking, some in industry, some in science. One a lawyer."

"I didn't know that Taiwan had laws," said Lily. They laughed. But none of them found it very funny.

Fong asked, "Which one was hung from the rafters?"

"The lawyer." Lily, the coroner and Chen had spoken in unison.

"So, just looking at victims, what does this add up to?" asked Fong. He waited for a moment but no one spoke. "All right. How about something simpler: Why were those men on that boat?"

"They were celebrating."

"I agree, Lily, but celebrating what? What had they

accomplished that merited the reward of a celebration?"

This was greeted by a silence. Finally Chen spoke, "I don't know, sir, but I've found something that I think might be important." They all looked at him. "I think there was a Chinese man who's not accounted for."

"Maybe he was tossed overboard?" said the coroner and spat again.

"Maybe he wasn't, Grandpa." Chen's voice was hard. Fong hadn't expected this in the young man. He was evidently tenacious once he got his teeth into something. Like a short stumpy rat, Fong thought. Fong liked that but warned himself to hold off any judgement of the young officer until he knew more about him.

"What's on your mind, Captain Chen?" asked Fong.

"The Taiwanese all stayed in Xian in one of the big tourist hotels. There were seven Chinese bodies found on the ship. They had reservations for eight rooms."

"An extra room for the whores?" suggested Lily.

"Two of them bunking together for unnatural purposes?" asked the coroner as sweetly as a child asking for a second rice cookie.

"All indications from the boat suggest heterosexual dalliance. Besides that would have made for the use of six hotel rooms not eight," said Lily, matching his smile with an innocent one of her own. "Having trouble with addition these days, Grandpa?"

"Grandpa from you too?"

"Seems to fit, Grandpa," said Fong.

"Fine. I accept. I also vote for the room of whores that Lily is suggesting."

"The hotel bill may have been picked up by the Taipei government, but I doubt that even those pimps would pay for an extra room for the girls." Fong turned away from them. He shivered as the mongoose circled the base of his spine. Tiny claws tore the ground with anticipation. Fong's teeth clacked. They did that now when he got excited. He looked up and they were all looking at him.

"Sharing time, short stuff?"

Before the coroner could complain again about the use of English in the Middle Kingdom, Fong replied in English, "Not yet — tall glass of water." Lily's confusion pleased him. Then in Shanghanese he quickly said, "You're up, Lily."

Lily hesitated then laid her notes on the table in front of her. She liked the spotlight. "The boat was filled with clues, but some of the investigation at the crime site is debatable. Whoever this specialist was, he knew his stuff, but the locals are amateurs." Before Chen could defend himself she added, "It's probably not Chen's fault, but soldiers are soldiers and cops are cops." She looked at Fong, a churlish smile on her face. In English she said, "East is East. No?"

Fong had no idea what she was trying to say. So he responded in Shanghanese, "I'm sure you're right." Then to the men's querying looks, he simply shrugged his shoulders. A gesture a Chinese man uses in circumstances varying from learning that his wife has given birth to quintuplets to being told that the bus he is waiting for is going to be late.

The other men shrugged back at him. It was used for that too.

Lily didn't shrug. She threw an evidence bag with two spent cartridges on the table. It landed with a thunk. Then she splayed seven photographs of the large bar indicating exactly where the cartridges had been found. Chen picked up the evidence bag and turned it slowly in the light.

"Give that to your grandpa. You're way too young to identify those."

Chen handed the bag to the coroner who held it at a distance from himself to get a good look. Fong marvelled that the man's vanity still prevented him from wearing glasses. Fong wondered when vanity finally left a man alone. Gave him some peace. Then he realized that when vanity left, so did a part of life — a part he wasn't ready to let go of just yet.

"These belong in a museum," the coroner said. "I'm surprised they actually fired. Doesn't gunpowder deteriorate or something?"

"It does, Grandpa," said Lily.

"So, how did they fire?" asked the coroner.

"They're new," said Lily.

"What? He just said they were ancient, Lily," Fong said.

"They were. And Grandpa is right that gunpowder deteriorates. These were the original shells — probably from the 1860s or 1870s. I'll have to check that. But they've been recharged with modern powder, although no doubt fired from the original weapon. If you look at the markings on the shells, I think they were made in Japan, Tokugawa era or some such."

"Why? Why bother? Weapons aren't that hard to get. Why bother filling old gun shells with new powder? Why would Triads bother with that?" asked Chen.

Fong was happy when the coroner jumped in, "More important, why leave them there to be found?" His old face was a mask of confusion. "There were at least five gunshots fired in that bar room. But the specialist only found these two shells. Why? And look where the shells were." He shuffled through the photographs and found the wide-angle shot of the room with the two shells circled on the floor. "Right in the middle of the room. Why would they end up there? It doesn't make sense."

Fong felt their eyes move toward him. He kept his face as neutral as he could but his mind was racing. The bar room. The faceless Chinese men. Each countenance one large dark mouth, screaming. Gunshots. Knife wounds. A man hog-tied and allowed to bleed to death from the wounds on his face — one awful red cry.

"Good questions," said Lily. "Here are some more mysteries to ponder. The splatter patterns on the walls of the bar indicate that some of the other shots were from modern weapons. The distance between the deceased and the marks on the mirrors indicate that a high-powered, definitely modern, handgun was used. Without the real bodies, we'll never be able to know exactly what kind of weapon it was. Apparently the lake is filled with eels. By the time they'll be able to retrieve the bodies there won't be enough left to bury, let alone autopsy. But the issue remains. The splatter marks indicate that there was at least one high-powered weapon on the boat. Why bother using an antique when you have a modern gun?" Without waiting for discussion, she reached into the box with the evidence bags at her side. She tossed the bag with the Triad medallion on the broken chain onto the table. "Typical '14K' stuff. I'll check, but my guess is that it's pretty low in the hierarchy. A foot soldier would be my guess. Then there are these." She tossed out the four photos of the amulet on its chain. "A lot of pictures for. . ." Lily never completed her thought.

"Film's cheap. He took a lot of pictures of all the Triad markings," said the coroner.

"Next," said Fong, not wanting to deal with Triads just yet.

Lily pulled out the Hong Kong video and tossed it onto the table. "Standard issue pornography — of the hetero variety. I guess we could track down where in Hong Kong it was made but I doubt that there's anything to it." She looked at her male company. "Just guys having their boyish fun."

The men averted their eyes as if looking at the black rectangle implicated them somehow in the event.

Lily held the plastic bag with the set of Parisian glasses taken from the Japanese man. "I have no idea why the specialist insisted that they be itemized. There are no doubt prints on them but whose is beyond our ability to determine. Same for the CD from the runway room." She tossed it onto the table.

Fong picked it up. It was American. He wasn't much on Western music but Fu Tsong had insisted that he listen to all sorts of things that her lover, the Canadian director Geoffrey Hyland, had given her. He allowed the thought to dissipate into the thinness of the air. It'd been a long time since that jealousy had haunted his thoughts. He looked at the CD and forced himself to remember his English sounds. Somehow they were easier when he spoke than when he read. *Counting Crows.* He wondered if that was the name of the artist or if it was a group. Surely "Counting" was an odd first name. His English didn't extend to bird nomenclature. He had no idea what "recovering the satellites," which was written in odd print on the cover, meant. He turned the casing over and read the names of the songs. His eyes landed on title after title: *"Angels of the Silences," "Daylight Fading," "Children in Bloom," "Millers Angels," "A Long December."*

The shiver again — the mongoose was running.

Fong understood synchronicity. He understood it in his bones. And he didn't believe totally in human will. At times he knew that accidents were caused by nature. That two things in one place often meant something. He would totally deny that he was superstitious — but serendipity was a way of conveying meaning. Angels, silences, children, bloom and December — clues as far as Fong was concerned.

He put the CD back on the table. "What does it say?" asked Chen.

"Nothing important," Fong answered.

The coroner laughed deep in his throat. All eyes swung to him. "I just love the way he lies, don't you?" he said. "What does it say, Fong?"

Fong translated every word on the CD. "Satisfied, or would you like me to translate the liner notes, too?"

"No, I think that's enough, Fong." But the coroner was smiling as if he'd been lied to.

"Who cares?" demanded Lily. "Some girl took off her clothes while that stuff played. What's the difference what the songs were?" Her vehemence ended the discussion. She tossed a bag of dirt on the table. "That was found on the runway. Again I'm not sure why the specialist thought it was important." The bag was handed around. Fong made a point of hardly looking at the thing and handed it on to Chen.

"What else do you have, Lily?" asked Fong, making sure that he didn't look back at the bag in Chen's hands.

"A stack of clothes that I've only begun to catalogue. Seventeen wallets. All of which identify who these guys were but little else. Drivers' licences, picture IDs, pictures of grandkids."

"No visas or passports?" asked Fong.

A silence descended on the room. Everyone knew what the question meant. If these men entered China without visas or passports, then they were government guests and this whole thing was even bigger than it already was.

"I've asked Chen to check their hotel in Xian. It's possible that the men left those kind of documents with the front desk, I guess," said Lily.

Fong wanted to leave this behind for a while. There was more than enough fear to go around without the possibility of government involvement. Although they all knew that was silly. There was government involvement in everything that was important in the Middle Kingdom. It was just a matter of how much involvement . . . and who in the government.

"What else have you got, Lily?"

"Just a roll of film from one of the Japanese men's cameras. The other camera had no film in it."

"So what's on the film, Lily?"

She switched to English despite the obvious anger of the coroner. "I don't know, Fong. No black room here, safe."

Quickly, he responded in Shanghanese, "There is nothing secret here, Lily. Why do you think they put us up in this abandoned factory? It's got to be bugged. Just get the pictures developed. There's nothing else we can do." He turned to the men. "Lily was concerned that she couldn't find a secure darkroom to develop the film."

"No, sir. Miss Lily was concerned that I am untrustworthy," Chen stated.

The tension in the room mounted exponentially. Fong got to his feet. "That's enough, Captain Chen. Lily was wrong. It was nothing more than a mistake for her to use English. Apologize, Lily."

Lily glared at him.

"I said apologize, Lily."

After a moment of resistance, Lily bowed her head slightly. A gesture so old that Fong sensed the Earth growing beneath her feet, her legs up to the knees in dung-filled water, a peasant's hat on her head. Fong was always astounded how vibrantly alive the old ways were even in the likes of modern women like Lily. "For this insult I ask your forgiveness, Captain Chen."

Chen waited for a beat then snapped his head down then back up quickly. The tension was gone. Through the ritual, forgiveness had been found. Through the old ways.

"Can I see the shots of the Japanese again?" Fong asked.

Lily pushed twenty-odd photographs across the table to him. He sorted them quickly.

"What, Fong?" Lily asked, but Fong wasn't answering questions. He was staring at the wide-angle photo of the runway and its six chairs. Five of the six were occupied by the dead Japanese men, but the sixth sat empty at the head of the runway — the best view. "If this had been a banquet," Fong thought, "the head of the fish would have pointed in that direction — the place of honour. An empty chair. An extra room at the hotel in Xian. One and the same?" Fong rifled through the photos again. The man with the ill-fitting expensive glasses was to the right of the empty seat. The men with cameras were both to the left. "From the missing piece, deduce the whole," he told himself. He allowed words into his mouth, "Cameras, empty seat, glasses. Glasses, empty seat, cameras." Seeing. All about seeing. Yeah, but seeing what?

Fong looked up. They were all watching him closely.

Fine. But he was leading this meeting. He signalled to the coroner that it was his turn.

"Why don't you call me grandpa, Fong, everyone else seems to think it fits."

"Fine, Grandpa, your turn."

The coroner started by lamenting the nature of the search and then tossed the specialist's request for a toxicology scan on the table. "A wee bit late for that now. There was no doubt alcohol on board. Maybe opium or hashish. Whatever it was it. . .it had to be pretty potent to subdue that many men. Seventeen men are a lot of men to execute. The others would have to have been either restrained or drugged while the murderers got on with their butchering."

"Your best guess, Grandpa?" Fong asked.

The coroner waggled his head back and forth a few times. "It's an agricultural area, there's always the possibility of adding that government insecticide crap to their drinks."

Swallowing the tasteless insecticide was the most common means of suicide in rural China. But it was a woman's death choice. Fong thought it more likely that the eel farming in the area provided better opportunities for toxins. There was always the possibility of local concoctions. Poisoning had a long history in China.

Poison in drinks had a particularly long history.

"Perhaps that explains why there were no half-empty glasses found anywhere on the boat," suggested Fong with a wry smile.

Lily, Chen and the coroner reached for the photos and

scanned them quickly. Not a single glass appeared in any of the shots. Lily looked up at Fong. "You noticed that."

"Crime sites consist of what is there and what isn't, Lily."

"Very good, Fong."

"Thanks, Grandpa. What's next?"

"The cut marks are interesting if your delectations move in that direction. The Japanese were gutted in a mockery of that thing they do over there whenever someone burps after dinner or some such silliness."

"Hari Kari," said Lily.

"Yeah, whatever they call it. The men who did this knew how to butcher things. It's like the Japanese were 'dressed' for an exhibit or something."

Fong was sure to let his breath out slowly. His pulse was racing. The mongoose was in furious motion.

"What do you make of the way the Koreans were shot?" asked Chen.

Fong looked at the young man.

"Again, you're too young to know about this kind of thing. At the end of the war before our glorious libera-tion," his sarcasm was so thick that the air in the room seemed to hover for a moment, "Korean gangs made major inroads in our cities. They spread terror by shoot-ing people beneath the armpits and then hanging them from beams. It takes a long time to die that way. Shooting someone from right to left pretty much guar-antees that the bullet will stay in the body, but it will not kill immediately. Just pain. Lots of pain."

"Koreans are good at that." The flat statement from Chen surprised everyone. Fong added it to his mental "Chen file."

Fong nodded for the coroner to continue. "The knives were sharp but beyond that I haven't got a thing to go on. But these . . . ," he tossed out several close-up photographs of the face-less Chinese men, "are interesting. Take a look at the top of the cut mark. The guy who ordered these pictures really knew what he was doing. See the angle he's guiding us to look at?"

As the others looked, Fong considered grandpa's last remark: ". . . he's guiding us to look at." Could it be that the specialist knew that they, or someone like them, would come to investigate further than he'd been allowed to? Is it possible that he arrested those three men knowing full well that they weren't the real criminals? Were they left by him as possible clues for investigators like us to follow? Was the specialist actually, somehow or other, still guiding this investigation from wherever he was?

Fong returned his attention to the coroner as the old man said, "The stroke was definitely from top to bottom as indicated by the bevel at the forehead and the overlap on the chin." He felt his own chin and pulled on the single long whisker there. "And it was done with one stroke." A dark look passed his features. Perhaps an undigested piece of beef. "So what we're looking for," he concluded, "is an incredibly sharp weapon that's wider than the widest of these faces."

"A kind of axe?" Lily asked.

"None that I've ever seen."

"How about a long knife or machete?"

"No, it would leave a slant from whichever side it was used. This was used straight up and down."

"Like a hoe?" Chen asked.

"Some hoe," the coroner chuckled mirthlessly.

"Let's not dismiss that," said Fong.

"Fine," said the coroner. Chen made a note on his pad. Lily glanced at Fong, but Fong looked away. He stood and stared out the filthy slanted windows, his back to the table. When he sensed that all their eyes were on him he spoke. "What do you know about *chi*, Grandpa?"

"The black mania? Chinese madness?" the old man was clearly offended. "Western nonsense."

"Perhaps." He turned toward them and spoke slowly, knowing the danger of the territory that he was entering. "In May of 1920, huge posters appeared everywhere in Beijing . . ."

"Kill the foreigners, throw them in the sea, China for the Chinese," said the coroner wearily. "We all know the story."

"Do we really, Grandpa? Thousands of foreigners were killed in two days. Heads were switched on white men's bodies and Chinese collaborators were hog-tied and bled to death. Sound familiar?"

"Fairy tales, Fong," grunted the coroner.

"I was born in the Old City, Grandpa. These were the stories of my youth. Perhaps elaborated. Perhaps. But my grandmother witnessed the event. She was amazed by the bravery of the revolutionists. The complete disregard for their own safety. She called it, 'So un-Chinese.'" An image of his grandmother yelling at him to get over his typhoid and stop embarrassing the family welled up within him. He shrugged it off. "And she wasn't one to be easily impressed." Lily looked at him strangely. This was new information. But he avoided her eyes and went on, "She brought back one of the red kerchiefs they wore. It had the word *Fu* emblazoned on the front."

"Happiness," Lily said in English as she turned away in disgust.

"Did they succeed, sir?" asked Chen.

"No. Their ferocity grew beyond their understanding. They leapt from tall buildings, frothed from their mouths uttering incomprehensible omens of doom and prophecies of the future. One leader, in his ecstasy, sliced his daughter into pieces and threw the bits to his followers. They were so taken by their furor that bullets only slowed them. Death was their companion."

Lines from *Measure for Measure* leapt into his head:

If I must die, I will encounter darkness as a bride,
And hug her in mine arms.

Fu Tsong loved those lines. An awful thought flitted through Fong's consciousness.

No one spoke. They could hear the hum of the building's air intake system.

Finally Fong broke the silence. "You three can take a look at the recreation now. But be forewarned. The model's potent." Fong returned to his notes. "Lily, you

take the film in the camera, try to get an analysis of the
dirt from the runway and I want you to find out more
about American patent law. If you need to get information in English, Lily, show me your translations before
you send them off. Captain Chen, take the specs on that
hoe thing and find out whatever you can on those old
cartridges and the gun that might have fired them. Then
locate the ship owner and try to figure out where the
crew was during all of this. Maybe the owner supplied
girls as well. Grandpa, find what you can about those
ligature marks on the arms. Let's see if we can narrow
down the type of wire they used, if nothing else. Then
get me as much data on the knife wounds as you can. As
well, you can interview the restaurant owner who supplied the food." Fong glanced down at a picture of the
brown blotch on the rug near the bar room door. "Ask
him about alcohol on board. While you're with him,
maybe he can address your complaints about the local
cuisine. Let's start with that."

Chen got to his feet, but the other two didn't move.
Fong knew perfectly well what Lily and Grandpa were
waiting for. At last he spoke. "I'm going to begin with
the local Triad. I want to ask them about the burn
marks."

"The what?"

"The burn marks." He paused for a second then continued, "After all the killing was done, the boat was
torched. It was only the shoal and the ice that kept it
afloat for a few days." He tossed close-ups of the hull's
scorch marks on the table.

"Why, Fong?" asked the coroner.

Fong chose his words carefully. "When I look at that model and the photos I'm struck by many things, but the one impression that is strongest for me is that the entire crime site looks carefully planned. As if it's an exhibit. I think it was done as a warning. I don't think there's any doubt that it was meant to be seen."

"The positions of the victims, you mean?" asked Chen.

"That and the way they were killed. The whole thing looks like a bizarre object lesson."

"That goes with the Triad motto on the overhead mirror," said Lily.

"So, some hoodlums play show and tell. So what? What does that have to do with burn marks?" pressed the coroner.

"Maybe nothing," replied Fong, "but why go to all that trouble to create an object lesson — then try to sink it?"

No one had an answer for that.

Fong walked toward the rusting barrels at the far end of the factory. He felt wobbly, as if something terrible was just around the corner — just far enough back in the shadows that its true form remained secret — for now, at least.

Without looking back he said, "I think its time I met with the local gangsters, Captain Chen."

"You mean the Triads, sir?"

"Yes, the Triads," Fong said; but what he thought was, "Even Chen realizes that there are many kinds of gangsters in this part of the Middle Kingdom."

"Why didn't the specialist just arrest some token Triad guys? The Triad leaders wouldn't have cared," said Lily.

"That's another good question, Lily," Fong said; but to himself he added, "That was *the* question." Then he tried to put Lily's question together with "Why design an object lesson and then try to burn it down?" And couldn't.

CHAPTER TEN

SMOTHER. MURDER. PATENTS

Inspector Wang couldn't tell if he was awake or dreaming. He was seeing himself from above. He looked like a silkworm chrysalis in its hanging cocoon — fighting, battling, tearing — to get out. He took a deep breath. Silken threads filled his mouth and lungs. His screams were muffled by the wadding.

A light glared. He was suddenly on the bed looking toward the ceiling. Through the gossamer he saw a figure in white. A woman. A girl. She reached out and somehow touched his forehead through the material. Her hand felt cool. Lovely.

The syringe stung as it entered his arm. Then relief. As if the cocoon had been slashed apart, ripped open. And air entered him. He tried to say thank you, but nothing came out.

"You're welcome," she said. "I can read your lips. Remember?"

He nodded.

"Use the button at your side next time. They're putting you under again. If you need my help, you'll have to use the call button. I can't know you're in trouble unless you buzz me. Understood?"

She wrapped his fingers around the shaft of the call button.

Don't let go of my hand, he wanted to say. But all he did was look up at her.

She was a nurse, a different one. He didn't recall being brought to the hospital this time. He'd lost track of the days. All he knew was that he was being put into some kind of time suspension again, that a vain battle against his passing was being fought. But despite these efforts, he was dying and he knew it. And his only hope for life was the plan that he'd set in motion in far-off Lake Ching. A plan that, because he was given so little time at the lake itself, needed a very talented investigator to complete.

Fong got out of the Jeep, more than a little startled where Chen had driven him. They were several kilometres into the countryside. The lake was well to their east. The road was crowded as they approached what looked like an animal theme park.

"The head of the Triad is going to meet me at a zoo?" he demanded.

"The leader, the Shan Chu, won't be there."

"I know that, Chen. Who is it, the Hung Kwan?"

"No. The White Paper Fan and the Incense Master."

The Incense Master (Heung Chu) was in charge of ritual indoctrination and the White Paper Fan (Pak Tsz Sin) was the financial officer of the Triad. They were third and sixth respectively in the hierarchy of Triad command. Not bad, Fong thought.

"I asked them for higher up, but . . ."

"But we take what we can get when it comes to local Triads, huh, Chen?"

"At least they didn't send the Grass Sandal."

The Grass Sandal (Cho Hai) was the Triad's mouth-piece. Fong had found in the past that the hardest thing about dealing with a Triad Cho Hai was stopping himself from knocking out the man's teeth. Dental work was not Fong's favourite topic, so he dropped the thought. "How deeply set is this Triad, Chen?"

"Deep. They were early in leaving the Kuomintang and aligning themselves with the People's Liberation Army."

"They could smell the winds that long ago?" Fong thought. He reminded himself to keep his cool with these men. He needed information, not more enemies. A man needed allies to survive in China.

Chen showed his ID, and he and Fong walked past a large line of Chinese men and women waiting to pay and enter the grounds. Naturally, many grumbled at Fong and Chen's obvious queue-jumping, but few made noises loud enough to attract attention. Clearly, Chen and Fong were police officers — most Chinese citizens knew better than to make trouble for themselves with the local authorities.

The grounds were crowded but well laid out. No small cages here. Open pens, large grass-covered knolls surrounded by moats to keep the animals from the spec-tators. A welcome relief from the claustrophobic horror of old-style zoos.

Fong put his hands in his pockets and drank it all in. So many people. So much chatter. Families. Then he noticed that something was missing.

"How far are we from Xian?"

"A forty-five-minute drive, maybe less."

Fong turned a full circle then asked, "Where are the tourists? There's not a single white face in the entire crowd."

Chen hung his head a little and said, more to his chest than to Fong, "This isn't really a zoo, sir. It's not on any tourist map. I doubt that they'd allow tourists in."

That surprised Fong. He looked anew at his surroundings. At the edge of some of the containment areas, Chinese men and women held fishing rods with food at the end of the line. He watched as animals approached and grabbed the dangling treats. Apples for apes and monkeys. Chunks of meat for tigers and lions. Slabs of fish for bears.

Well, that was new to Fong. "What? They pay extra for the right to feed the animals or something?"

"Yes, sir."

"I still don't get it, Chen. What could the Triads want with a place like this?"

"Well, sir, it's not so much the animals here, but rather the ones over there that are the Triad's business concern."

Chen was pointing to a large windowless building set back behind the containment areas. As they walked toward it, the crowds thickened and a kind of expectan- filled the air. It reminded Fong of the feeling he had at the one hanging he'd been forced to witness. He and his team had tracked down a pedophile who had fled Shanghai to a small town north of the Pudong. The man had made the mistake of trying to kidnap a young Australian boy from his parents. As a crime against foreigners, it had fallen into Fong's jurisdiction. The man was clumsy. A fool. He left a wide, easy path to follow. Fong had made the arrest himself. The man was hiding beneath his mother's bed. Fong had no doubt that the man was a danger to children. He also had no doubt that the man had the mental capacity of a ten year old and should have been put in an institution, not jail. Fong was forced to testify. At the trial, it quickly came out that the man had also sodomized several local children. The crowd outside the court was apoplectic with anger. The judge brought down his verdict without bothering to take a recess.

The hanging took place that afternoon. As the arresting officer, he'd been forced to walk the man to the scaffold. The man cried and peed his pants. He grabbed onto Fong's arm and begged to be allowed to go home. He promised to be good. That he knew he was a bad boy. That he was sorry. That he was frightened of all the people around him and he didn't know what was happening to him. When they put the noose around his neck, the crowd cheered. The man smiled as if he were being feted. Then a gunshot rang out. Everyone ducked. The boy slumped, held up by the noose around his neck.

The boy's mother stepped forward and surrendered her firearm. How had she managed to get a gun?

No one spoke. She walked away. Fong often wondered what had happened to her. Surely the only crime she had committed was saving the State the need to hang her son. But she had shot her son. She had shot her son — he would never forget her face.

Well, the expectancy in the crowd around this big building was the same as it had been at the hanging that day. Chen led Fong to the entrance and past the ticket taker. Fong was surprised by the price of admission to the building. It was twenty times greater than the cost of getting into the park itself.

Once inside, Fong followed Chen up a wide set of steep concrete steps. They climbed up and up and up and then followed a widening concrete tunnel to the bright light beyond.

Before them was a completely round space with seating on the second and third levels. The hard benches on the second level were completely packed. Fong guessed that there had to be more than a thousand people, almost all men. The comfortable upholstered chairs on the third level were two-thirds full. On the ground, there was an open concrete circle with a large drain in the centre. Around the outside of the concrete floor were barred cages.

Fong looked to Chen, who shrugged a particularly enigmatic shrug. "It's very popular, sir."

Fong was prevented from asking, "What's very popular?" by a cheer that erupted from the stands. A goat had been released from one of the cages. It let out an angry grunt as it raced into the centre of the ring. Even from a distance, Fong could see its nostrils flaring and hear its little sharp hooves clatter across the hard concrete.

Then another cage opened on the far side.

A full-maned lion strode out slowly and scented the air. The goat turned to see the danger. The crowd, as one, rose to its feet. At first, the lion seemed uninterested and pawed his way slowly around the perimeter. Then it turned and raced at the goat. The smaller animal dodged the attack and wheeled to face the second assault, but was too slow. A wide, taloned paw caught it along the flank. A slash of blood sailed six feet into the air and splattered to the concrete. For one horrific moment, the goat seemed to stare directly into Fong's eyes, then fell and the lion was on it.

The crowd cheered. Money passed hands. "There must be some sort of betting associated with this," Fong thought. A small tractor, its driver protected by thick metal meshing, came out into the arena and shooed the lion back into his cage. The goat's carcass was tossed in after the animal. Then, as several men with hoses washed down the arena (hence the drain in the centre), twenty Chinese girls dressed like cheerleaders came out and did a cheap imitation of something that some would call dance and others would call lewd. Fong called it neither.

Fong looked to Chen. "Let's get this over with. Where are they?"

Chen pointed to an enclosed luxury box overhanging the top of the stadium. They walked up a set of carpeted steps. At one point, Fong turned back to the stage.

The girls were finishing with a flourish. He'd never seen cheerleaders before and had no idea why anyone would dress this way. Yet another foreign influence that he could well live without.

At the door of the box Chen identified himself. Two large men frisked Chen and Fong. When one found Fong's ankle bracelet, he looked up. Fong said, "Everyone who is anyone has one of these in Shanghai."

For a moment the man pondered that. Then he smiled and checked Fong's crotch with much more force than was necessary. Fong did his best not to wince.

Once they passed inspection, they were guided through the door. Fong and Chen stepped into the room. It was air conditioned and, for China, extremely antiseptic. Two men sat in cushy leather chairs facing the arena.

A cheer went up from the crowd.

Fong couldn't resist taking a peek. A wild boar came racing out into the arena. Its deadly, cutting tusks were already smeared in blood. It kicked the concrete with its vicious hooves. The clacking sound snapped through the air of the arena.

"Do you like the games, officer?"

Fong swung back to face the speaker. He was a middle-aged man with smooth, handsome features and a cultured accent. This must be the financial officer, Fong thought. "Pak Tsz Sin," Fong said with the slightest nod of his head.

The man acknowledged the correct use of his title but said, "Not really all that hard to guess though, is it,

Detective Zhong? After all, I'm too young to be the Incense Master, aren't I?"

Be cool, Fong reminded himself, but couldn't resist saying, "You are that — too young, that is."

"But I am not," said the second man who turned in his chair to face Fong. The man was Fong's age and had deep pools for eyes and rage so clear that it sat on his skin like a sunburn. The man rose from the chair. He looked frail.

A second roar from the crowd announced the arrival of another beast.

"Go ahead, have a look, Detective Zhong. You want to. It's only human to know who has entered the ring."

"Who?"

"As you prefer — *what. What* has entered the ring."

Fong looked. The black panther was sleek and powerful. A full-grown male with bloodshot eyes and a shiny coat. He circled slowly, never taking his eyes off the deadly tusks of the wild boar. Fong forced his eyes back to the Incense Master.

The man had moved from his chair and was now halfway across the room, eyeing Fong.

"You want to talk about the boat." It was a statement not a question.

"I do," Fong acknowledged.

"Not our style, Detective Zhong."

Fong had always found it odd that gangsters thought they had style of any sort. Women, yes. Money, yes. Power, sometimes. But style, never.

"You mean killing's not your style?"

The Incense Master smiled. "Killing is such a condemnatory term, don't you find?"

"I wouldn't know about that."

"We are in business, Detective Zhong. We do what is good for business. Killing those foreigners on that boat was not good for business. We were already partway to an understanding with them. We'd offered the necessary protections for working in this part of the world."

"You mean you'd already settled on your extortion fees."

"More condemnatory terms, Detective. And no, we hadn't settled on terms. We were close though to an agreement that benefited all. In fact, as a show of our good faith we offered to supply the entertainment for the party on the boat."

"What was the party for?"

"A celebration, I believe."

"For what?"

"That was the foreigner's business — not ours."

"Yours was extortion."

The Incense Master smiled.

"So, you supplied the girls for the party."

"Women," he corrected Fong.

"But none of your men were on that boat?"

"Not a one."

"Explain this," Fong said as he threw him three pictures of the Triad insignia on the outside of the boat.

"Explain?"

"Yes, I assume you know the meaning of the term."

"I do. My explanation is that anyone with a brush and

paint could have marked the outside of that boat with our emblem."

"And this?" he threw him a photo of the Triad warning on the ceiling mirror of the dead American's room.

"That? That you'd need not only brush and paint but also a ladder. Do you have more pictures, Detective Zhong?"

"No."

"What a relief. I was beginning to think you were going to publish a book. Everybody does these days, don't they?"

"I wouldn't know. I do have this." Fong held up the Triad medallion on its broken chainlink.

The Incense Master laughed.

"What?" Fong demanded.

"Where have you been, Detective? Open the drawer over there."

The young financial officer opened the drawer for Fong. There were hundreds of medallions there. "They're big sellers, Detective Zhong. The tourists love them. They are a fine source of income for our business, as well as unpaid advertising. Like putting Tommy Hilfiger on a shirt, wouldn't you say?"

Fong didn't want to admit that he didn't know who Tommy Hilfiger was, but was saved the embarrassment of asking when a huge cry went up from the arena.

The panther had leapt at the wild boar, which had met the challenge by raising its cutting tusks. The sharp things had pierced through the underside of the panther's chin sending howling cries from the injured cat.

The boar then pushed hard off its tiny feet and pressed its advantage, trying to drive the tusks through to the panther's brain. The move, however, exposed the boar's underbelly. The cat raked the belly with its back claws. The boar roared and drove forward, its intestines falling as it moved. Blood shot from the panther as its head hit the concrete.

Boar tusks and panther claws did the work for which they were designed. Both animals twitched in the final throes of their lives. Then amid the mess and stink and offal, they died — and the crowd cheered.

Fong dragged his eyes from the event. Both Triad men were looking at him. Finally, the financial officer spoke. Indicating the arena, "That is what we do, Detective. We are here to make money, not scare it away. There was no money to be made in killing those foreigners. There was money to be made in 'assisting' the foreigners. Not in killing them."

"So you had nothing to do with it?" Fong said, feeling stupid.

"Oh, we had something to do with it, officer."

"What?" Fong demanded.

"As I said, we supplied the women." With that, he reached into his pocket and took out a fistful of gaudy-coloured business cards.

Chen took them.

The Triad man stared at Fong but pointed at the cards in Chen's hand. "Those women, Detective Zhong."

*   *   *

The coroner held the bar room section of the model in his hand. The tiny body of the eldest Chinese man swung gently from the rafter, his face a red blotch.

For an instant, the coroner felt the cut that severed the Achilles tendon then the yank that pulled the old man from his feet. No. They would have cut his face first. Then hauled him up into the air.

Keeping him upright would mean he'd bleed to death more slowly. With those facial wounds, he'd bleed out quickly if he were inverted. But he wasn't. It was meant to last.

The coroner had seen much of his countrymen's nastiness in his seventy-odd years. He had pulled apart the remains of more men than he cared to remember in an effort to find out how, if not why, anyone would inflict such damage on a fellow species member.

Little surprised him. He accepted much. He understood the deep nature of anger that resided in the Chinese heart. He condoned certain acts of vengeance as just human — just part of the darkness of being.

But the swinging man was an expression of something else. Perhaps not *chi*, but something other than anger. This was rage, a fury born of something very old, that is stored deep in the heart of humankind.

He replaced the section of the model, took a white cloth from his pocket and swabbed his face. He was clammy with sweat. He began to refold the cloth, but stopped suddenly when he saw to his shock that it was encrusted with rust-red deposits.

*   *   *

Chen pulled the Jeep out of its parking space and made his way through the crowd at the animal park by honking at anyone who dared slow his progress. When he finally got to the gate, he turned to Fong, "Do you believe them, sir?"

"Do you, Captain Chen?"

"I'm afraid I do. They had more to gain by the foreigners being alive than dead."

"And they are about making money, aren't they, Chen?"

"At least they have been for quite some time, sir."

"I actually think the most telling thing is that they didn't offer up some of their foot soldiers. Pin it on them. It would have been so easy, but they didn't."

"Can you figure out why, sir?"

Fong could, but the answer appalled him, so he kept it to himself.

Chen waited for a response then realized that none was forthcoming. He wasn't pleased but decided to change the topic. "What should I do with the women's business cards, sir?"

"Check them out." Chen nodded. "You saw a broken-down bus with young women on your way to the lake that night, didn't you?"

"Yes."

"Them?"

"That would be my guess, sir."

"Mine too, but make sure. Match the cards to accounts at the bus company. Who knows, we might get lucky."

"Do you believe in luck, sir?"

Fong didn't bother answering that either.

Lily stared at the model section of the small runway room. She glanced at the photos of the Japanese men on the chairs with the rags of intestine dangling between their legs staring up at her. She fought down her disgust both with the men and their demise. Then she felt for the girl who must have been on the runway — dancing to the music of the American rock band, Counting Crows.

Lily imagined her.

Up there.

Alone.

Lily often teased but never like that. Never like that.

The phone in the Jeep rang. Fong grabbed it. He listened for a second then shouted, "What?" Then quickly, "When?" He listened for a moment then cut the man off. "When exactly? Never mind. Don't let anyone near that cell. I want the whole place put off limits and I want all the men on duty prepared to be interviewed. Is that clear?"

Fong turned to Chen, "One of the islanders died in his jail cell."

Chen spun the steering wheel and pressed down hard on the accelerator.

The young warden who met them at the prison entrance was filled with excuses and apologies, clearly fearing that he'd be blamed for the death that had taken place on his watch.

Fong ignored the man and demanded to be brought to the cell. The remaining two brothers were in the basement isolation lock-ups. All that was left in the original cell was the dead man. Fong recognized the nervous man he'd interrogated two days ago. For a moment, he couldn't recall his name. Then he did. Hesheng, meaning: in this year of peace. He remembered that he'd made a joke about it — no one had found it particularly funny — not even those who watched the process.

The dead man sat with his back against the bars, his head slumped unnaturally far forward. Fong pushed open the cell door and stepped in. Hesheng's colour was already souring to that of a Caucasian. There were no overt indications of cause of death. There were no signs that a struggle had taken place. Just a man suddenly deep in sleep and not about to ever awaken again.

Although he knew that Hesheng was dead, Fong said, "Get me a pocket mirror, Captain Chen, and call the coroner, I want an autopsy done on the body. I want to know how he died." Fong felt, more than saw, the young officer leave. He wanted to be alone with the corpse.

Fong knelt down and moved his hand beneath the man's nose. No air movement. Dead men still don't breathe. Fong examined Hesheng's face. He seemed young. He seemed peaceful. Fong put his hand to the man's neck and pushed gently. The head moved. No rigour, so it hadn't been too long.

Then he sensed a movement. He couldn't tell where, but something was in motion. For a long moment he questioned his own perception, and then he saw it again. The man's shirt moved. Slid.

The mongoose leapt up his spine.

Fong jumped back, knocking a metal pitcher from the low table in the centre of the cell. The pitcher and a metal cup clattered to the floor.

The serpent emerged from the space between the top buttons of the dead man's shirt. Its slender yellow head pivoted with a sensuous ease, its tongue flicked out and tasted the air. The eyes, flat omens of death, slowly panned toward Fong, and then the head followed.

The mongoose turned and feigned indifference, although Fong sensed it ready to fight.

Fong tried to move, but slipped on the liquid that had spilled from the pitcher. In the back of his mind he noted that the water was slightly oily.

The mongoose flexed its knees and prepared to spring.

The serpent slithered down the front of the dead man, its eyes boring holes in Fong.

Fong rose slowly and moved away from the yellow presence. "Don't ever trap an enemy or it will have to fight." *The Art of War* phrase leapt into his mouth as he continued to back away.

Then the snake was in motion. Fast.

The mongoose pushed off Fong's spine and was instantly airborne.

Fong planted a foot and tried to leap away, but the oily liquid on the sole of his shoe made him slide and he crashed to the ground. For a second his head filled with blackness. When he snapped open his eyes, the lethal yellow head was within inches of his mouth.

Fong felt the serpent's breath on his cheek. How odd that death's breath should be so soft. So inviting.

Then the snake's head disappeared beneath a heavy boot.

Fong looked up.

Chen stood there squashing the last of the life from the surprisingly small reptile.

Fong sprung to his feet. He immediately sensed the mongoose was no longer with him. He glanced at Chen; the squat man seemed to have a lithe grace about him that wasn't there before. Fong understood. The mongoose had saved his life and moved on. He put his hand on Chen's shoulder. The man was shaking. "It's dead. Leave it."

Chen wanted to protest, but Fong was already searching the wall of the cell and calling to him, "There's got to be a hole." Fong ran his hand along the base of the wall. "There." He raced out of the cell yelling, "Collect a sample of that liquid on the floor."

Fong shouted at the two guards in the front to follow him as he ran around the side of the jail and counted cell windows until he got to Hesheng's. He approached the wall while holding up his hand to stop the two cops from following him. "Cordon off this entire area. It's a crime scene now. Tape it!" The guards looked at one another, not sure what the Shanghai cop was talking about.

Fong looked back toward the road. Nothing much

there. A tall-fenced landfill, a deserted industrial site. A good place to dig a tunnel and deliver a snaky message. For a moment he wondered if the message was for all three men. Then he rejected that. It was for Hesheng, and somehow it had found its mark.

It was for Hesheng because the man was becoming frightened.

Fong remembered the man's fear. It hung like a cloud before him. Fong had seen it. And so had they — the politico and Chen and the thug and the warden. They'd all seen the fear, and he'd added to that fear. He cursed himself, his stupidity, his vanity, his involvement in another death. His wife's — his friend Wang Jun's — and now Hesheng's.

Fong hitched up his pant legs and got down on all fours. He ran his palm along the base of the wall. The hole had to be there somewhere. Something gave beneath his hand. He pulled away some litter. At first he couldn't see it. Then he did. A single piece of dislodged mortar had fallen inward. He carefully removed the other pieces. The gap in the wall was almost square, cut by a sharp tool. He measured the square by spreading his fingers. The hole was wider than his outstretched fingers. He brought his hand, fingers spread, to his face. His fingers reached past his cheekbones.

A sharp cutting tool wider than a face — for an instant an image of the hanging man on the boat came to him — the face, one bloody scream.

He forced himself back to the present and cleared the area of debris. He looked into the passageway. It was grooved both top and bottom, about eight inches in diameter. As if it had been dug by a long corkscrew. Fong traced one of the grooves with his hand and imagined the yellow serpent rolling gently in the contours as it moved toward its prey.

An extremely long, sharp-tipped, corkscrew-like instrument, with an eight-inch diameter. Like the wide-bladed hoe they postulated was used to remove the faces of the Taiwanese men on the boat, this was another implement Fong had never seen.

Back at the factory, Fong filled in the others on the murder at the jail. The phone beeped the code for an incoming long distance call.

As Lily went to answer it she said, "A whole lot of death for a little place."

"I agree," said Fong.

"Where are the two brothers who avoided the serpent?"

"They didn't avoid it. They'd been moved several hours earlier," Fong replied. Before they could question him he added, "That's why there was only one cup by the water pitcher."

"More with the cups. You've become a specialist in disappearing drinking devices, Fong."

"Who took the brothers out of their cells, sir?"

"Don't know, Chen, but until it's answered I've ordered the brothers kept in holding cells apart from each other."

"Do you think they had something to do with this

snake thing, Fong?" asked the coroner. "Fuck, who kills with snakes?"

"Farmers," said Chen. "Farmers kill with snakes. By the way, the water on the floor was laced with insecticide."

"As a backup," asked the coroner, "in case the snake got tired or something?"

"The snake wouldn't get tired. It would have been starved for days to get it ready to kill on sight," said Chen.

"Snake through the wall, insecticide through the bars," Fong said softly.

"What's the sense in that?" asked the coroner.

"Hesheng was ready to talk. He had fear in his eyes when I interrogated him." Fong failed to mention that he hadn't insisted on being alone to interview the man. Others had seen Hesheng's fear. The politico, Chen, the warden and the thug. Chen had just saved his life so Fong was disinclined to finger him. The warden was just a labourer in a uniform. That left the politico and the thug. The old team reunited.

"What, Fong?" asked the coroner.

"Snakes from outside, insecticide from within. Dead bodies set up to be seen, but the boat torched," thought Fong. "Parallel patterns," he muttered.

Before anyone could comment, Lily snapped into the phone, "Are you sure?" That drew every eye. She nodded her head. "Thanks. As long as you're sure!" She waited for a moment, nodded again then hung up.

"What is it, Lily?" Fong demanded.

She raised her shoulders with a "here's another

mystery" look on her face. "The two American lawyers specialized in patent law dealing with DNA."

Chen asked Lily to clarify what she had said, but Fong wasn't paying attention. He was staring out the grime-encrusted windows. The sun was fading. Another day was ending. More questions had presented themselves. Good questions. But it was a bad day. One more dead body. One more soul on his conscience.

Fong divided up the assignments for the next day and retired to his sleeping mat. From his time west of the Wall he was used to falling asleep shortly after dusk and rising when the sun came up. But Lily had seldom been outside of Shanghai. Her day was only beginning when it got dark.

She wandered around the grimy, emptied factory unable to find sleep. Somehow, the men had all managed to drift off without a problem. Their snores attested to that.

Without thinking about it, she found herself in the far corner of the factory, where Fong had laid out his mat. She sat on the floor beside him and watched. He slept with his lids slightly open. It was eerie when his eyes began to move rapidly beneath. Eerie, but beautiful.

She still remembered the day he had held her in his arms after she'd been assaulted. She remembered how he had tried to help. His rough, tactless kindness.

She reached out and moved a strand of hair away from his forehead. Her nail traced a thin red line that appeared and then disappeared into his skin. Like love, she thought.

His eyelids fluttered, then opened. He looked up at her. "Thanks for the telegram," he said. Then his lids closed and his breathing deepened.

"He looks older," she thought. Then she reached out and touched his face. His head rolled over, nestling his cheek in her palm. As she watched him sleep, she had only one thought in her head: "Why had they let that telegram get through. She'd sent many others and all had been turned back. But that one got through. Why?"

CHAPTER ELEVEN

PARALLEL PATTERNS

The vigorous old man shifted on his sitting mat and stared through the open doorway at the terraced fields of the island. He and his had built those terraces from nothing. Brought something — wealth — from barrenness. Every ridge they had built. Every water barrier. Every path hewn from the stone. Even the soil they had made. They had put into the land and then reaped from that land. And they had kept to themselves. For centuries they had kept to themselves. Unwanted by their Han Chinese neighbours on the mainland, they had turned inward. For their sustenance. For their mates. For their lives. The wind off the lake momentarily swirled into the hut. The dense aroma from the fermenting pails of human fecal matter wafted into the room. "Must never forget that we are nothing more than the stuff that passes through us," he thought. Then he laughed. His many, many years entitled him to laugh without explaining why. The others waited.

Finally he spoke. "You're sure it was necessary, Jiajia?"

"Hesheng was losing hope, Iman," said his first great-grandson.

"And it is now done?"

"Yesterday, Iman." The old man looked at Jiajia. Many years divided them. Many years. But Iman felt for this one above his many other progeny. He had insisted at the boy's birth that he be placed on the highest, most exposed, hill of the island for a full day — sundown to sundown — his life or death to be determined by his own strength. And Jiajia, unlike many others, had survived — without a whimper — just as Iman himself had done all those many years before.

Like him, Jiajia had made contacts on the mainland as faraway as Xian. He was a patient learner and had a keen ear and sharp eye. He was even able to break down the sullen barriers of secrecy erected by the devious fishermen who lived on the island's south shore.

Then Chu Shi, Jiajia's intended, became infatuated with the off-islander, took him as a lover, became ill and suddenly died. It had changed Jiajia — made him stand up to Iman on that matter of taking her from the Earth. Made him almost uncontrollable. But he had come around lately. Although his face was now hard and almost unreadable, Iman believed his first great grandson to be loyal, and reliable, and resourceful, and smart. "Like me," Iman thought, "like me."

"We must collect Hesheng's body," Jiajia stated. "He must be buried with us." Then he added, "Especially at a time like this."

Everyone in the room knew what that meant. A long silence entered the room like an unwelcome guest. Finally the old man spoke, "I will see to this." He held Jiajia's eyes.

"It is the least we can do," spat back Jiajia.

Iman was shocked by the openness of the challenge in the younger man's voice. Was it what happened or the unearthing of his beloved Chu Shi that bothered Jiajia most? It was the unearthing. The other seemed to have brought him back to life. A cold, angry life, but one that Iman understood. Loss did that to young men.

Jiajia broke the silence. "Will Madame Minister . . . ?"

"We are not slaves!" Iman shouted, furious that Jiajia dared to presume. "We made our island. We make our own choices. We will act in our interests, not those of any minister in Beijing. Is that clear, Jiajia?"

Still stone-faced, Jiajia got to his feet and leaned against the mud wall of the hut.

The old man shifted in his squat and waited until all eyes turned back to him. "Is everyone prepared for the arrival of this policeman?" Affirmative grunts in many forms came from around the room. "Good. The ever-neighbourly townsfolk of Ching will no doubt point him in our direction shortly. More now than ever be wary of the fishermen; they are never to be trusted."

Many nods. "We believe that others have arrived from Shanghai to help this police officer."

The old man nodded slowly, "He's amassing his forces." Iman didn't bother saying out loud, "just as I would." He grunted then asked, "What's this police-man's name?"

"Zhong Fong, Iman."

"They brought this man here then drugged and beat him?"

"So it seems, Iman, but he appears to be in command now," his youngest great-grandson replied. The other men in the hut nodded agreement.

"Fong?" They nodded. "He's got a simple man's name?"

"Yes, Iman."

"I'd like to know more about him." He tilted his head.

A middle grandson looked at a first cousin. "It will be done." The two men left.

"Do we go for Hesheng's body now, Iman?" asked his first-born.

"No," the old man replied and pushed himself to his feet. "Now we plant." He strode out of the hut with remarkable agility and unhooked the two metal cans of shit on his doorposts and then slung them over his shoulder. "Six days of fermenting is enough. Now even this works for us," he announced. His large brood laughed and grabbed their farm implements. They fell into line behind him, shovels, rakes, hoes and a collection of small hand-forged tools slung over their shoulders.

As they headed toward the raised terraces of the island, Iman and Jiajia looked back at the beach. Two cormorant fishermen were readying their young birds for a first session on the water. Sensing they were being watched, the fishermen looked up. Wary nods were exchanged. The farmers and fishermen lived in a complicated truce worked out over the years but unsealed by marriages between the two groups.

On the fifth terrace level, the men passed a small

graveyard. Barely twenty discreet plots. Oddly small for a place that buried its own and had done so for as long as anyone could remember.

One of the graves was freshly dug. The men looked away as they passed as if looking at the turned earth would bring Jiajia's intended, Chu Shi, back to haunt them yet again.

After two hours of grilling Hesheng's brothers, Captain Chen and Fong met in the warden's office to compare notes.

"So, do you think they knew about this?" demanded Fong. The younger man hesitated. "Take a guess, Captain Chen!"

"You really want me to guess, sir?"

Fong looked at his ugly young colleague. He'd seen farm animals that were more attractive. But it was possible that Captain Chen was honest; maybe he'd been born that way. Maybe that's why the mongoose chose him. "Yes, Captain Chen, I want you to guess."

"Fine. I guess they both — the two of them — they both knew and didn't know."

Fong would have put it more elegantly, but that was his assessment too. "I agree."

"You do?"

"I do, Captain Chen. I think they both knew that Hesheng was in danger, but neither knew how or when or even if an attack was going to take place."

"They didn't murder their brother, then?" There was obvious relief in the statement.

"Not by anything they did," said Fong. "But that's only my guess."

Chen's anxiety increased. "Did they know about the insecticide in the water?"

"No. I don't think so." Fong looked away, anxious that Chen not read his face. When he turned back, the ugly young man was staring at him.

"Why bother bringing me along if you don't trust me?"

"Do you trust me, Captain Chen?" Before Chen could answer, Fong continued, "You remind me of a young detective in Shanghai. His name was Li Xiao."

After a breath of silence the younger man asked, "Was he a good cop?"

"Yes, Captain Chen, he was a good cop." Fong nodded, momentarily lost in a memory. He shook it off and said, "He was the chief investigator into my wife's death. In fact, five years ago, his testimony was central to the case that sent me to jail. So I ask you again, Captain Chen, do you trust me, a convicted felon?"

Captain Chen was cowed by Fong's admission. He sat and looked at his stubby fingers. When he finally opened his mouth, his usually dark voice was light — breathy — as if he were about to faint. "I don't think the world is a simple place, sir. I've often thought I should hand in my shield. I see both sides of everything. I can't begin to understand how justice works."

Fong sensed that it was unusual for Chen to speak so openly, so personally. He took advantage of the moment to plumb for information on this strange young man.

"Are you married, Captain Chen?"

"I am, sir."

"What kind of woman is your wife?"

"She's a sad woman, sir."

"Sir, he called me sir," thought Fong, "but this time, like I was his . . ." Before Fong could complete his thought, the young man spoke again.

"She can't seem to get pregnant. She wants a child. She blames me."

Three thoughts. Three short sentences. The end of a marriage — something that Fong knew a great deal about. Fong reached for a platitude and then rejected it. Instead he said, "I think we have two killers at work, Captain Chen. One sent the snake. The other poisoned the water."

"Both at the same time. A little far-fetched, isn't it?" His voice still had traces of falling in it.

"It was the first opportunity. It was the prisoners' next scheduled shower, after my interrogation. The shower facilities only allow for two at a time. It was Hesheng's turn to wait while the other two cleaned up."

"How did . . .?"

Fong held out a prison schedule.

Chen took it, saying, "And anyone could get hold of these?"

"Anyone who knew someone in the prison or even knew the basic workings of the place." Fong sat in the wooden chair and drummed his fingers on his knee.

"So there was opportunity. What about motive?"

"I may have supplied that."

Chen's mouth dropped open. He had bad teeth as well as everything else. "How did you . . .?"

"You saw me interrogate Hesheng the first time. I was out of practice but anxious to show everyone that I hadn't lost my skill. Well, I hadn't totally lost my skill and you all saw. Saw Hesheng about to break. After all he'd been through, I just nudged him over the edge. Everyone knew I'd be back for more. And when I came back he'd tell me everything. He had that much weariness in him. It was like he was holding a terribly heavy rock high over his head. His knees were shaking from the strain. He wasn't capable of bearing the load much longer."

Chen let Fong sit with his thoughts for a moment then said, "So both groups were set into motion at the same time."

"That's how I see it, Captain Chen. One responded with the snake, the other with the poison."

"You asked me to guess, so I guess that the one who used the snake killed those men on the boat and set it up as an object lesson. The poisoners tried to burn the boat," said Chen. His voice had returned to its lower register. "It's just a guess, sir."

Fong looked at the younger man and smiled. He could learn to like this ugly fellow. Silently he congratulated the mongoose on his choice. "So let's go find out who they are."

Chen smiled and said, "And administer a little justice?"

"No, Captain Chen, let's leave justice out of this. Let's just find out who did this."

"Then what?"

"Then . . . then we'll see what to do next."

A chorus of shouts and wails in the corridor drew their attention. Fong opened the warden's door and peered out. Three women and a vigorous old man were shouting at the officer. The gist was clear. They wanted Hesheng's body for burial. The officer looked to the warden who in turn looked to Fong.

Fong nodded.

"Don't you want Grandpa to open him up?" Chen whispered over his shoulder.

"It's not necessary. We know how he died and why he died — all we don't know is who killed him," said Fong as he continued to stare at the old man.

While an officer cleared the corridor, the warden returned to his office. "Who was he?" Fong asked.

"He's the elder out there on the Island of the Half-wits. They call him Iman."

Fong looked away. He didn't need the mongoose to tell him that danger was near. Iman's coal-black eyes were enough. But it wasn't just danger he sensed. It was something else. Something ancient. Wordless.

"Who the hell kills with snakes?" screamed Madame Wu in her Beijing office. Then she remembered her youth. Of course — farmers killed with snakes. *The fools acted on their own,"* she thought. "Call the warden," she ordered her assistant, "the body's not to be allowed to return to the island." *"Idiots,"* she thought, *"they don't know where this could lead."*

As her assistant made the call, Madame Wu looked out at the capital. How far she had come from her peasant roots. How desperately important it was that they all go back to those simpler times.

Her assistant hung up the phone and turned to her. He kept his eyes down. "The body's already been released, Madame Minister."

"Well, that might bring this Zhong Fong to the island," she thought. "Perhaps that's best." She raised her eyes to meet the assistant's. "I want Zhong Fong's file on my desk." The man looked like he was about to kow-tow. "Now!" she shrieked.

As the man scrambled from her office, all she could think was that when she screamed she sounded like her mother, hands burnt from the boiling water from which she plucked the silkworm cocoons, and angry — her mother, so angry at her wasted life.

Then she picked up her private line and hissed, "Find Chen — find my son."

Chen turned the factory lights off, plunging the space into darkness, then joined Fong, the coroner and Lily at the oval table. Once the coroner's grumbling died down, Chen turned on the first of his overhead projectors. The transparency of the wide-angle shot of the bar room appeared full size against the wall east of the table.

The image was startlingly clear. "So that's what a transparency does," thought Fong.

Chen turned on his second projector. The image of the

two murdered Americans lying on the bed filled the west wall.

"Who'd have guessed that the fire plug is mechanically inclined," snarked the coroner, but there were traces of admiration in his voice.

Chen turned on the last two projectors, bringing to life the video room with the dead Koreans on the south wall and the runway room with the mutilated Japanese on the north wall.

Fong rose. He found himself literally surrounded by death. The bar room, the bedroom, the video room and the room with the runway — and him in the middle.

"Turn them off," Fong said. His voice was harsh.

All four images disappeared. There was a moment of darkness then Chen turned on the factory lights, "I'm sorry, sir, I just thought . . ."

"Don't be sorry, Captain Chen."

"Shall I take down the projectors, sir?"

"No, leave them for now. Your work is good. Very good. But it gets us ahead of ourselves. Right now, I want the reports I asked you to prepare." He looked to the coroner. "Well," said the coroner, opening the notebook in front of him, "the guy who supplied the food for the boat party claimed that a boy came with the order and the money."

"Did he have it delivered to the dock?" Fong asked.

"Yeah. And the guy was pissed off that they wouldn't use his sons as waiters. The bandit claims he threatened to cancel the whole order."

"And the Pope wears a dress," said Lily sarcastically

in English. All the men, Fong included, turned to her with questioning looks on their faces. Lily smiled. It occurred to her that this would be more fun if there were another woman around. She laughed to herself. What an out-and-out lie that was. She nodded and said in Shanghanese, "I don't believe the restaurateur, do you?"

Fong compared "I don't believe the restaurateur, do you?" with "And the Pope wears a dress" and, despite his comprehensive knowledge of both languages, could not find a single point of commonality between the two statements.

"Who was the boy who came with the order and the money?" asked Fong.

"The asshole didn't know him. Said he looked retarded," said Grandpa.

"From the island?" asked Fong, suddenly interested.

"Who knows?"

"So he cooked the food and brought it to the boat, right?"

"He *prepared* the food, Fong. Yes, he was very precise on that point. He *prepared* the food." Each time the old man said "prepared the food" he lisped a little more.

"You make a terrifying homosexual," said Lily. In response, the coroner added mincing to lisping.

"Who received the food at the dock?" asked Fong, trying to keep his temper in check.

"Not just food. Food and substantial quantities of liquor."

"Okay, food and liquor. Who received them?"

"No one."

"What?"

"He was instructed to leave it in a cart by the wharf."

"Could he describe the cart?" asked Fong.

"He could and did — wood frame, wooden wheels, long timber poles to attach to an animal's harness."

"Great, that narrows it down to every farmer within a day's ride," snapped Fong.

The coroner began to chuckle.

"Something funny, Grandpa?" Fong demanded.

"Have you ever drunk champagne, Zhong Fong?"

"No. Why?"

"Well, this restaurateur was asked to supply champagne for the festivities."

"So?"

"So, he was asked to supply it in bottles with twist-off caps."

"So?"

"So, good champagne doesn't come with twist-off caps. They have sealed tops and corks," said Lily. Everyone looked to her. "As an attractive and available Han Chinese girl, on occasion I am treated to the delectations of the West — by boys."

Fong was happy she hadn't tried to say that in English. But he was concerned that things were getting out of hand. "So what, I repeat."

"So," Lily said in English. "Twist-off cheap, cheap. Why cheap, cheap for boat guys? No sense makes."

Bad English or not, Lily's point was made.

Fong began to nod his agreement as Chen and the coroner complained loudly about Lily's use of English.

In the midst of Lily's repetition of her sentiments in Shanghanese, Fong said, "That's how the poison got on board."

"That would be my guess," said the coroner. "Of course, it's possible that the local cuisine killed these guys without the use of additives. It's sure doing its work on me." At that the old man's flatulence filled the air.

"Nice, very. In a lady's front, no less," shouted Lily in English.

Fong grinned. Lily did not.

After a brief recess, literally to allow the air to clear, it was Chen's turn to report on his conversation with the boat owner.

"May I point out something?"

"No," snapped Fong, "just do what I asked, Captain Chen. Tell us exactly what was said when you interviewed the boat owner?"

"Exactly?" Chen asked.

It appeared to Fong that the man was blushing. He couldn't guess why, so he bulled forward, "Word for word."

Chen coughed into his hand to hide his embarrassment. Then he flipped open a notebook and read from his notes.

Q: Are you the owner of the boat that sank in the lake?

A: No.

Q: No?

A: This is China. No one owns anything.

Chen said, "He laughed then." Under his breath he muttered, "He laughed a lot."

Q: Are you in charge of the rental arrangements for the boat that sank in the lake?

A: Who the fuck are you?"

Q: I'm a police officer investigating the events that transpired on board that ship.

A: You talk funny and you are a seriously ugly puke.

"He stopped at that."

"Did you threaten him, sewer rat?" asked the coroner nonchalantly.

"No," Chen said threateningly.

"Let's get on with it," said Fong. "What happened next?"

"I showed him my ID."

"Not the picture one, I hope," gulped the coroner.

Chen looked to Fong. Fong shrugged in the coroner's direction, "He's overexcited because he's out of town. What did you ask next?"

Chen took a deep breath and started again.

Q: So are you the person in charge of the boat?

A: I was.

Q: Was?

A: It's sunk, gone, no more. So I'm not the person in charge of the boat anymore, am I? You going to write all this down?

Q: Yes. Who rented the boat from you?

A: A guy.

Q: Which guy?

A: The guy who rented the boat.

Q: You always such a smart ass?

A: Your face always look like a pimpled ass?

"Hide you ass," Lily said in her personal variant of the English language.

"So 'Hide you us' means *hideous*. Swell." Fong thought. But what he said was, "What did you learn from this turd, Captain Chen? What did you learn that we need to know?"

Chen put aside his notebook. "The guy had all the necessary clearances to give the boat to foreigners. His men got the boat out onto the lake, handed the controls over to the Taiwanese guy with the pilot's licence then took one of the lifeboats back to shore."

"Did he or his men see anyone, other than the dead men, on board the boat?"

Chen hesitated.

Before Chen could speak, the coroner piped up with, "Shit."

Chen smiled. The smile sat oddly on his features.

"May I add my information now, sir?"

"Certainly, Chen," Fong responded testily.

"Thank you, sir." He took a breath, enjoying the moment then said, "They saw the girl."

"Which girl?" asked Lily.

Captain Chen's smile increased. He reached into his pocket and took out one of the business cards the Triad man gave him. "This one." He flipped the coloured business card onto the table.

"Nice picture," the coroner said.

"Doesn't that ever go away," Fong thought. "What about the writing, Grandpa?" he asked.

The coroner moved the card far from his face and read in a booming voice: **"Sun Li Cha — Mistress of the Ancient Arts.** Then some foreign scratching."

Lily grabbed the card. "It's English, I think," she said in Shanghanese. The coroner looked at her. "English speaks me. It doesn't read me," Lily told him.

Fong took the card and read the English. "**Sunny Lee — Mistress of the Cervical Arts**." Fong didn't have a clue what that meant. But Lily was suddenly on her feet, pacing.

"I know that reference in English. I've heard it before," she said in Shanghanese. "I've seen it on TV."

Fong stared at her. Unless television had changed drastically during his years on the other side of the Wall, he doubted that Sunny Lee's artistry had ever been seen on a television set in the People's Republic of China.

"Got it!" Lily announced. "Got it! It's that game the British play with sticks and balls on a green table. The announcer calls it (here she switched to English) 'The Academy of Cervical Arts.'"

Fong briefly wondered if Lily knew any English at all. Then he recalled dealing with a rape case early in his time with Special Investigations in Shanghai. He remembered his embarrassment when he was forced to learn the English names for female private parts. In many ways, it was an education for him since the Chinese names were more fanciful than scientific. He remembered nodding like an idiot as the doctor briefed him on the assault. Then he took the doctor's report home to Fu Tsong. They were eating a meal he had prepared when he chose to ask his questions. She'd at first found it funny then slowly realized that Fong was deadly serious. Embarrassed, but deadly serious. So she led him through — part by part.

It had bonded them even closer together — had made her infidelity even more devastating.

Fong spoke. "Let's leave it that she was part of the entertainment on board ship, shall we?"

Chen took the card from Fong and flipped it over. "Personally, I thought this was of more interest." He pointed at a phone number. Fong swore under his breath.

"It's a local Xian number."

"It's probably just a cell phone," said Grandpa.

"She'd have to register an address to get a cell phone," said Chen.

"And I'm sure she gave an accurate account of her lodgings to the authorities, fart face."

"Get her name and picture to Xian vice. Xian's a big tourist town, they're bound to know her," said Fong.

Chen nodded, was about to say something then thought better of it.

Fong said, "Well done, Captain Chen."

"Thank you. I can complete the transparencies if you want, sir."

"Complete how?"

"With more projectors I can detail the floors and ceilings to go with the walls."

"Do it, Chen."

Chen nodded and headed out.

The coroner spat a wad across the room then said, "So who does he work for, Fong?"

Fong didn't respond. Everything about Chen was

confusing. A good cop, but a yes man. In charge, but obviously a junior officer. Fong could see him as a party man, but there was something wrong about that too. It didn't sit well. "Didn't stack well" was the phrase that came to him and, with a smile, he filed it away. "I don't know, Grandpa. What's your guess?"

The coroner cleared his throat. "He's connected, but not like the commissioner back in Shanghai or the guy who put that leg cuff on you."

"Then how is he connected?"

"Have you been to Beijing, Fong? No, course not, you're just a stupid cop when all is said and done."

"Thanks."

"Think nothing of it." Something sad crossed the old man's features. "Beijing is set up in boxes, Fong. Then boxes within those boxes. And each box is kept apart from all the other boxes. Mao understood revolution, after all. And he, and those who followed him, knew how to prevent further revolutions. Stop the boxes talking to each other and make them do all their communicating through the chairman's office. Then be sure that only the chairman's office deals with the outside world. But sometimes boxes get it in their heads that they can make their own connections without the chairman's office — first to other boxes and then to the world beyond boxes — beyond Beijing. Sometimes they even try to spawn boxes of their own. They're called rogues." He said the word *rogues* a second time but this time it was in a hoarse, pained whisper. "Very Chinese if you think about it. I was called once from one such box." He paused as if something sour had touched his tongue. When he spoke again, his voice was thin. Uncertain. "A man had been decapitated in a party hotel suite. The wife had called me. She was a powerful government minister. Head of a box." He chuckled briefly, but the sound was as dry as the air from a hot kiln. "She'd found her husband down in Shanghai with a younger woman or a boy — it really doesn't matter. What matters is that I was called in. At first I thought it was through official channels. But quickly it became apparent that wasn't the case. The wife was acting on her own — as a rogue. She wanted a death certificate stating death by natural causes. I laughed at her and told her, 'Sure — he came so hard his head fell off.' She didn't laugh."

The old man paused. Pain passed over his features like a cloud obscuring the sun. He spat angrily.

"I'm a diabetic. She knew. She told me that if I didn't give her the death certificate, my supply of insulin would be cut off."

Fong thought he'd never seen anyone look so old.

"I signed the papers. I got the insulin. I'm still here." His voice was light as dust in the wind.

Fong thought about it. The coroner had covered up a murder. A crime. But if he hadn't, he'd have died a long time ago. Would it have been worth dying to punish the party woman? Fong didn't know. In the years since the incident, the coroner had been invaluable in bringing hundreds of cases to successful completion. Without him — who knows? Fong shook his head, but said nothing. He just filed it under "another case of relative justice."

"So you figure Chen may be on a leash from one of those Beijing boxes, Grandpa?"

"I don't know, Fong."

Fong didn't figure Chen to be with the people who set up the exhibit on the boat and killed Hesheng with the snake or with the people who tried to burn the ship and poison Hesheng.

Then a bit of logic that had escaped him fell into place. Someone sets up an exhibition of dead foreigners. What would the reaction be to that display? "How far are we from Xian?" he asked.

"It took us two hours to get here from the Xian airport," answered Lily.

Before she could question him further, Fong continued, "And there are lots of foreigners in Xian. No?"

"Yes, stupid foreigners like clay Chinese better than living ones," the coroner commented, smirking.

"What about foreign press?" Fong asked.

"Got to be some there," said Lily as she leaned in closer to Fong.

"So, whoever killed those foreigners on the boat and set them up as an object lesson would want the world outside of China to know what they did. Agreed? The dead were all foreigners, after all. Chinese wouldn't care. This would have to be for foreign consumption."

Heads nodded slowly. Carefully.

"And what would be the world's reaction to this sort of thing?" Before anyone could reply, Fong answered his own question, "They'd freak. All their suspicions about us, their fears of us would rise to the surface."

"And they'd pack their bags and head back to wherever they came from," said the coroner.

"Taking all their money with them," added Fong.

That settled in the air of the room like something hot and heavy.

"Not something the Triads would encourage," said Lily.

"Not at all."

Fong's teeth clacked.

"So, whoever did the killings on that boat and killed Hesheng with the snake wants foreign money out of China?" asked the coroner.

"Whoever did the killings, Grandpa, or whoever in Beijing *induced* the killings to be done," hissed Fong. His anger surprised the others. It crackled in the air.

"A rogue," said the coroner in a sad voice.

"That makes sense to me," said Fong.

"I'm not sure . . ." The coroner didn't complete his thought. He didn't need to. Everyone in the room understood. The coroner wasn't sure that this was worth pursuing, that he wasn't up to another meeting with a Beijing rogue.

"And the burn marks on the ship, Fong?" asked Lily.

They all realized that they were near something very dangerous.

When Fong opened his mouth, he spoke slowly. "Beijing wants to bring foreign money into China. That's been the government's party line since Deng Xao Ping." Fong folded his arms and thought, "The order to burn that boat could have come from the highest levels in Beijing."

"How does it work, Fong? What's the sequence?" asked Lily guiding them away from the terror of the big picture and back to the actual events of a crime.

"Chen gets the report, Lily, about the ship . . ."

"Or he claims to get the report, Fong," said the coroner.

Fong nodded. "Agreed. He reports back what he finds — what the rogue in Beijing did — or had done — the dead foreigners set up, awaiting an audience of journalists to spread the word around the world. Beijing has a problem. Seventeen dead foreigners. Influential foreigners. No way to hide it. But seventeen dead foreigners is better than seventeen dead mutilated, gutted, castrated and decapitated foreigners."

"So Beijing tries to burn the boat, hoping to claim that the seventeen died in a boating accident?" asked Lily.

"Right, but they got unlucky with the ice storm and the sharp rocks of the shoal."

"So Beijing brings in the specialist and blames the three half-wit brothers?"

"So why were you sent for, Fong?" asked the coroner. "To prove they're serious to the foreigners?"

"No. I don't think so."

"So who sent for you? The murderers or the burners? The rogue or official Beijing?"

"The burners — Beijing."

"Why, Fong? Why would the ones who burned the boat send for you?" asked Lily.

"Because they want to know what really happened out there," stated the coroner and looked to Fong. Fong didn't reply.

"So you can find the murderers, right, Fong?" asked Lily.

"In a way. They want the murderers found. But not because they want to see justice done. They want the murderers so they can trace their way from the murderers back to who ordered the murders — the rogue — in Beijing."

The heaviness in the room deepened. Everyone understood what Fong was saying — that they were just being used in a much bigger game. That no one gave a shit about the dead men. Or maybe even who killed them. Or maybe even the Western money. The only thing Beijing wanted was the path back to the rogue in their midst.

"It would help if we knew who the specialist worked for, Fong," said Lily.

Fong looked at her. How very much he admired this strong young woman. What a good cop she was. How her loneliness touched him. But Fong hesitated to share what was in his head because he was reasonably sure that the specialist was from yet another Beijing box — perhaps a box of one. Fong wondered if he was ill. If he was dying. If he was alone.

Fong kept it all to himself. "Whoever killed those men would want the foreign press to know about it. They must have contacted them. Lily, you follow that."

"It's bound to lead to Xian."

"No kidding," Fong said. A lot seems to lead to Xian . . . and to the island.

"So, while Chen's looking for the hooker and Lily's

investigating the Western press, what are you going to be doing, Fong?" asked the coroner.

"I'm going to a funeral, Grandpa. Want to come?"

The moment the words were out of his mouth, Fong regretted them. He had embarrassed an elder in public. Fong bowed his head slightly. The coroner waited for a beat and then acknowledged the apology. But he had no comeback. He turned from Fong and shuffled out of the dirty factory.

Fong began to follow, but Lily stopped him. "Don't, Fong," she said gently. "It must be terrible to be old and know as much about death as he knows."

Fong looked at her. Sadness, like spring weeds after a storm, blossomed in her eyes.

CHAPTER TWELVE

AN ISLAND FUNERAL

ong didn't want to be late for Hesheng's funeral rites, but he delayed his departure as long as he could. Even the thought of a boat ride made him queasy. But islands, by their nature, required the crossing of water. Finally he went down to the docks and gingerly boarded the boat that Chen had arranged to take him to the Island of the Half-wits. The boat rocked. They hadn't even left the dock and Fong already felt sick. But any impulse to step out of the boat and back onto dry land was stopped because so much pointed toward the island — and Xian. "What did the Island of the Half-wits and Xian have in common?" he asked himself. "An isolated island in a big lake and the ancient capital of China's first emperor. What could they possibly share?" The boatman pushed off and the voyage began. Although the morning had brought a cold wind, Fong found himself quickly slick with sweat.

He took a deep breath and made himself examine the boat. Something, anything to distract himself from the vaulting nausea in his gut.

The vessel was a Chinese-style gondola designed for fishing and carrying cargo. The boat's owner stood at the stern and moved his oar back and forth to propel and steer the boat. In typical Chinese fashion, why use an oar and a rudder — just lengthen the oar and it can act as both. Also, typically Chinese, all the power needed was generated by human muscle. No motor here, just an angry-faced boatman.

As they got farther from shore, the water on the large lake became more choppy. Fong dearly wished he'd skipped the breakfast porridge. At one point he was sure that he was going to lose the contents of his stomach, but a terse threat from the boatman made it clear that if he did he'd have to clean it up — with his tongue. So Fong kept his mind off his stomach and held on tight.

"How long till we get there?" he asked through gritted teeth.

The boatman shrugged and reiterated his threat to make Fong lick up anything he "left" in the boat. Fong was about to reply that he was a police officer and the man had better remember that, but he was afraid to speak. He kept his peace — and his mouth shut.

Fong turned away and spotted a cormorant fisherman far off to the port side. The old fisher had just released one of his elegant birds and was preparing a second for the day's work.

When young, Fong, like most Chinese children, had been told stories about the famous fishermen who used trained cormorants rather than hook, bait and rod, but he'd never seen one before.

He noted the lantern stands at the front and back of the fisherman's boat.

"Do they fish at night?" he managed to ask.

"Night, day, winter, summer — they're always there," the boatman answered with a sour sneer. Fong assumed he didn't like cormorant fishermen. Why should he? He didn't seem to like anything else. Why should cormorant fishermen escape his venom?

As Fong watched, a mature cormorant hopped up onto the fisherman's boat and waddled over to the old man. The man's gnarled fingers reached out and stroked the bird's long neck — from its beak down to the glinting metal ring at its base. The bird cooed and released a fish from its throat. The plump thing flapped on the seat of the boat for two beats then disappeared to the floor. The fisherman fondled the bird again and fluffed its feathers before committing the animal once more to the lake's cold waters.

From a distance, the cormorant and the old fisherman appeared to be ideally fitted — two halves of a cross-species partnership. At least that's what the children's stories would have one believe.

"There," said the boatman in a guttural exclamation from behind Fong. He was pointing to the right.

The island had come up quickly. Fong looked at his watch. They'd been on the lake for just over an hour — a personal best that he had no desire to challenge.

There was no wharf on the Island of the Half-wits, just a rocky beach where several fishing boats rested at cocky angles. One was flipped over and two men were re-gumming the starboard side of the keel with a dark resin. Women sat on some of the larger rocks cleaning and dressing fish. Children walked beside baby cormorants that picked their way carefully among the sharp stones. The whole scene struck Fong as oddly domestic — like Shanghai on Sundays.

To the north along the rock-strewn beach, tendrils of smoke came from the fishermen's huts. Past them, a gravel path led steeply upward to what Fong guessed was the farmers' enclave.

As he approached, eyes followed him. Just like in the village west of the Wall. But something was different here and Fong felt it the moment he'd left the shoreline and headed inland. It was as if he'd left China. Not just modern China, but China altogether.

Like every other conquering power, the Communists made deals with local power elites. Over the years, Mao and his successors had reneged on, or renegotiated, a great many of those agreements. But China is a vast country and during the War of Liberation, thousands, perhaps tens of thousands, of virtually autonomous regions formed. On the whole, if a region was small and self-contained, the Communists left it alone. Clearly this island, the Island of the Half-wits, was such a place.

As Fong moved farther inland, the place got somehow older and definitely more foreign. Even the pattern of the farmers' huts hit an odd chord in him. The only familiar objects were the pails of night soil hanging on either side of every doorway. As he passed them, their scents told Fong how long the material had been ripening.

Old skills never really die — they ferment.

Then he heard the braying of a horn and the slash of a cymbal.

Fong followed the sound to the back of the huts. A procession was forming. It seemed that the whole village had assembled. Not the whole island, he noted. The fishers stayed to themselves.

Four young men lifted a scarlet-sheeted body above their heads and started up the path. The red cloth was the most intense red Fong could remember.

A long line of vigorous, work-toughened men walked slowly behind the body. They were dressed from head to toe in white. The old man Fong had seen at the jail — Iman — led the procession.

Fong scanned the men. They shared similar facial features. Almost all were the same height, all had the same square body type — shit they even used the same shambling gait.

The women followed the men. Once again led by an elder. Once again in white. The women were as rugged as the men and resembled them closely. They looked like they'd all sprung from the same set of loins. But there seemed to be no mental deprivation here. Only a sameness — and an undeniable vigour.

The rhythm of the cymbals increased and the procession picked up speed heading straight up the terraced hills toward the centre of the island. As they passed by terrace after terrace, the procession began to sing. The words were ancient. "Death is ancient," Fong thought. "It invites us all with cymbal and horn — like a Peking Opera performance."

By the time the body reached a dry terrace, two-thirds of the way up the mountain, Fong had fallen far behind. He knew they'd seen him, but when he crested the final rise he was surprised to find them lining either side of the path. The singing had stopped. The only sound was the blare of the mournful horn — and Fong's wheezing efforts to supply his lungs with oxygen.

Fong walked slowly between the rows of faces. Up close he saw that some were so alike that he was sure he wouldn't be able to tell one from the next even after concerted study. Then he was there — at the end of the line of islanders — facing the one called Iman. Behind the vital old man stood the four younger men with the crimson-swathed body of Hesheng on their shoulders. Suddenly, Iman snapped his head downward in a gesture of submission as old as the land upon which they both stood. "You honour us with your presence."

Fong wouldn't have been more surprised if the old man had whipped out his penis and sprayed his name in the dirt. Fong nodded slightly, careful to keep his head above the level to which Iman had lowered his. Iman's eyes held Fong's for a long moment.

The interment began.

Some of Fong's acquaintances had passed away, but none of them had been formally buried. No one was put in a box and dropped into a hole anymore in the great Communist state. Even funeral ceremonies were frowned on.

A shallow grave had already been scraped from the moist ground. The body in its scarlet swathing lay beside the hole. The trumpet sounded and the cymbals crashed a-rhythmically. Then Iman raised his hands and cried out, "Take Hesheng back to you. We commit him to your care. We honour you, our ancestors, and now him, by committing him to your care. Take Heshing back to you, our ancestors."

"Why are rituals always repetitious?" Fong wondered.

Iman paused. His mouth opened then shut.

Fong took a step closer, anxious to hear what Iman would say next. But he said nothing. "Why?" Fong thought. "A man of Iman's advanced years must have recited the burial ceremony dozens, if not hundreds, of times." Yet the man stood stock-still, clearly lost as to what to say next.

Finally, Iman signalled that Hesheng's body should be put in the ground.

Fong backed off and climbed a slight rise at the back of the graveyard. He looked around him. The place was small. Few plots.

Then his eye landed on a grave directly beneath the wall. The soil on top had not yet settled. Night soil–laden dirt did that — took a long time to pack. He looked up. Above him was a hand-hewn terrace wall that no doubt held back an upper paddy's water. In the rainy season it could overflow, depositing night soil in the graveyard. Night soil.

He looked at the grave. It had been dug recently.

He crossed over to it and picked up a handful of dirt. He let it run through his fingers. Memories of his youth flooded through him — and of the bag of dirt the specialist had taken as evidence from the sunken boat's runway. Dirt on the stripper's runway. Night soil–laden dirt. Like the dirt from this grave.

Fong felt a tendril of cold slither up his spine as a possibility — a shocking possibility — presented itself. Then he looked behind the grave's headstone. And a piece fell into place. There on the ground stood a small column of free-standing stones, one balanced perfectly on the next. Four stones. Stacking stones. "The stones are a way of marking time, Detective Zhong. A way of noting its passage. One stone for each . . ."

"Of my visits," Fong said aloud. Xian and the Island of the Half-wits — Dr. Roung the archeologist from Xian, and whoever was buried in this grave.

As he reached out to touch the head stone, a foot kicked his hand aside. "Don't touch that!" The command's sharp nasal tones broke the silence.

"I intended no . . ."

"Do you want her dug up again?" There was something odd in the voice. Fong caught a glint in the young man's eyes that he'd seen before in violent men. A madness. A spiralling; anger that had no floor. Fong marked him closely. He looked like the other islanders, but there was something different about him. Something to be feared.

Fong stepped back. He didn't want to fight this man.

"Jiajia!"

Both Fong and the younger man looked up. Iman strode briskly toward them. "This man is a guest on our island, Jiajia."

There was a tick of silence. Jiajia gave Fong a hate-filled look then said, "Yes, Iman," and stomped away.

Iman turned to Fong then glanced at the grave. "Her name was Chu Shi. She was Jiajia's wife." Fong nodded. "Death is hard on the young." Iman made his face into a rough approximation of a smile then returned to the others who were lowering the crimson-sheeted Hesheng into the ground.

Fong watched Iman move — *lope* was the word that came to him. "When I get old, I want to be that healthy," he thought.

Fong took a last look at Chu Shi's headstone, and then at Hesheng's. Hesheng's name was on his and the date of his passing, but no other dates. There were no dates at all on Chu Shi's grave marker.

Fong began down the terraced mountain, suddenly anxious to be alone with his thoughts.

As he approached the waiting boat he didn't know which was worse — the shocking possibilities he'd found by Chu Shi's grave or his imminent lake voyage back to Ching.

Dr. Roung stood on the shore of the great lake and watched the sun set. In the distance he could just make out the figure of a lone worker in an upper paddy on the Island of the Half-wits. Well, not really the worker. Just the glint of the fading light off his broad trench-hewer. Then the glint faded. Like everything else on the island. A brightness, a hope, and then no more.

The island. The place that had changed his life.

Lifted his eyes from his concentration on small pieces. Showed him new possibilities. Great possibilities. The chance not to recreate but to create — to create something that could last and last. Not for as long as the terra-cotta warriors, but long. Long and alive. Something that was his and could very well carry his identity, his very self, forward through time. As he thought the word — *time* — he elongated the vowels.

Far to his right was the shoal that had first brought him to this place. The shoal was also the structure on which the luxury boat had floundered and from which it had eventually entered, ice-covered and scorched, into the inky winter water. A lone fisherman with two cormorants on the gunwhales of his boat glided directly toward him. How did he always know? Everything.

This fisherman had discovered the artifact. One of his cormorants had returned to the boat with something caught in its throat. The fisherman had stuck his hand all the way down its lengthy gullet. What he came up with, after considerable tugging and much cursing, was a moss-encrusted object that he would have tossed back into the water, accompanied by the appropriate obscenity for wasted effort, had he not noted the dull sheen of metal. It was no doubt that hint of brightness that had first attracted the bird.

The old schemer pocketed the object and took it home. There he carefully chipped away the growth then polished the object which, after much attention, revealed itself to be a startlingly accurate depiction of a horse's hindquarters and rear legs rendered in bronze. It was just over three inches in length and beautifully done — a fact that escaped the fisherman.

What didn't escape him was the possibility that the thing might be worth something.

It took him several months of judicious asking around before he found out about Dr. Roung, the archeologist in Xian, and another few months before he made his way to the ancient capital. He'd never left the environs of the lake before. But profit was a powerful motivator.

One chilly morning, the smelly man was ushered through Dr. Roung's office door. The archeologist had been examining the medieval Italian's book about China that had so long puzzled him. He didn't like puzzles he couldn't solve. But he never considered conceding defeat. He took a last look at the book and returned it to the shelf. Without turning to face the fisherman he said, "My assistant tells me that you have something to show me?"

The fisherman looked around, not sure what to say or do.

The archeologist looked at the old man.

"Would you like a drink?"

The fisherman's eyes widened. Dr. Roung never drank himself, but had found strong Chinese wine a useful enticement with the locals. He poured a glass. The man sat down.

Two glasses later, the man was ready to talk. "Excellency. Do you purchase ancient things? Small, ancient things?"

"From time to time I do."

"It's small, though," the man said tentatively.

"Size is seldom an issue."

The fisherman smiled then screwed up his face as if what he was about to say would cause him great pain. "What if it's broken?" There was anxiety in the fisherman's voice.

A brightness flashed for a moment across Dr. Roung's face, then was gone. He took a breath. Then, with his anticipation concealed safely behind his eyes, he asked, "Cracked, you mean?"

"No, Excellency, broken — as if in half."

The archeologist looked away from the fisherman. A few months earlier, he and his team had begun the third phase of the reclamation of the terra-cotta warriors. During the dig he had come across six small half-sculptures. All horses. All the front end — the emperor's end. "Is it of a horse?" he asked as casually as he could manage.

The fisherman emitted a hiss.

"It is of a horse, isn't it?"

The fisherman stumbled to his feet. "He thinks I'm a witch," Dr. Roung thought. "Good." He took a breath then said, "It's worthless, old man." He unlocked a drawer to his desk and took out the six half-horses and put them on the desk. "Worthless," he repeated.

But the fisherman was canny. Over his many years he had done much bartering for fish and on occasion for cormorant chicks. "If they were worthless, why keep them under lock and key?" he thought. But he said nothing. Just bent his shoulders and turned toward the door.

"Show me your find, old man."

"Why, Excellency?" The old fisherman locked eyes

with the archeologist. "It has no value."

"Show it to me." Dr. Roung allowed a threatening tone into his voice. The fisherman heard it and backed off. Slowly he reached into his pocket and pulled out a dirty rag. Holding it in the palm of his left hand, he unwrapped the tiny thing.

The archeologist had to control his excitement. The perfect hindquarters were the first he had ever seen. His fingers itched to fit it together with one of the six frontquarters he had. His keen eye quickly eliminated the chance of a match with the first three of his horses. But horses four and six were real possibilities.

"Are there more where this came from, old man?"

The man scratched his neck, but didn't answer.

"If you know where this came from, and are willing to show me, I'll pay you handsomely."

"How handsomely?" snapped back the old fisherman.

Dr. Roung stepped past the man and left the office. Moments later, he returned with a packet of kwais. He held out the bulging envelope and said, "More money than you'll earn in ten years."

The fisherman reached for the packet, but the archeologist pulled it away. He extracted ten 100-kwai notes and dangled them from his fingers.

The fisherman held out the small statuette.

The exchange was made.

"Now show me where you found this, old man, and the rest of the money is yours."

*   *   *

The fisherman guided Dr. Roung to the lake. The archeologist had never been there before. He didn't even know there was a large lake so close to Xian. The water was clear, and there, just off the side of the fisherman's tippy boat, not four feet down, was a large mound. Clearly it had been man-made. The formation of the stones was very similar to those he'd unearthed with the terra-cotta warriors. It was possible that the shoal was in fact the tip of another tomb. He took out the hindquarters that the fisherman had given him. Qin period for sure. Could this be the tomb of one of the first emperor's generals? That was who had the back end of the horses. The emperor Qin Shi Huang had kept control of the movement of troops by having these split horses made. The emperor kept the front half of each. The hindquarters were given to various generals. When a messenger arrived bearing the emperor's part of the horse that completed theirs, the general supplied troops. Troops were power. Control of power was everything.

The archeologist saw that the fisherman was clearly uncomfortable. "Ah, he wants his money," he thought. But he was wrong.

The obligation of hospitality is real in rural China. Despite not wanting anything to do with the archeologist, the fisherman was duty-bound to offer him a meal. Grudgingly he asked, "Would your Excellency honour my humble home by taking some food?" The archeologist was duty-bound to accept the offer.

Dr. Roung noted the landmarks to be sure he could find the shoal again, then nodded.

It was on landing that first time on the Island of the Half-wits that he saw her. Chu Shi — Jiajia's intended. She was stooping to fill her wooden pails with water from the lake. With square shoulders and weathered skin, she was far from the elegant Han Chinese women that he'd known. Her hands were big and rough. But there was depth in her eyes.

Then she smiled at him.

He felt himself falling, somehow the ground beneath him had suddenly shifted and he was plummeting down a great chasm.

The old fisherman stared at him, a faraway look in his eyes. A knowing, no, an understanding look.

"Who is she, old lecher?"

For a moment the old man seemed openly offended and then he softened, "Not one of us. One of the farmers. One of the half-wits. They keep to themselves, Excellency." His voice was off-centre. He took a step forward and said as casually as he could, "Perhaps Excellency would like to meet . . ."

"I will double your fee if you arrange it."

The fisherman's face creased with a slow, oddly sad smile that exposed his rotted teeth. "Give her this," said Dr. Roung, holding out the small statue that he'd just bought from the fisherman.

*　　*　　*

That's how it had begun. He requested and received permission from Beijing's powerful minister of the interior to start excavating the sunken shoal to cover his approaches to the island — to Chu Shi. The fisherman arranged the meetings with Chu Shi but each time he seemed a little sadder, a little more wistful.

The love between Dr. Roung and Chu Shi had been fast, secret and more important to him than anything that had happened before. With her he seemed to understand things. He felt part of the great flow of the black-haired people. He felt her connect him to the past and the future. He began to dream of their child — somehow living forever.

He had kept the ministry in Beijing abreast of his progress at the shoal, which he had intentionally slowed. Then, in the sixth month of his work, he was surprised to receive a personal communication from the minister of the interior herself asking to be kept strictly up-to-date with his work and a request that he find out what he could about . . . the farmers on the island.

He didn't know what to make of the request, but he didn't care. It offered him an official reason to visit the island regularly.

It was on one of these sanctioned visits that he found himself alone with Chu Shi in her family house.

"This is my room, but this is my father's home." Her eyes twinkled.

"It could be ours when he passes on."

Chu Shi turned away from him, the dim light of the hut somehow making her even more alluring.

"I meant no offence."

"I know," she said still looking away from him. Then she turned back and smiled.

"What?"

"It's odd to be alone in this place. Usually there are so many others."

"Little privacy, huh?"

"We islanders are not prudish." Her smile broadened. "You may have noticed that."

He smiled. "I have."

"Good," she said. "Now take off your pants — Excellency." Her voice danced around the final word but her eyes devoured him.

Their bodies fit together as if they had been made from one piece that had been separated by the Maker.

Later, lying naked and enwrapped, he ran his fingers along the rise of her hip. "Do you have the gift I first gave you?" She nodded and reached across him. His fingers traced the strong muscles of her back as she extracted the small statue of the horse's hindquarters from her clothing on the floor. She lay back and, smiling, placed it on her left breast. Then looked at him.

He rose from the bed, naked, and crossed to his pants on the far side of the room. He put on his delicate French glasses then knelt and dug into his pockets. She loved to watch him. He was so different from the islanders. So different from Iman's favourite, Jiajia, to whom she'd been promised, and who constantly sought her attention.

He returned, knelt over her and repositioned her statue. Then he opened his hand and showed her his matching statue of the horse's frontquarters.

She bent her head forward to get a closer look, but he

held her still and placed his bronze figure on her right breast.

She shivered. She'd never seen anyone look at anything the way her lover looked at her now. Finally, after what seemed forever, he gently moved her breasts together. The figures slid toward each other. They touched, then interlocked — perfectly — every plane of one fitted to every plane of the other.

She was about to giggle when she looked up. He was staring deep into her eyes. "Do you see how they lock together."

She nodded, a little lost.

"I want us to marry. To have children."

She moved so quickly that he was lucky to catch the bronze pieces before they crashed to the ground.

As she shoved a leg into her pants she said, "It's not possible."

"Why?" he demanded.

She turned to him and held his eyes. "Because, here, on this island, we marry our own."

Then she was gone.

He held the completed bronze horse in his fingers for a longish moment. Then he detached the hindquarters and left them beneath her pillow.

As he put on his clothing he wondered what he would do next. What life would be like without Chu Shi.

He did his best to wrap up the excavation of the shoal. It was proving much more difficult than he had originally thought. He faced little resistance from the ministry.

Then the foreigners arrived. Foreigners from several countries. Elderly men asking questions. Asking about the family backgrounds of the islanders. Not from the fishermen; only from the farmers.

He dutifully followed the foreigners to the island and then reported their activity to the interior ministry. He was surprised to get an urgent message ordering him to continue excavating the shoal and to go to the island and report back everything that he could find about the interaction between the foreigners and the farmers of the island.

Despite Chu Shi's rejection, he obeyed the orders from Beijing and went to the island. He talked to as many of the islanders as he could. On his way back to his boat he saw Chu Shi in the darkness down by the beach. He was about to approach when a young man broke from the nearby thicket and ran into her arms.

Jiajia, Iman's chosen. Her betrothed.

The weather turned suddenly cold as he returned from the island. Early for it. He bundled up as he sat in his room and wrote to the Ministry of the Interior.

MADAME MINISTER:

Two weeks ago, the Islanders, after an initial resistance, accepted sizeable sums of money from the foreigners in return for which, Iman, their leader, agreed to give the foreigners the family histories they wanted.

Why the foreigners would want the islander's family histories is a mystery to me.

Now the foreigners want to take blood samples from the islanders. Iman categorically refused and violence was only narrowly avoided as the foreigners had to be escorted off the island by local police.

Work on the shoal is proving almost impossible. Could I request, with all respect, a return to my work in Xian?

C.

Madame Wu received the communiqué just as she was finishing another long day in her office. Her old eyes read the words and sensed their meaning. The man's love affair was over and now he wanted to go home. He may be exceptionally talented, this one, but he acts just like every other male.

Madame Wu felt her assistant's steely eyes on her. Had she spoken aloud? No. Absolutely not. She returned the stare and the man backed off. "Perhaps it's time to get myself a younger, prettier assistant. It had been a long while since someone young and pretty had been her companion.

"Madame Minister?"

"Respond that he is to stay at Lake Ching until I tell him that it is time for him to go. As well, tell him that he is not to presume. That all normal formality shall be used in all his communications."

The man quickly left the office.

Madame Wu turned to the window. Police were already on the island to help the foreigners. So the danger was near. For a moment she thought about her son. Then about her mother.

So many ghosts these days. But this is an important time. A time of change. They were dangerous times for individuals. The good of the country came first. The future needed to be addressed — no — forged. What could she care for a dead mother and a son who was lost to her.

Two days later the archeologist was surprised to see the old fisherman approach the shoal. He was wrapped in rags to keep out the cold. "What now, old man?" he yelled.

"They're scaring off the fish!" the old man barked.

"Who is?"

"The visitors! Don't you know anything!"

Dr. Roung was about to rise to the bait when something told him to hold his temper. "Are the foreigners back, old man?" It came out awkwardly — half-question, half-accusation.

"Worse than that." What could be worse to this man than foreigners? "Government people. Beijing government people."

This was new. "Take me." He reached into his pocket and threw a few bills at the older man. The fisherman did a good impression of a cabbie who thought his tip was too light.

Chu Shi wasn't happy to see him when he entered her hut. "I'm a married woman now."

"I know."

She started to leave, but he reached for her. At first he thought she was going to scream. Then he thought she was going to hit him, and then, somehow, their clothing lay in piles on the floor and he flowed into her as she sang his name over and over. When they were done, she handed him his clothing and his expensive imported glasses. They dressed slowly staring at each other.

Then suddenly she was crying.

He held out his arms to her, but she shook her head.

"I need answers to a few questions." A look of shock crossed her face. It was almost comical.

"You came here to ask me questions?" she blurted out.

"No. It's the only way I think I can get to see you again."

"Don't try to see me again." But her fingers were interlocked with his.

"Who are the new people on the island?"

"Government people," she answered.

"Police officers?"

She looked away. When she spoke, her words came out slowly as if their very sounds were dangerous. "No. Different. Government people from Beijing."

"You're sure?"

"Yes."

"What do they want, Chu Shi?"

"They threatened Iman that if he doesn't agree to give blood samples to the foreigners they'll remove our people from the island. They claim we never had any right to be on the island in the first place."

"Will Iman give in to the demands?"

"He already has."

That night in the cold, haunted silence of his room in Ching he wrote again to Madame Minister Wu.

This missive she received while attending a formal state banquet for the Japanese ambassador and several of that country's leading industrialists. Toasts were exchanged. History forgotten. A swollen future embraced.

"Just like before the liberation," she thought as she raised her glass. "Foreigners everywhere, owning everything."

Madame Wu sipped the heated saki. The air conditioning puffed out the silk of the woman's blouse across the table from her.

Silk!

Throughout her youth, Madame Wu had been forced to carry silkworm eggs strapped to her body. It kept the eggs warm. Many nights she was awakened by her mother screaming at her not to roll over in her sleep and crush the precious eggs. Other nights she awoke feeling a feathery movement on her skin. One ounce of eggs produced twenty thousand worms. They'd hatch in the night. She hated having to stand naked and still as her mother picked them off her.

The worms had to increase their weight ten thousand times before they spun their cocoons. Since noise was harmful to their growth, the house was a place of silence. But in the silence was intense anger.

It was always a relief when the worms finally began to spin their cocoons from the loose stalks of straw that the family had provided. The two or three days needed to spin were the happiest times in the house. But it was short-lived. Once the cocoons were spun, the chrysalis had to be killed.

Boiled.

Her mother's hands, an angry red from fishing the cocoons out of the boiling water and carefully unravelling the still-wet pouches, were the stuff of her childhood nightmares. And it had all been done for a silk factory owned by the very Japanese they were toasting here tonight.

Traitors.

The men who run this country are traitors to the people of China — to the memory of her mother.

But they will not get away with it. Her family will see to that.

The Japanese ambassador was speaking. Something about business bringing our two great countries together. Madame Wu sipped at her saki again. She grimaced. The taste made her angry. Yet another foreign thing to be swept out of the country. Then she looked at the saki and a slow smile crossed her features.

Dr. Roung was surprised when the case of wine arrived with the note from the Interior Minister:

> *Please present this to the Islanders with my compliments on their new business venture. Enclosed please find a requisition order to cover your expenses for the banquet that should accompany my gift.* — M.W.

He stared at the case of ceremonial wine. Then at the note from Madame Wu. This was definitely her writing style. But something was wrong. Why send a case of wine from Beijing? Although he didn't drink himself, he was pretty sure this wine was available in Xian. But before he followed this line of inquiry he saw that this presented another opportunity to see Chu Shi — and all reason vanished before the onslaught of desire.

It took little persuasion to get the islanders to accept Interior Minister Wu's offered banquet. Shortly, the archeologist was dressed in his best clothes, his thinsulate vest beneath his coat, and on his way to the island.

The light was dying as he crossed the lake. Through the murk and far to one side, he saw a cormorant's head pop out of the water and crane around. "As if searching for him," he thought.

It was bitterly cold. He looked past the cormorant and scanned the horizon for the fisherman who always seemed to be there. Always seemed to know when he was coming. But he couldn't see him or the lanterns of the boat, although he knew some fisherman had to be near. A cormorant was a valuable asset and never allowed too far from the boat. Of course, should the bird decide to fly away, its newfound independence would soon give way to starvation. The metal circlet on its neck made it impossible for the animal to swallow fish — its only natural food. Once the circlet was in place, the bird could only receive sustenance from a narrow lengthy dropper, and that could only be manipulated by a man's hand. "We're all on a leash of some sort," he said aloud. His boatman ignored him. Just another city person who talked to himself.

The banquet was set in the large communal hall halfway up the central terraced hill. The building was a storage place for the upper level crops at the three harvest times. In the winter it was seldom used.

Tables had been made from planking set on crude wooden cubes. Lanterns were lit and hung from poles. Dung burned in the metal braziers. The place, like so much of the island, literally smelled like shit. But the archeologist didn't mind. Chu Shi had just come into the room with her husband, Jiajia. She wore a woven shawl to keep out the chill of the night. Her eyes were focused on the floor.

Something was different with her. What?

The room was filling quickly. The whole island seemed to be here. Just the farmers not the fishermen, he corrected himself. Food was piled high and savoury on the central table. The braziers and lanterns added to the smoke from the islanders' harsh cigarettes which featured such fanciful names as snake charmers, bullet proofs and smacks.

He rose. All eyes turned to him. He delivered Madame Interior Minister Wu's congratulations to the islanders on their business acumen then opened a bottle of her gift, the ceremonial wine. He filled glass after glass as they were presented to him. When the last bottle was almost emptied, he looked up. Even the young had glasses in their hands. They awaited him. He raised his glass and was about to speak when he saw Chu Shi. She seemed very close to him although she was far across the large crowded room. The smoke in the room made him dizzy. He lifted his glass a little higher and shouted, "To the future."

The room filled with cheering. Glasses were emptied and exclamations filled the air. He took the opportunity to tip his glass over onto the hard mud floor. He was no drinker. The wine seeped into the ground like a brown slug seeking the dark.

It felt as if the evening zoomed by. He didn't get to speak to Chu Shi. Before he knew it, he found himself back on a boat, frozen stiff, heading toward Ching.

He spent that night, that seemingly endless night, wrestling with his loneliness.

Two days later he was by the shoal, leading the beginning of the excavation of the south end of the mound when he looked up to see the old fisherman sitting in his boat not twenty yards away. His birds were on the gunwales, not in the water. He wasn't fishing. The archeologist took the paddle from the floor of his own boat and made his way out to the fisherman.

"What?"

"There's sickness."

"Where?"

"The farmers. Many are sick. Deep sickness."

"Influenza? What?"

"She may die." There was no need to name Chu Shi. To Dr. Roung's surprise, the old man's sadness seemed to be aimed at himself. As if he was to blame somehow. Without another word, the fisherman grabbed his oar and headed toward the island.

Dr. Roung sat dead still, his boat bobbing gently, the creepy-crawly of fear dancing on his spine.

Three days later, on December 1, the archeologist was shocked into waking by a hand pressing down hard on his chest. Four men were in his room. Islanders. Before he could speak, Iman stepped forward. "Chu Shi is dead."

Dr. Roung didn't know what to do.

"We are not foolish people, Excellency. We know about you and her."

"Then why didn't . . ."

"We stop it?" Iman completed the archeologist's question. For a moment he was lost in thought. Then he shrugged. "The others are getting better, but she died from the sickness."

Dr. Roung's head filled with questions as he felt himself falling down a great pit of blackness. Then Iman closed off the light at the top of the pit. "She died carrying your child." He didn't see Jiajia's blow coming. It caught him full on the face. Only Iman's presence saved his life.

He was not allowed on the island for the burial. No one from outside was allowed on the island anymore. Rumours on shore spread that the islanders blamed the sickness on the foreigners with whom they had done business. That giving blood had caused the sickness. That all business deals were off.

Blood was sacred to the islanders in many ways.

Fires burned constantly on the uppermost parts of the island. Rumours became fact when two of the islanders' foreign business partners arrived and were chased away at gunpoint.

Twenty-four hours later, special assault units of federal soldiers were helicoptered onto the island. Stories. An exhumation. The foreigners insisted. The islanders resisted. The army backed the foreigners. Several islanders were shot. The islanders came out in force and fought a pitched battle with the federal forces. Then another helicopter, this one a small, modern, single-passenger model without markings, landed on the far side of the island. Away from the fighting. Iman and his best fighters stood silently waiting for the rotors to stop their lethal circling. When they did, the door slid open and Madame Minister Wu stepped out.

She looked at him, identified herself and canted her head slightly to one side.

He matched her gesture — this would be a meeting of equals.

Quickly, a small fire was built on the sandy beach and the two sat facing each other across the flames.

Jiajia stepped forward.

"Was it this young man's wife who died of this foul contagion?"

"It was, Madame Minister."

"My condolences, young man. Now let me have words in private with Iman."

Jiajia started to protest then stopped as he saw the flecks of rage the flames of the fire brought to life in Madame Wu's eyes. He turned and left the ring of light.

Madame Wu picked up a stick and poked at the fire. Iman watched her closely. Finally, she raised her eyes and said, "He is reckless in his grief." Iman nodded but said nothing. Madame Wu smiled. "But such men can be of use in times such as we are living through. Don't you agree, Iman?" Again he nodded. "Good," she said. "Now let us plan a response to these indignities the foreigners have heaped upon you and your people."

"We are already seeing to that," Iman said in a cold flat voice.

"By fighting with federal assault troops? Folly, old man. Folly." Before Iman could respond she added, "There is a better way of dealing with this . . . situation." She caught his eye. "Let them dig up the dead girl." Iman leapt to his feet. She shouted, "Sit down." He did. "One must get one's revenge when the enemy is not ready for it." She slipped a small, beautifully bound copy of Sun Tzu's *The Art of War* from her pocket and held it out to Iman. "Have someone read you the chapter on spies." She checked to see if Iman was offended. He wasn't. She went on, "Pay special attention to the part about lulling the enemy into a false sense of security — friendship even."

Iman took the book.

"I'm sure you will agree with me that letting the foreigners dig up the dead girl is the best way to proceed."

Madame Wu rose and walked out of the fire's circle of light. She didn't want him to see the hatred on her face.

As she allowed herself to be helped into the helicopter it occurred to her that having come all this way, maybe she should see her son, Chen. Then she dismissed the thought as bourgeois and sentimental. They'd been apart all these years. Why bother seeing him face to face now? She barked an order and the pilot engaged the engine. The rotors began to howl. She put her head back against the plush seat and closed her eyes. The islanders would do as she suggested. They were people of the land, just as she was.

* * *

Jiajia put down the minister's copy of *The Art of War*. He had just finished the brief chapter on spies. For a moment he looked at the cover of the book — so fancy, so decorated — so unlike war. He shook his head and strode out of his mud hut — at one time their home, his and Chu Shi's. He reconsidered Sun Tzu's advice as he walked quickly up the steep path to the graveyard. It seemed to him that Sun Tzu's instruction on the waging of war was flawed. It assumed a dispassion, a cold logic. He crested the final rise and stepped into the graveyard. He stood over Chu Shi's grave for a long time then he hawked up a wad of phlegm and spat it right at her heart.

Jiajia kicked at the grave's night soil-clotted earth then began to tear at the dirt with his fingers. As he did, he planned. Not as *The Art of War* had suggested. But then again, Sun Tzu was waging a military campaign. Not seeking revenge.

Jiajia flung aside clods of the thick dirt until he unearthed the edge of the crimson burial shroud. He leaned back his head and howled Chu Shi's name.

Revenge was not dispassionate. It was not cold and logical. It was human — and hot.

The next day Iman ordered the islanders to put down their weapons. A dead girl. A pregnant dead girl was dug up and transported to the mainland where her body was hacked to pieces in a secret foreign ritual.

So went the story.

Dr. Roung knew better. He didn't know what had changed the islanders' minds to allow it, but he knew that Chu Shi must have been exhumed so that an autopsy could be done. Probably in Xian. He assumed that the foreigners insistence on the exhumation and autopsy had something to do with their business deal. But again he didn't know what. And he said nothing. Did nothing. Just sat in the darkness of his Ching room wondering over and over again why the ceremonial wine had been shipped from Beijing. That night he awoke in a cold sweat, his mind crawling with fear. Fear that he knew the answer to the question. It was just past 6 a.m. He went out into the freezing darkness.

That was just before the frigid dawn of December 22. Seventeen foreigners had less than a week to live.

Half an hour after Fong's return from the island funeral, the hollow sound of his banging on Dr. Roung's workshop door echoed through Ching's soft spring night. Fong's shouts went unanswered. Finally an old woman came around the corner of the building.

"Gone, flat-head."

"What?"

"He's gone." The old woman cocked her head to the

side and stared at Fong's mouth. "Where'd you get your teeth?"

"Where did Dr. Roung go?"

"To Xian. Where else?"

Where else indeed. The island and Xian. Always the island and Xian. And finally the link between the two — four stones stacked neatly in a tower behind a dead girl's headstone — to mark time.

Fong turned on his heel and headed back to the Jeep. Over his shoulder he heard the old woman shout, "You really ought to complain. Those teeth look awful."

When he got into the car, Chen asked him, "Did she say something about teeth?"

"No," Fong said harder than he should have. Then he spat out, "Have you found out if there was an exhumation order executed on the island?"

"Yes, there was." Chen referred to his notes. "It was done December 21. How did you know . . .?"

"Seven days before the murders on the boat."

"Yes, sir."

"Was there an autopsy performed?"

"Yes, the same day."

"Where? Don't answer that — Xian? Right?" Chen nodded. Fong cursed under his breath. "I want the autopsy report sent to Grandpa."

"They won't send it."

"What?"

"I've already asked for it. They said it's confidential."

Fong knew the word *confidential* in China's bureaucratese meant "volatile." "Will they let him see it if we go to them?"

"Yes, they're okay with that."

"Fine."

"How did you know there'd been an . . .?"

Fong thought back to the grave on the island. The soil was still unpacked. The fecal material resisting decomposition, as it always did when disturbed . . . He shrugged. Why not tell Chen? Because admitting a knowledge of night soil would allow access to his past. And he wasn't prepared to discuss his personal history with anyone.

Chen reached in his pocket and pulled out a fax. "This arrived for you while you were on the island."

Fong spread it out against the dash:

HEY HO SHORT STUFF. BIG COOKINGS HERE IN XIAN. WHAT GUESS FOUND I? NO GUESS? TWO BAD. DNA PATENT FOUND I. DNA PATENT GIVEN TO DEAD AMERICAN LAWYER, DECEMBER 25TH - THINK NOT CLOSE TO PARTY TIME? - DO I? I DO. DO. DO. DO YOU?

Fong shivered.

They were nearing the edge.

He brushed some liquid from his chin. It was deep red. Somehow he'd cut himself and was bleeding. He looked at the red smear on the back of his hand. Blood without. Blood within. This all has to do with blood.

"Fax Lily. Tell her we've got to know exactly what the DNA patent was for."

"Yes, sir."

"And get Grandpa ready."

"For what?"

"Our trip to Xian. He needs an outing."

The alarm sounded loudly at the nurse's station. She'd been in Inspector Wang's room only moments before. Maybe he'd accidentally rolled over on the button.

Maybe he was finally dying.

The thickness was lining his mouth and had gotten up into his nasal passages. It was now extending down into his lungs, covering every inch — every tiny sack that could bring him air.

He struggled and thrashed as best he could. He grabbed the button and pressed with all his might. Then he stopped. Stopped fighting. Stopped fighting what he thought was the end. Images floated up at him. Sharp-edged crime scene lights threw everything into high relief. The pop of a sulphur match and the delicious flavour of cigarette smoke. Then a face close to his. Zhong Fong. He'd never had a son. Never married. Lived his whole life as an unbeliever. But here on the very brink of his time, just before he leapt from this earthly plane, he sent out a blessing. A final gift to Zhong Fong. Not as tactile as the telegram he'd arranged to get through despite all regulations against outside contact with the traitor. But more important. Or at least that's what the specialist thought — as his last act upon the Earth.

The white-clad nurse leaned in close to the old man's mouth. He was trying to speak. His lips forming sound-less words. She read his lips as she had so many times before. But what she read made no sense. "Bless you."

His lips formed a name she'd never heard before. "Make me proud. You are my pride. Deduce that it was me . . ."

The nurse recalled this man asking for communications experts a few months back. Just after he'd returned from Xian. Then documents from Shanghai. All quite a fuss. For what? She knew he'd been to Xian because he'd brought her back a small kneeling figure of an archer. He'd flirted in his wordless way. But despite all the time she'd nursed him, she didn't know much about him. In fact, she had no idea who this man was. Only that he was important enough to have a private room in a politburo hospital. That he had three serious gunshot wounds when he first arrived. Two in his back and one that had pierced his voice box. And the doctors were administering a treatment to him she'd never seen before.

But all that didn't matter now because he was quickly growing cold. If she'd known any Shakespeare, she might have quoted *Measure for Measure*: "This sensible warm motion" was quickly becoming "a kneaded clod."

But she didn't know any Shakespeare. Why should she?

Then again, those lines wouldn't fit a man — not dead — but put into a kind of suspended animation. Something new. Another way to cheat time. And all, of course, done without the knowledge of either Inspector Wang Jun or his doting nurse.

CHAPTER THIRTEEN

INTERVIEWS IN XIAN

Well before the Jeep reached Xian, Fong sensed the approach of the desert. A dry stillness seemed to suck at the air. Something from before time. Then the first structures of the ancient Qin capital, China's very first, materialized on the horizon. Shortly after, the wind picked up and fine grains of desert sand began to pelt their vehicle — grains of sand all the way from the mythologized Silk Road — the first conduit between East and West. Xian in its day had been the Middle Kingdom's port of entry. Camels crossing the torturous Silk Road brought the West to China 2,500 years ago.

Soon the Jeep entered the crumbling outer ring of the Old City. This was not the tourist Xian; this was the Chinese Xian. The Muslim quarter with its souk tents and dusted colours came first. It was bigger than Fong had expected. A small Tibetan sector abutted the Muslim quarter. The people there seemed sullen and angry. As the Jeep made its way toward the centre of the old place, it passed through many different communities. The faces in this city were composites. Clues. Hints of Mongol, Manchu, Turk, Afghan, Tibetan in the faces, but all Chinese now. Oh yes, they were all Chinese now.

The great ocean China salts every river.

The desert dust was blowing hard as Chen parked the Jeep outside the Xian central police station. Fong helped the coroner out of the car as Lily approached them. The wind-blown sand got into the old man's lungs and he let out a hacking cough that ended with him doubled over in pain. Lily was clearly shocked by his appearance. He looked awful.

The ride, like most such endeavours in the Middle Kingdom, was much more exhausting than expected. Twice they had to stop and let the old man out. Both times Fong walked at his side as Grandpa moved slowly along the road's edge, like an old dog looking for the scent he needed to defecate. At the end of the second stop the coroner hooked his arm through Fong's and allowed himself to be led back to the car. The man's touch had startled Fong.

"I've got our meetings set up, Fong. The news guys are expecting us later this afternoon. The vice cops are ready for us now," said Lily.

"Good," said Fong.

As they entered the police station he whispered, "Have you found anything more on that DNA patent?"

"Not yet. It's hard to get any exact information. But I'm still trying."

The vice cops were cordial enough and offered to pick up Sun Li Cha, the Mistress of Cervical Arts, for them. Fong declined the offer. "Just tell us where we can find her."

The possibility of seeing Sun Li Cha seemed to cheer

up the coroner. "An unexpected benefit," Fong thought.

The police began listing places to check.

Fong cut them off, "Does she have a home address?"

"Yeah," said the youngest vice cop, "but we've never found her there."

"Where does her mother live?" asked Lily.

Fong saw a flash of anger cross the officer's face. Perhaps the man didn't like being questioned by a woman or maybe he found it offensive to bring the mother into this. Xian was getting to be a big city; he'd have to learn that mothers are often the best way to daughters. Change is hard on us all.

Pockets of new wealth were in evidence throughout Xian. Although not pristine, the city was clearly maintained in such a way that Western tourists would find it acceptable.

Shanghai too Western? Chungking too crowded? Beijing too political? Don't worry, there's always Xian, real old Chinese. Foreigners certainly bought the pitch. They jammed the narrow streets. They were everywhere.

Sitting in the Jeep and waiting for Chen to return from his errand, Fong found himself put off. An old reaction. For years Chinese citizens had been fed a steady diet of hatred for the Westerners who had bled their country dry. It is hard to get over one's racial training. "We're all raised as racists," he said aloud.

"Even from you, Fong, that has to qualify as an unusual statement," croaked the coroner from the back seat of the car.

"Think about it," Fong replied. "You're born into a family. I sure was." He noticed Lily cock her head in interest at that. He pressed on: "The first training you get is that your family is better than the one next door. Then you get that your street is better than the one behind you. Then your village is better than the village to the north."

The coroner folded his arms across his chest, leaned against the door and closed his eyes. Fong continued, "Naturally enough, if all those things are true, your country has to be better than all other countries . . . and your race better than any other."

The coroner began to snore.

Lily spoke softly, "So, Fong, does that make us all bad?"

Fong heard the concern in her voice buried beneath the veneer of a casual question. "No. Having racist feelings and behaving as a racist are two completely different things. It takes an effort to overcome the training of your youth. Often the initial biases are overturned, but sometimes they linger despite our best efforts to erase them."

Fong looked in the rear-view mirror. The coroner had a gentle smile on his grizzled face. He began snoring louder.

In the other side of the mirror, Lily looked pensive.

"Lily?"

"Fong, we were all trained to hate Caucasians. There are still times when I can't believe how ugly they are." She stopped as if she were entering territory that was too complicated — perhaps too dangerous.

"You have a question, Lily?"

"I do."

"Ask."

"The white woman." Fong instantly knew that she was talking about Amanda Pitman, the wife of the New Orleans police officer who had been found chopped into small pieces in an alley off Julu Lu almost five years earlier. He'd spent four days — and nights — with her.

"What about her, Lily?"

Lily allowed her tongue to trace the front of her teeth. Despite the new thinking in China and Lily's almost constant exposure to Western media, she didn't know how to broach issues of male sexuality. Especially with Fong.

"What about her, Lily?" Fong repeated. His voice carried a definite edge.

She let out a deep breath then said in English, "No gain without a penny for a pound, right Fong?"

Fong had no idea what she was trying to say but decided to nod.

"You won't hate me in the morning?" she asked in English.

Fong was quite lost. Which morning? What had she done to be hated? He looked at her. She looked so earnest that he shook his head.

"You're sure?"

He shrugged.

"Okay. Good. Okay." She took a deep breath and switched back to Mandarin. "Did you sleep with the big white woman?"

Fong was shocked.

"Don't look at me like that, Fong. You told me it was all right for me to ask. So I asked."

Fong took his eyes from the mirror and looked out the front window. Chen was returning to the Jeep with a bag of steamed buns and about a dozen cheap Triad medallions dangling from his wrist. The timing of the gods was merciful for once. But as Chen approached the car, Lily hissed, "Was she good? Do you like big tits? What did she smell like?"

Chen opened the door and got in. "Sorry I was so long, the crowd was . . ."

"Just get in, will you!" Fong ordered angrily.

Chen didn't know what to say, so he apologized again.

"Don't apologize, fire plug. Your absence provoked a fascinating conversation," said the coroner with a big smile on his craggy face. "What kind of cop are you, Fong, to take snoring for sleeping? Hey, how about one of those buns back here."

Fong looked in the rear-view mirror. The coroner was laughing. Lily was not.

Then the coroner coughed — and coughed and coughed. Rattles deep inside him began to sound. A knell that everyone in the Jeep heard.

Twenty minutes later, Chen pulled the car out of traffic, headed down a side street and stopped in front of a modern building.

"Her mother lives in a government office block?"

"No, sir, this is where the autopsy was done on the

island girl who was disinterred. I thought Grandpa wanted . . ."

"Grandpa wants to see Sun Li Cha, that's what . . ." but the old man didn't get another word out as he saw the scowl on Fong's face. "Actually, a lively bit of scientific bibble babble beats meeting a mistress of the ancient arts any old day," he said, stepping out of the car.

As Fong walked with him toward the building he noted the greyness that seemed to be growing around the man's eyes. "Do you want me to stay with you, Grandpa?"

"No." The older man unhooked his arm from Fong's and climbed the steps to the building slowly but with a fierce determination. He stumbled and righted himself. He swore loudly — that gave Fong hope.

When Fong got back into the car he was smiling. "What did that old coot say?" asked Lily.

"Nothing much."

"So why are you smiling?"

"He's angry. As long as he's angry he'll be fine. Once he gets sentimental I'll begin to worry."

"Does his family know he's here?"

Fong almost responded, "He has a family?" then realized that saying it aloud would admit how little he knew about the old man. So he said nothing.

*   *   *

At first Sun Li Cha's mother wasn't particularly happy to see them, but she warmed up quickly. There was something of the old coquette about her. Fong had seen it many times before. Older people were ignored in the New China. A burden. Now, all of a sudden, she was wanted. People cared about what she thought. Were willing to listen to her stories.

Both Fong and Chen sat patiently as she claimed ownership of a very exciting, although totally implausible, personal history. It was Lily who finally brought matters to a head.

"Do you think we're idiots, old lady?"

"No, I don't, dearie. I think you're cops." She laughed so hard at her own cleverness that she snorted like a pig.

"Just tell us where your daughter is!" Lily demanded.

Fong could have killed Lily. All this patient waiting and smiling was meant to build up credit with the old lady so she'd do just that.

"How should I know? Young people have no respect anymore. Like you," she barked at Lily. "Sun Li doesn't tell me anything. Do you tell your mother where you're going, girl?" Before Lily could defend herself the crone continued, "Or that you sleep with these two men. Oh, I see the way they look at you. I'm not new to the Earth you know."

"Does your daughter have a boyfriend?" asked Fong gently, before Lily could tear a strip off the lady's old carcass.

"No."

"Come, Grandma, a girl as beautiful as Sun Li must have men around her all the time," said Chen gently.

The old woman softened. Fong looked to Chen who just smiled.

"Only beautiful mothers give birth to beautiful daughters," Chen added. Lily almost puked down the front of her dress.

The old charlatan reached over and touched Chen's arm. "True. Beauty begets beauty. Very true." She patted his arm twice more and then said, "Your mother must have been a real dog. Bow-wow wow-wow. Know what I mean?"

Fong was about to leap to Chen's defence when the younger man held up a hand. "What you say may be true, but I haven't seen my mother for many, many years. Perhaps she has become, like you, beautiful in her old age." He smiled.

She smiled back.

Then she said, "You could try the Humming Way bar in the Sheraton. Sometimes she's there." Then sadness crossed her face and she said, "She's an entertainer, you know."

The Humming Way bar at the Sheraton was dark and stank of cigars and expensive perfume. When Fong's eyes adjusted to the murk he saw many foreigners with Chinese women. The women were all overly made up and wore tight-fitting clothing.

"Westerners didn't understand us at all," Fong thought. These girls were openly disdainful of the men. Yes, their hands rested with seeming ease on the Westerners, but their body language spoke openly of their aversion. Why couldn't Westerners see that?

It was Lily who picked Sun Li out from the others.

"There," she said pointing at a back booth where a tall Han Chinese woman laughed loudly at something the Western man at her side had said. She touched his hand with her elegant fingers, but her body canted away. A second Westerner returned to the table, balancing three martinis. A small cheroot dangled from the side of his mouth.

"Chen, guard the entrance."

"Yes, sir."

"Lily, you take the door to the woman's toilet."

"Why?"

"This isn't a forensic lab, Lily," he snapped. "Just do as I tell you." Lily, surprised by his tone, didn't question him further.

Fong turned from Lily and surveyed the bar closely. He would be more careful with this interrogation than he'd been with Hesheng's. The image of the terrified islander's face came to him. He breathed it away.

Once Lily and Chen were in position, Fong strolled over to the booth. Sun Li Cha's right hand was beneath the table on the thigh of the young Westerner on her right. Her other hand held a half-emptied martini glass. The older man on her left had an arm around her shoulder, his stubby fingers dangling close to the top of her low-cut silk blouse.

Her laughter stopped when she saw Fong.

"What's wrong, honey? Who's this?" the older of the two men said in English.

In furiously quick Shanghanese, Fong spat out, "Tell them to go away."

"Is that accent real?" She smiled but a tiny crack appeared in her bon vivant mask.

"I won't ask a second time. Tell them to go." He almost added, "Tell them to fuck their own daughters, not ours," but didn't.

"Bug off, fella," said the younger one but before he could say more, Sun Li whispered something in his ear that made him glow with expectation. "It's a deal." She smiled as he got to his feet and signalled for the other man to follow him.

Fong slid into the booth. The buttery leather gave to accept his weight. Sun Li touched the lip of the martini glass, lit a cigarette. She had the most beautiful hands he'd ever seen. And she knew it.

She blew out a line of smoke and turned to Fong. "So?" Her voice was consciously low and smoky.

"I'm a police officer . . . "

"No!" she laughed. "Even before you came into the room I knew that. I could smell you. Hey, I got to pee first, then we can chat, okay?" Fong shrugged. She put a hand on his thigh and leaned in close to his face. "Won't be a second." She slid out of the booth adjusting her skirt just enough to cover the crease between her long legs and her nether portions.

As Sun Li moved toward the washroom, Lily caught Fong's eyes with a what-am-I-supposed-to-do look. He mouthed back, "Stop her."

The woman's toilet was brightly lit and spanking new. Three stalls. Beautiful swan head faucets. And to one side a partly opened window. Sun Li Cha kicked off her high heels and made a beeline for the window. She already had one of her long legs on the counter beneath the window when Lily, catching her off-balance, yanked her back to the floor.

"Hey . . ."

"You're a suspect in a multiple murder case, Miss Sun. Consider yourself lucky that I don't charge you right here. Get back out there and talk to Inspector Zhong."

Sun Li Cha slowly put her heels back on then looked down at Lily. "I like your blouse, where'd you get it?"

"Could it really be about clothes," Lily thought. "Sleep with men to get money to buy good clothes so that men will want to sleep with you?"

Sun Li Cha's beautiful hand touched Lily's arm.

Lily shrugged off the hand. "Huai Hai Road."

"What about Huai Hai Road?"

"It's where I got the blouse."

"Swell." Sun Li Cha reached out, allowing her fingers to linger on the top button of Lily's blouse. Lily didn't know what to do. The whore smiled at her discomfort but she didn't remove her hand. She said languidly, "I think I'll go out and talk to your boss now — or is he something more, honey?" The whore's fingers expertly undid the button exposing the strong sinew of Lily's neck. "Sweet," Sun Li Cha whispered then turned and sashayed out of the toilet. Lily found her eyes drawn to the whore's retreating figure. She felt a surge of envy followed by a flush of anger.

"Good pee?"

"Yummy. What can I do for you, Inspector Zhong?"

"Three months ago you were on a luxury boat on Lake Ching."

"Was I?"

Fong tossed Sun Li's business card onto the table. "You left this there," he lied smoothly.

"You can get one of those at the front desk of dozens of hotels."

"Perhaps, but I'm sure the fingerprints on the back of this one would match yours and at least one of the men on that boat. Now, we can throw you in jail for the five weeks or so it will take to finish the fingerprint analysis or you can talk to me here. Your choice."

After briefly considering her options she smiled and said, "I guess I was there." Fong nodded. "I said I was there," she repeated. Fong simply nodded again. She smiled. "So is that it? Anything else in your cute little head?"

"Tell me about it."

She fluttered her beautiful hands just long enough to attract Fong's eye. "It was cold. They told me to wait on the dock and greet the foreigners who . . . who were there."

"Did you?"

"Yeah. So what?" Fong saw fleeting lines of fear cross her face then disappear. Surely she'd heard about the murders on the boat. There it was again. Fear. Like an animal realizing it was trapped. "I didn't do anything," she barked. Fong didn't respond. She reached for her purse and lit a cigarette, forgetting that she already had one smouldering in the ashtray. Fong stubbed it out. She smoked Kents. If he ever took up smoking again, he'd definitely change brands. "Besides, they arrested those three peasants for . . ."

"Do you really think three peasants are capable of planning and executing the murder of seventeen foreigners on a boat?" Fong snapped.

"Well . . . maybe . . ."

"So you greeted the foreigners on the dock?"

"Yeah."

"Then what?"

"I went on board the ship when they told me to."

"Who told you to?"

"The Chinese guy who was in charge."

"The boat owner?"

"No, the old Taiwanese who piloted the thing."

"Then what?"

"The boat got out into the middle of the lake and I served drinks."

"Champagne."

"Yeah," she said, surprised that he knew that. "Just champagne."

"Were there any other kinds of liquor on board?"

"No."

"That didn't strike you as odd?"

"Well yeah, but it was none of my business. I was being paid. So I did what I was asked to do. I served them drinks. I danced for them on this corny runway thing then I spent some time with the two Americans." She paused then added, "You know . . ."

That hung in the air for a bit. Fong asked, "Did you have any champagne yourself?"

"No. They wouldn't let me."

"When did the crew leave the ship?"

"Just after I finished with the Americans. They were . . . well, sort of too drowsy to . . . you know. So they didn't do anything."

"How long after you left the dock was that?"

"A guess? Maybe an hour and a half . . . two, tops. Then the other guys came on board." Fong held his breath. She shrugged, "You know, those odd-looking peasant guys."

"Why do you say they were odd-looking?"

"Well, they all sort of looked the same, you know. Weird. Looked like the old guy who was on board. Farmers, you know."

"Of course," Fong thought, "it was a celebration. Iman would have been invited." He smiled at her and asked, "How many of them were there?"

"Dozens. Hundreds. A lot — counting's not my idea of fun. They seemed to be everywhere. I don't think I've ever seen that many up close. You may have noticed, I'm a city girl."

She touched his arm. He shrugged her hand away. "How do you know they were farmers?"

"They carried tools."

Fong saw the scraped-off faces of the Chinese men in the bar. He closed his eyes and asked, "Hoes?"

"I don't know what you call them. The wide, short, sharp things used for . . ."

"Hewing. Building terraces. I've seen them," he said almost in a whisper.

"If you say so — how would I know what they are?"

But Fong wasn't listening to her. He had retreated into the recesses of his mind. A terrible truth sat there. All the island farmers did the killing onboard that ship.

Dizziness threatened to engulf him but he breathed it away and asked, "And these farmer types took over running the ship?"

"I guess. The guests seemed really sleepy, except for that old guy who they all looked like."

His mind supplied the unwanted image of islanders entering the rooms, slashing blows of the hewers, gunshots, gutting, castration — fury — *chi*. He looked up at her. "How did you get away?"

"The fisherman."

"What?"

"I was out on the deck and a fisherman . . . you know, one of those guys with the birds, yelled at me to jump. I thought he was nuts. The clothes I was wearing cost me a fortune. Besides, I don't swim much."

"How did he get you to jump?"

"When I saw how excited he was I figured that maybe I'd better listen to him. Know what I mean? Anyhow, I didn't have to jump, he brought his boat in close and helped me down. I didn't even get wet." She stopped for a moment. "I didn't kill anyone. Shit, I didn't even fuck anyone. Or any other stuff. I just took off my clothes. Is that a crime in the New China? If so, since when?"

They were on their way to the China news agency across town as Fong finished telling them about his conversation with Sun Li Cha.

"It makes no sense, Fong. One girl for seventeen foreigners." With a smile she added, "Chinese women are extraordinary, but seventeen to one seems . . ."

"You forget the girls pushing the broken-down bus Chen saw outside of Ching that night."

"Russian craftsmanship strikes again," added Chen.

"That breakdown probably saved their lives."

"Sorry, sir, I didn't mean to be . . ."

He never got to complete his apology. "So how did Sun Li Cha get there, Fong?"

"She drove, Lily."

"She has a car?" Lily asked, astounded.

"Evidently her business is thriving." Lily frowned. He didn't. "Are we getting close to the news bureau, Captain Chen?" The younger man nodded. "Who are we talking to there, Lily?"

"There's a Reuters correspondent, a CNN guy and an Associated Press stringer."

"Were they all there in December?"

"Not the Associated Press guy, but the other two were."

"They're all covering the story of the murders?"

"Well, they were until the government threatened to remove their credentials."

"So there's been no coverage overseas of the murders?" Fong asked incredulously.

"There was a furor for a while, then came the arrests.

The recreation model was displayed prominently to the press as proof that prosecutions were imminent."

"And now?"

"I think not much."

"But that's not the point, is it, Fong?" asked Lily. "Isn't the issue how they got word of the story in the first place?"

"It sure is Lily, which is why I think maybe you ought to conduct these interviews."

"Me?"

"Who else knows CNN and that other Western stuff better than you?"

Lily thought about that for a moment. "True. But I can't meet them looking like this."

"What's wrong with the clothes you're wearing. They look fine to me. Right, Chen?"

Chen blushed. "Maybe Lily has different standards than we do, sir."

It had never occurred to Fong that Chen would be attracted to Lily. Well, why not? The young man's marriage was falling apart. And Chen was a lot closer to Lily's age than he was.

"Turn here, Chen," Lily said, indicating a street at the right. It led to an area of high-class restaurants and fashionable shops.

"There." Lily said, pointing at a large, Western-style store. "Stop the car, Chen. That looks promising." She hopped out and leaned in the window. "What's my budget?"

Fong had no idea if they even had a budget. Chen

reached into his wallet and withdrew a credit card. "It's got about four hundred American dollars left on it."

As Lily took the card, Fong stared at Chen. "Left on it?"

"It's a smart card, sir."

Fong nodded as if he understood what was said to him. But he didn't. He'd been on the wrong side of the Wall for a long time. How could a credit card be smart — or dumb for that matter?

The store spread out before Lily like a cave freshly opened to the light. She stood on the entry dais some six feet above floor level. The Western influence was evident everywhere. This was a place for the privileged. There seemed to be more shopgirls than buyers in the store. To one side a few Western women were speaking too loudly as their bored husbands tried their best to be interested in more than just the price of their wives' selections.

Two Chinese women moved with cool precision through the aisles, careful not to catch each other's eyes. Each knew the compromises necessary to have the money to shop in such a store. Neither was anxious to broach the subject. Both were beautiful. Both were young. Both made Lily feel ugly and old for a moment. But only for a moment.

A shopgirl approached Lily and bowed slightly. Lily put on her best I'm-a-ranking-party-member look and moved past the girl who obediently followed in her wake.

Lily didn't look back. She liked the unobstructed

view. She liked shopping, especially on someone else's budget — no, not someone, the government's.

The selection was not as varied as in her favourite shops in Shanghai, but the quality of the merchandise was extremely high. The prices were shocking.

"Good," she thought, "Beijing owes me something for my trouble."

She paused by a display of eyeglass frames made in Paris. Such things were still extremely hard to find, even in Shanghai. A small sign indicated that these glass frames were for display purposes only but the frames could be ordered and that delivery would take between three and five months. "Probably closer to a year," Lily thought.

At the end of the next aisle she saw one of the Chinese women looking at an array of mannequin torsos displaying lacy bras from Los Angeles. The woman's beautiful figure hardly needed the accents offered by the expensive lingerie.

"Would you like to look, also?" asked the salesgirl from behind her.

"I'll call for you when I need you," Lily announced contemptuously. But the moment she'd spoken, she wished she could take back her words. This was a country girl. Pretty. Trained, but a country girl. Not a hardened Shanghai store clerk. Lily turned around. "Perhaps you can help me."

The girl's eyes lit up.

Lily came down the stairs of the store like a queen descending from her throne. The two shopping bags dangling from her arms swayed to the rhythm of her hips.

The men were standing by the car. Chen stared openly at her, his mouth a little too agape. Fong examined her as he would a work of art. His eyes were not easily deceived. The black silk shirtwaist was delicately embroidered with silver threads. The garment accentuated her narrow waist and the length of her slender upper body. The leather skirt just peeked out enough to announce its presence. Her long elegant legs were silvery grey in sheer stockings that led the eye to black pumps with high heels. She was a corporate vision in black and grey. Her always-deep eyes were now alive and bright.

She raised her hands and executed a half-turn while keeping her eyes on the men. "So?" She looked at Chen, whose mouth had opened even a little more than before. "Good," she murmured, "You may comment if you wish."

"What's in the bags?"

"My old clothes, Chen," she snapped. Then in her sweetest voice she said, "I take it that you approve of my choices."

"I do." Chen did his best to collect himself.

"And the older member of our team?"

For a moment Fong thought she was referring to the coroner, then he remembered that the old man was at the morgue. He did his best to hide his disappointment. "Your choices are excellent for our purposes."

"You sound like a Russian."

"That bad?"

"Yeah." Then in English she pleaded, "Tell you me like it. Please."

Fong was touched — and relieved. In English he replied, "I like it Lily. I really do."

She smiled and handed the bill and the card to Chen. "I wouldn't try using that thing until it's refuelled. Oh, by the way, in case you didn't know, you have overdraft protection on the card. Had overdraft protection," she corrected herself. "I used that up too."

*   *   *

Fong's decision to have Lily lead the interrogation at the China news agency was a good one. The three Westerners were charmed by her and answered her questions without a moment's hesitation. On occasion her Shanghanese accent puzzled the men, so Fong translated into English.

"On the night of December 28 you were contacted?"

The eldest reporter, the one from Reuters, brushed at the coffee stains on his expansive white shirt, as he answered for the others. "Two of us were. Me and him." He pointed at the handsome CNN reporter. "We were the only ones here then."

"Who contacted you?"

"Beijing."

"Beijing's a big place."

"It was a woman. An older woman. She called and told us that there had been a massacre of foreigners on Lake Ching."

"Did you go to the lake?"

"We tried, but our usual drivers had been told not to take us out of Xian. Even our gypsies had been grounded."

Lily spoke in highly colloquial Shanghanese so the Westerners couldn't follow, "So someone called them to tell them about the murders then someone else made sure they couldn't get to the lake?"

"That would be my guess. Parallel lines again." Fong turned to the reporters. "When did you finally get to the lake?" Fong asked in English.

"Late January. And there was nothing to see."

After the specialist came and the boat sank.

"Except that incredible model."

"Very fancy, but who could tell dick from that?"

Lily wore a puzzled look, "What means *who could tell dick*?"

"Richard. Dick. Remember?"

"Oh," Lily blushed. Fong thought she looked lovely when she was a little off-balance.

Chen tapped the elaborate display on the telephone on the reporter's desk. "Did the call come to this phone?"

"Yeah," said the Reuters man.

"This has call display, doesn't it?"

"Sure."

Chen flipped over the phone and read the Chinese inscription on the bottom. "It has memory."

"So?" demanded Fong.

"So maybe it still has the number that called you from Beijing."

The new world. It was as if he'd been asleep for a hundred years on the west side of the Wall.

Chen followed the digital instructions to the memory. He punched in 12/28 and three punches later several blinking zeros appeared in a neat digital line.

Chen was about to apologize, but Fong cut him off and turned to the reporters. "You keep a phone log don't you?"

"Yeah, but . . ."

Fong followed the man's eye line to a well-thumbed notepad on the desk. He flipped it to December 28. There, logged in as the sixth call of the day, was an eight-digit number preceded by the Beijing area code.

"Hey!"

"We're taking this as evidence." Before anyone could complain further, Fong headed toward the door with the phone log under his arm. He had already memorized the number. Fong repeated the number slowly to himself. Was this a way back to a rogue in Beijing? Probably not, but at least it was a place to begin. He looked down at the tracking bracelet on his leg. Its single red eye blinked up at him. "A way to be free of you, you cyclops," he thought. He didn't dare think it might be a way to get home, back to Shanghai.

Half an hour later Chen pulled the Jeep up outside the Xian morgue. The coroner looked ancient. He was sitting on the poured concrete steps with his pants rolled up exposing his bony pale shins. Fong got out of the car and went over to him.

"You asleep, Grandpa?" The coroner looked up at

Fong and shook his head. "Sick?" The old man looked away. "What then?"

The coroner spat on the pavement. Then said one word: "Typhoid."

Fong suddenly felt he was sweltering with fever, his grandmother looming over his bed. Her words hot with anger at his sickness, his weakness: "*Die boy if you're going to, but be quick about it.*"

Years later a ragged man had come to the rooms he shared with Fu Tsong at the theatre academy and announced that Fong's grandmother was gravely ill and had requested his presence. He'd slammed the door in the man's face. Then he warned Fu Tsong not to question him about this. Not about this!

He shook himself free of the memory and asked, "This girl from the island, this Chu Shi, she died of typhoid, Grandpa?"

"That's what the autopsy report says," he said, struggling to his feet.

"But that can't be. They've been farming with feces as manure for ages. Why would typhoid all of a sudden break out?"

"It didn't, Fong."

"It didn't . . . what?"

"This was a cultured strain of typhoid."

"A what?"

"Cultured strain." On seeing Fong's lost look, the old man spat on the pavement a second time and said, "It was grown in a lab, Fong. This strain can't naturally occur in nature. It was grown. Planted. It was cultured."

He moved past Fong toward the car, his figure even more bent now than before. As if the extent of human evil were weighing him down.

CHAPTER FOURTEEN

WITH A PIECE OF CHALK

Fong insisted that they drive back to Ching immediately. Lily and Chen protested, but Fong was
adamant that the work could only be completed near
the lake. He refused to specify what work. Chen drove;
Lily sat beside him. The coroner sat in the back. He had-
n't spoken since his announcement about the cultured
typhoid on the steps of the Xian morgue. No one spoke
much.

Fong closed his eyes. His thoughts bounded from
image to image as the Jeep bounced along the pitted
road. He didn't open his eyes until they stopped in front
of the abandoned factory. It was already dark.

When they entered, Fong saw a large stack of boxes
by the door.

"More projectors, sir. I thought they might help," said
Chen.

Fong nodded. They couldn't hurt.

After a quick meal, Fong sat by himself beneath the
bare bulb that illuminated his wide, flat-topped desk.
Lily sat in the far corner, a book on American patent law
on her lap. The book looked like it weighed in excess of
forty pounds. The coroner dozed in his chair. Chen was

spending the night at home with his "sad" wife.

Memories of his office on the Bund in Shanghai flooded through Fong as he slowly cleared his desktop. He took out the box of chalk Chen had brought him shortly after he arrived in Ching. That seemed a long time ago.

He selected a piece of chalk. This was his own private ritual. Something he didn't share — not even with Fu Tsong. She would have laughed at him. He couldn't have borne that.

He rolled the piece of chalk in his fingers.

A piece of chalk was the only gift he'd ever gotten from his grandmother. She claimed his father had been able to draw with "stupid things like this." Landscapes. Gossamer impressions of things he'd never seen. Fong couldn't draw a straight line — with a piece of chalk or without it. But he could think very well with a piece of chalk in his hand.

He turned on the projectors. Images of the death rooms surrounded him. After a moment he flicked them off and stared at the bare desktop as if its ancient wood grain would spur him to thought. Then he drew a large circle at the top. In the circle he wrote the words *DNA PATENT WANTED*. In smaller letters beneath that he wrote *From the Islanders*. Then in bold letters he wrote **WHAT KIND OF DNA?**

It all started there somehow.

At the bottom he drew another circle and was about to write in it but changed his mind and drew a circle two-thirds of the way down. In this circle he wrote the words *SEVENTEEN DEAD FOREIGNERS ON A BOAT.*

"They were not the end, just a means to an end," he said aloud. Lily glanced in his direction then returned to her tome. "And Hesheng — the man whose name means 'in this year of peace' — was murdered because he might lead us to that end."

He drew a line from the *DNA PATENT WANTED From the Islanders* circle to the *SEVENTEEN DEAD FOR-EIGNERS ON A BOAT* circle and then continued the line down to the circle at the bottom.

The empty circle at the bottom. There was always an empty circle to be filled at the bottom.

Then he drew two parallel lines from top to bottom on either side of the page. Fire and ice. "Where do parallel lines meet?" he muttered. "Never," he said aloud. Then he rethought that. No. No law defies death — or endless life. "Hesheng — in this year of peace," he whispered. Then he smiled, looked at the piece of chalk, almost said thank you aloud, and set to work.

An hour later he had almost filled the desktop with circled words and connective lines. A maze of interlocking events finally began to yield up their pattern — evidently parallel lines do meet.

At the very bottom of the diagram in the empty circle he wrote in heavy letters *HOW DID THE GIRL GET TYPHOID?*

Then he recircled it three times.

"Why all the lines, Fong?"

He hadn't heard Lily approach. In fact, he didn't realize that she had put a hand on his shoulder. Then he did and felt awkward but pleased. She sensed his discomfort and removed her hand. "Why does the girl who died from typhoid get so many circles, Fong?"

"She might be the link back to the rogue in Beijing, Lily."

"That's what they want you to find for them, isn't it, Fong?"

"Yeah. They sure as hell didn't bring me back from west of the Wall to find out who committed these murders. They really couldn't care less who slaughtered those men. All they want to know is who their opposition is — the name of the rogue in their midst."

"That phone number in Beijing?"

He nodded, but there were still big pieces missing, pieces that fit in smoothly. Pieces that joined it all together. He stared at the diagram. A phrase popped into his head. Aloud he said, "And they fish in all weather."

"Who does?"

"And one of them helped the whore Sun Li Cha to safety." Suddenly he was in motion. As if the building had tilted and he was loping down a slope. He would have been surprised to know that the piece of chalk in his hand was spinning rapidly between his fingers.

"Drawing pictures, Fong?" The coroner had been stirred to waking by Fong's pacing, but his words were slow and his cough a hoarse rattle.

Fong looked down at the tabletop. It was as if he'd never seen the diagram before.

The coroner coughed again. Another rattle. Fong looked at him and his heart sank. "I owe him so much and I've given him so little," he thought. "A parting gift's the least I can do for this man whom I've known so long but know so little."

"I need the two of you to go to Beijing," Fong said quietly.

"Why?" Lily demanded.

"To find out whose phone number that is in the phone log from the China news agency office. Right?" The coroner's words were slurred.

"Wrong, Grandpa. That number'll be no more than a place to begin. I can't imagine anyone would be stupid enough to use their own phone."

"But you want to pursue it anyway?" asked Lily with more than a hint of suspicion.

In English he answered, "Think of it as a free trip to Beijing, Lily." He allowed her to see that he was asking for a favour and nodded toward the old man. "Don't ask any more questions — please?"

Lily nodded and replied sadly, "Okey-dokey. Next time Hong Kong, okay?"

Fong was surprised that the coroner didn't complain about their use of English. He had gotten to his feet, which seemed to shuffle although he didn't move. "Where'll you go, Fong?"

"Fishing." Before they could question him he added, "Then back to Xian, Grandpa."

"But we just got back from there."

Fong moved to the old man. "True, but there are connectives between that island and Xian which I think I missed. And I think I know what they are."

The coroner looked at Fong for a long time. "You mean who they are, don't you, Fong?" Then he reached out and touched Fong's face.

Fong felt a pang of sadness. The old man was being sentimental. "I do, Grandpa."

"Be careful, Fong."

"You fly safe, Grandpa."

"China is beautiful from the air," said the coroner and returned to his chair. He sat erect but his eyelids were shut, heavy with fatigue.

Fong watched him for a moment. Was he asleep or had he just closed his eyes for a second? Or was he float-ing?

CHAPTER FIFTEEN

CORMORANTS

I t wasn't hard to find the local labourers who had worked on the excavation at the shoal, where the sculpture of the half-horse had been found. At first they were reluctant to answer Fong's questions, but when it became clear that his only interest was in the cormorant fishermen they spoke more freely.

Over and over again they mentioned one specific elderly fisherman who came by the shoal. Who talked to Dr. Roung, as one of them put it, as if he owned him.

Through his binoculars, Fong saw the elderly fisherman sitting very still in his bamboo-wrapped boat as he waited for the cormorant to emerge from the deep lake. The lantern on the boat's stern swayed slowly with the roll of the water. Fong thought the man looked like an aged bird himself.

Fong put down his binoculars and climbed cautiously into the boat that Chen had supplied for him. He rowed slowly out to the older man. By the time Fong neared the cormorant fisherman's boat he was breathing heavily. He waved a greeting. The old man spat in the water and muttered, "City idiot." Fong let it pass and smiled. The old

241

man didn't return his smile but did signal Fong to keep his distance. For a moment Fong didn't understand, then he did. The cormorant was still beneath the water, fishing for his master.

About ten yards to Fong's left, the cormorant broke the surface. Its elegant head swivelled to see who was in the new boat. The bird's eyes found Fong and stared at him. Fong returned the gaze and watched the beautiful bird instinctively try over and over again to swallow the fish in its throat. Only when the cormorant broke its eye contact with Fong and headed toward the elderly man did Fong see the glint of the wire that had been twisted around the bird's neck to stop it from eating its catch.

Some called the relationship between cormorant and fisherman symbiotic. Fong knew better. This was indentured servitude. The cormorant fisherman is present at the hatching of the bird. The first thing the animal sees is the grin on the fisherman's face. For days the fisherman never leaves the baby cormorant's side. The bird comes to know the fisherman as warmth, as the source of all food, as his master. After ten days the bird begins to walk. It follows the fisherman around like a gosling does a goose. It is two months before the fisherman takes the bird on his boat. It sits on the fisherman's lap and watches the other cormorants work. After two years the slender wire is slipped around its neck and tightened so that the bird cannot swallow its catch. In return for two years of child care, the bird works its entire life for the fisherman. Twenty years of service for two years of apparent kindness. The bird will breed as well as fish.

And finally, it will die in the lake.

Chinese, Fong thought. Very Chinese. But not kind. Fong's two years in the country had taught him a lot about the rough realities of living, the rareness of kindness in the wilds.

The old man put his hand on the cormorant's neck just above the tightened wire and squeezed. The bird gave up its catch and then was committed to the water once again. When the fowl disappeared, the old man looked to Fong. "What?" His voice was oddly high and singsong.

He'd already guessed that Fong was a cop.

"Can I ask you a few questions?" Fong began.

The old man didn't answer.

"I could impound your birds." That got the old man's attention.

"I could tip your boat and no one'd know that your stupid ass had sunk to the bottom of the lake," the old man growled. "Dumb flat-head." The man lowered his lantern to the merest glow and began to row away.

Darkness quickly enveloped Fong. The old man could easily do what he threatened. Then anger swept through Fong. He was from Shanghai. He wasn't some dumb country cop. He wished they'd given him a gun. Then he wished that he'd never been taken from the quiet dustridden village west of the Wall. Then he wished that he knew how to swim. Then he noticed that the ripples of the fisherman's wake were disappearing, so Fong grabbed his oar, cursed the water and pulled.

After ten minutes of hard rowing Fong saw a lantern

flare. The old man was going in a large circle. Of course he was! The cormorant was valuable and it was beneath the water fishing. If it emerged and the fisherman wasn't there — well, Fong didn't know what would happen in that case; but he did know that the fisherman was Chinese and Chinese people did not walk away from valuable investments, which is exactly what the cormorant was. So Fong turned his boat and backtracked. Sure enough, the shadowy presence of the fishing boat appeared only moments later.

The old man wasn't pleased. His assumption of the basic urban dumbness of the cop had proven wrong.

"You row your boat like a girl."

The man's accent was so dense that it was difficult for Fong to understand him.

"A girl?"

"A girl, a whore, who's just had every orifice filled."

"Like the girl on the lake boat?"

A shadow crossed the old man's face. Or was it anger? And what kind of talk was it for an old man to refer to women's orifices being filled?

The cormorant broke the surface with a plop. The fisherman reached down and lifted the sleek bird into the boat, which rocked gently.

Fong changed tack. "It's a beautiful bird."

"It's my last."

Fong wondered if that was because of age or something else.

"Is it a good bird?" Fong asked.

The fisherman relieved the bird of the contents of its

neck — two small fish — then recommitted it to the deep. The man's hands trembled as he released the creature. Fong was surprised by the gentleness. But it fit somehow and led him to his next question. "Have you got a daughter, Grandpa?"

The old man turned so quickly that his boat almost tipped. The glow from the swinging lantern picked up the rage in his eyes. He reached over and slapped the side of his boat with his open palm. Two quick thwacks. Seconds later the cormorant surfaced and headed toward the boat. There were no fish in its throat. The fisherman lifted the bird into the boat then stared at Fong. "Go away, stupid man. Go home. Or to hell. Just go." Before Fong could answer, the old man snapped the glass shut on his lantern. Instantly the darkness was complete.

Fong couldn't see his hand in front of his face. He strained to hear the man's oar but couldn't. The man must be sitting in the dark staring at him. Fong settled back and waited. An odd connection grew between the two men. Finally Fong repeated his question. "Do you have a daughter, Grandpa?"

The plunk of an oar broke the silence. Fong reached for his oar and tried to follow the sound, but every time he paused to listen the noise seemed to be coming from a different direction. Finally he stopped rowing and just listened. He didn't hear anything.

Hours later Fong managed to reach a rocky point of land. He had no idea where he was. He got out of the boat and did his best to hook the bowline to a tree stump.

He sat on the smooth rocks and listened to the lapping of the lake.

Then, as if from the water itself, the fisherman appeared — a spectre from the nether worlds. He didn't get out of his boat. He just sat there lolling with the waves and stroking the cormorant. Finally he spoke.

He told Fong everything. The small statue of the horse's hindquarters he'd found in the cormorant's throat. Meeting the archeologist. The man's affair with Chu Shi. The coming of the foreigners. The resistance to them. The Beijing people. The acceptance. The taking of blood. The party high up on the island terrace. The wine. The typhoid. The death. The disinterment of Chu Shi. The celebration on the lake boat. Finally, of saving the whore, Sun Li Cha.

When he was finished, Fong sat quietly looking at the great lake with the island just coming to light in the dawn. All he could think of saying was, "Thank you."

The old fisherman shrugged and began to row away.

"One more question?"

The old man stopped. "What more could you possibly want to know?"

"Just one thing — why did you tell me?"

A long silence followed. The old man looked away from Fong and stared at the dawn. When he spoke, something had broken in his voice. Something had given up. "You ask why I told you all this — because I have no children left. Because I'm old. Perhaps, because I'm a fool." He patted the cormorant. The bird nuzzled its beautiful head into the old gnarled hand. Then the man sighed and finally unleashed his burden. "Because Chu Shi, the girl who died from typhoid, was my daughter. Her mother and I met — once — when I was young." A smile softened his ancient features.

Fong nodded but didn't speak.

The fisherman reached down and picked up something from the floor of the boat. Then tossed it to Fong.

Fong caught the object and turned it in the light.

It was the small bronze of the hindquarters of a horse. "What . . .?"

"I found that thing, down there." He pointed vaguely toward the shoal. "I gave it to Dr. Roung. He gave it to Chu Shi. She arranged to get it back to me before she died. I think that thing killed her. No, I lie. My greed killed her."

He sat very still for a moment then turned away from Fong, toward the rising sun. His shoulders lifted and dropped convulsively. Fong heard nothing but assumed the man was sobbing.

CHAPTER SIXTEEN

IN THE AIR

The coroner had the window seat. Lily sat beside him, her head buried in a fashion magazine she'd bought at the airport. As soon as the plane levelled off, he leaned his forehead against the cool Plexiglass — and drank it in.

China.

Home.

Bands of colour melded into the patterns of intricate tapestries — then into rainbows. Hills became the contours of women's bodies. Space became infinite and soft. Things that do not meet, met.

Then clacking. Clacking. An express train slowing as it passed through a local station. Then him, seated on the express train, looking at the platform across the way through the windows of the stationary local train.

A young man and a woman. Standing on the platform. Holding hands. She facing the tracks, he turned away — peeing through the boards. Simple. Just holding hands and peeing.

"Are you done?" she asked.

He looked up into her round, calm face, into her coal black eyes and nodded.

"Then button up, the train's ready to go."

"Is it far?" His voice was surprisingly young.

"Beyond the mountain," she said and smiled.

"That far?"

"It's not far, dear. In fact, it's always been very near."

He wanted to look at her but found himself looking at his hand. And her hand. And recognized it — his mother's hand. He looked up into his mother's proud face and grinned.

"You know the way?"

"I do." She touched his forehead and brushed away his hair. "Do you?"

He felt himself smiling and crying at the same time. He took a deep breath then said, "I do."

Then he let go.

Lily saw Grandpa's tears running down the window-pane. She heard him mumble. She heard him take a deep breath then let out the air in one long single line of life. In the reflection, deep in the double Plexiglass win-dowpane, she saw the smile on his lips. She felt his hand. It was cold and so very still.

When the plane landed in Beijing, she sat beside the dead man until everyone left their seats. A steward came down the aisle to them. "Is he all right?"

Lily looked at the young man. She didn't know how to answer his question.

* * *

Within six hours Lily had the basic information on the telephone number and was back on a plane to Xian. This

time it was she who stared out the window at the terrifying, intense beauty of China from the air.

A small porcelain vase with a sealed top sat on her
lap.

CHAPTER SEVENTEEN

ALL ROADS LEAD BACK TO XIAN

A great desert storm cloud enshrouded Xian as Fong approached in the Jeep. There was no water in the dingy cloud, only darkness and sand blown all the way from the vast desert to the west. "Here the West is to the west of you," Fong thought. "At home, in Shanghai, the West is to the east. Old and new."

Fong guided the Jeep carefully into the darkness. It was colder than he thought and the streets were empty. Gaudy tourist hotels, then crumbling Chinese buildings momentarily pierced the gloom as the vehicle's headlights swept past them.

Fong took a corner and suddenly emerged from the cloud. He stopped the Jeep and hopped out to glory in the beauty of the night sky. Brilliantly bright stars, pinpricks in the black, black dome of the heavens shone down on him. On the horizon, a perfect crescent moon.

For an instant he considered getting back into the Jeep and driving as hard and fast as he could in any direction. Just drive until the gas gave out. Then walk until his legs failed him. Then crawl until — but only for an instant. He checked his street map and got back into the Jeep, slamming the door. He liked the angry sound of the metal against metal. It bespoke action. Maybe even justice.

Dr. Roung wasn't particularly surprised when Fong barged into his office, but he was definitely not pleased. The man excused himself and went out of the room, leaving Fong alone. Fong fingered the small bronze statue in his pocket. It and the four stacked stones linked the archeologist to Chu Shi. Xian to the island. But he still needed the link back to the rogue in Beijing.

Fong's eyes scanned the broad desktop and landed on the small bronze of the forequarters of the horse sitting to one side.

Then the man's cold hand touched his shoulder. Fong hadn't heard him return. Or perhaps he hadn't actually left. Just stepped toward the door. Before the taller man could speak, Fong said, "I have a few questions I'd like you to answer."

The archeologist raised an eyebrow. "Evidently you do." The light glinted off his heavy steel-framed glasses as he tried to learn what Fong had seen among the objects on his desk. But he wasn't able to discern what had drawn Fong's attention.

Fong noticed and smiled openly. He ran his tongue over his smooth teeth.

The archeologist smiled back. That twinkle again.

Fong stepped away from the desk, careful to keep his eyes away from the small bronze statuette.

The older man watched him carefully, then nodded as if he'd made up his mind about something. He tapped the top of an odd-looking, square machine sitting on the office floor. "Do you know what this is, Detective Zhong?"

Fong looked at the squat grey thing. By its bulk and open ugliness he assumed it was Soviet in design, but he couldn't begin to guess what it was. "World's most impractical doorstop," he suggested.

"No, Zhong Fong, it's a shredder." A knowing smile blossomed on the man's face as he added, "A Soviet-made shredder."

Fong was disconcerted by the latter comment — it was as if the archeologist had read his mind. "What does it do?" Fong demanded, a little too forcefully.

"It shreds things, Detective Zhong." The man's smile grew to offensive proportions as he took a large map of Shaanxi province from his desk and placed it in the feed bin. He pressed a button. A flurry of metal blades made a racket for a few seconds then hundreds of odd-shaped pieces vomited out into a tray. The archeologist tilted the contents of the tray onto his desktop and spread them out flat. He didn't bother turning over the pieces that were face down. For twenty or so seconds he studied the array before him. Then he began. In less than five minutes he had reconstructed the entire map. As he fitted the last piece of the puzzle, he looked up. "It's a unique talent. I was born with it. I never worked at it. Never thought about it. Just used it. My talent."

Fong wanted to say, "I'm impressed," but didn't. "I assume you use the same principles to piece together the terra-cotta warriors?"

"I do, indeed," the archeologist asserted, as if he were

being challenged on some fundamental level. His smile was no longer warm. His eyes were piercing. "You too have a unique talent, Detective Zhong. In some ways we are very similar."

"I don't follow that."

"Really?" Dr. Roung's voice arched upward. "I piece together puzzles. You piece together puzzles. I am treated differently by the Chinese state than most other Chinese males and so are you. After all, how many murderers are allowed to return to the civilized side of the Wall?"

Fong didn't respond.

The archeologist wasn't put off by Fong's silence. "You do agree, don't you, Detective Zhong?"

Fong tilted his head slightly. Not a real agreement — but enough.

"Good. Then perhaps you'd help me solve a puzzle that's been bothering me for a very long time, Detective Zhong." The man seemed suddenly joyful.

Again Fong tilted his head, wondering where this was leading.

Dr. Roung crossed to the shelf behind his desk and pulled down an old, leather-bound book from an upper tier. "Have you read the Italian's account of 'discovering' China?"

"Marco Polo?" Fong asked. Dr. Roung nodded and handed over the well-thumbed text. Fong felt the heft of the thing. It was pleasing.

"Such an odd name, Marco Polo, don't you agree? Sounds like a child's food."

Fong allowed himself a smile despite being totally at a loss as to what was going on. He handed back the book. "Yes, I read this in English. It was part of my training in that language."

"So you are perfectly prepared to help me with my puzzle." The man seemed gleeful.

"If you say so," Fong said warily.

"I do." He clapped his hands once loudly. "Well, every Chinese person who reads this silly account knows in his heart that it's a lie. A joke played on some European master by this person with a name that sounds like baby food. Do you agree?"

"Yes," Fong said without hesitation.

"Good. I hoped you would. Now, tell me how we know that this book is a lie? Know in our heads, not in our hearts."

Fong thought for a moment. "Because of what Marco Polo left out."

"Because of what wasn't in the text?" the archeologist asked, openly fascinated by the idea.

"Yes," Fong said slowly.

"Like what, Detective Zhong? What was missing in the book?"

Fong looked for a trap but couldn't find one. Finally he spoke, "How could a man from the West who claimed to have lived in the Middle Kingdom for almost ten years fail to mention in his books the Great Wall, our character system of writing or for that matter, the tiny, bound feet of aristocratic women? How could these fail to impress him? How could Marco Polo have been here and not seen fit to include them in his account? Don't you find that odd?" He was happy to be asking the questions.

"I do, Zhong Fong." Dr. Roung smiled warmly. "Now that you mention it . . . I do." He laughed. An odd, honest laugh. "But before you brought it up, it had escaped my attention." He took a deep breath as if he was about to cross an invisible divide. He reached up and took off his army-issue spectacles. "I create whole things from their many pieces. It is my gift. Yours, Zhong Fong, is to create whole things from those pieces that are missing. It is another kind of gift. A photo negative of my gift, if you follow."

Fong considered Dr. Roung's statement and found some truth in it. More important, for the first time he sensed the man's deep need to talk. To talk to someone he saw as an equal.

Fong hesitated. Unsure how to lead the conversation.

"Would you like to see my terra-cotta warriors, Zhong Fong?" Dr. Roung said in a surprisingly gentle voice.

It wasn't lost on Fong that the archeologist hadn't called him detective. "I would. I would like to see your warriors."

As Dr. Roung walked ahead of him, Fong realized that he was following a man who had secrets — dark secrets that he needed to share with an equal — with someone who understood his worth.

With the simple flip of a light switch Dr. Roung brought

the great sleeping contents of pit #1 to life. Row upon row of standing and kneeling men. Archers, horsemen, foot soldiers — each with its own face. An eerily silent army just about to move or having just moved, only to be stunned into immobility by the rising of the light. The famous terra-cotta warriors — the lasting memorial of Qin Shi Huang, China's first emperor.

Fong and the archeologist stood on the gallery above the ranks of frozen men. "In April of 1974 I was called by the Ministry of the Interior. Some stupid farmer outside of Xian had reported discovering a few artifacts in his field," Dr. Roung chuckled. "I thought it would take me a week at most to deal with what I assumed was a useless piece of junk. My first night here I was brought to a peasant's hut. The old woman had two terra-cotta heads set up beside her fireplace. She was worshipping them as gods. And you know what, Zhong Fong?" Fong looked at him. "I understood why she'd do that. In my heart it seemed to me that those two old heads were as worthy of adoration as anything I'd ever seen — up until that time." The final words were only wisps of sound — the heart's breath.

Fong repeated the final four words: *up until that time.* He'd never heard any admission of loss so deep. He looked at the man. Tears were coming from his eyes.

"It took two years, but by the middle of 1976, my team had unearthed three full pits. A fourth was found late in 1977, but it was empty. Pit #1, down there, has thirty-eight columns of soldiers. Naturally, they all face east. There were originally over six thousand figures.

We've managed to restore just over a thousand warriors and horses. Pit #2 has fifteen sections. We opened it to the public in 1976 then closed it down."

Fong was about to ask why when the archeologist beat him to the punch. "You always leap ahead, Zhong Fong." He wiped the tears from his cheeks with a fine linen handkerchief. "I may get to that in time. Working on the Qin Dynasty warriors teaches patience, if nothing else. Do you know your history, Zhong Fong?" Before Fong could reply, he continued, "Qin Shi Huang declared himself China's first emperor in 221 BC — this is his tomb. He must have been quite a man. He defeated the six major warring states of China and ascended a throne that he built. He quashed all resistance from the nobles and set to work unifying a land mass that had never been unified before. He established the civil service system complete with examinations and meritocracy, which lasted over two thousand years, right up to the fall of the Manchu government in 1911. He codified weights and measures to permit commerce in the country. He standardized the written language that you and I use to this day. True, he burned any books that were in opposition to his rule, but then again the world has a long tradition of book burners, doesn't it?"

Dr. Roung reached into his pants pocket and took out a greenish-bronze coin. "He instituted the use of currency. This bronze *ban liang* coin was his creation. We found thousands of them in the pits. They were good for commerce — and taxes, of course. So much easier to collect money than rice. Qin Shi Huang built the Great Wall to keep them away from us. More recently, you, Fong, from me. And he raised a great army by the use of this clever little invention." From his pocket he produced the small bronze statuette of the frontquarters of a horse that Fong had seen on the desk. He must have palmed it before they left the office. Fong wondered how he'd missed that. "He gave a half to each of his generals. They could only raise troops when they were met by the emperor's man who had the other half that fit his. In a time of limited communication it allowed the emperor to control the most important communications — those that led to the raising of troops — of potential insurrection."

Fong noticed the delicate way Dr. Roung handled the bronze and thought he saw a subtle further fall in the man's features. He resisted the impulse to reach into his own pocket and touch Chu Shi's statuette. Then he thought about "potential insurrection" — and a rogue in Beijing.

"Of course, Qin Shi Huang's achievements required huge taxes and hundreds of thousands, maybe even a million, forced labourers. We are sure that more than seven hundred thousand artisans and workers worked on the tomb for thirty-six years. But on some level it was worth it, don't you think?" The archeologist turned toward the lines of soldiers in the pit. Fong followed his gaze. "A creation that withstands the very movement of time."

Fong found it both beautiful and appalling. An achievement, no doubt. But at what cost? Over seven hundred thousand lives dedicated to what? Fong felt Dr.

Roung's cold hand on his shoulder again. "Let's not start here. I think I know how you would best be introduced to my terra-cotta warriors, Zhong Fong."

With that, he flicked off the switch and the place went ghostly dark.

Fong followed the archeologist out of the building and down a back alley. The night air was quick and chilled. A desert night. Fong found himself happy that Dr. Roung was setting a fast pace in his walk.

They moved through the silent dark for more than half an hour before the man stopped in front of a large, corrugated metal building. He pulled out a set of industrial keys and opened the sheet-metal door. The interior smelled of things old and dusty. Then Dr. Roung hit the light switch. No soft folding light here. High-intensity overhead beams turned night into a glaring day. And brought to life a tableau of a world in pitched battle between birth and decay.

Fong stepped forward without invitation. The huge space was littered with partially completed terra-cotta warriors. Many seemed as if they were trying to rise from the dust, pulling limbs still caught by the very time of the Earth. Others lay on their sides as if arms and parts of legs were being sucked down into the ground. Then heaps of body parts. And finally, a pile twice Fong's height and maybe twenty feet wide of stacked heads. Some looking wistfully toward the harsh light as if the false sun could rejuvenate their long-lost lives, while others were bidding their final adieus to a cruel world.

Fong turned and saw the archeologist sitting at a large glass-topped table. On the surface were thousands of shards of fired clay. Dr. Roung moved his hands above the pieces as he had done with the shredded bits of map in his office. Even in the cold light, Fong couldn't deny the beauty of the man's arched back and long tapered fingers. The man's left hand reached out and snatched a piece from the table and snapped it perfectly into place with another piece that was by his side. He turned to Fong, a simple smile on his face.

"This man is happy here," Fong thought. "He should never have ventured out of doors."

"There are millions of pieces yet to be fitted." That seemed an immensely pleasing fact to the archeologist. "Each of the pits was covered by a heavy wooden roof. They all collapsed. From the char marks, we surmise that they were burned. Probably by the rebels who ended the Qin Dynasty's short-lived rule. Well, the roof beams smashed all the figures. The kneeling ones, often archers, were least damaged. Things were in pieces, you might say. Beijing called on my services. No. They needed my services." He nodded at Fong, "As they have now called on your services." Fong nodded back.

"We call this place the fitting room — apt, don't you think." He pushed back his seat and crossed to a computer on a side table. As he typed he said, "Every piece is coded. Each side of each piece carries a sub-code. When we find a match we enter it in the computer and the computer helps find similar shards that might fit what we now have. But the final fitting can't be done by machine. It needs a human hand. It needs talent." He finished his entry and looked at Fong. Then he raised a single finger and pointed to a side room.

Fong followed.

In the room was a fully completed figure. Naked. Partially painted. "We use a glue made from sharks' lungs to keep any flakes of the original paint in place. Then we make old-style pigments from minerals and bind them with animal blood and egg white. Charcoal is used to tint the hair, hemp for soles of the shoes and braided hair for the archers. The torsos and limbs are generic; there are thirty-two different styles, but the faces are unique. No two match. Of all the mysteries here, and yes, Fong, there are some extremely interesting mysteries here, the fact that Qin Shi Huang went to the trouble of giving each soldier an individual face stands out as most interesting to me. Of course, that's just my opinion. Others find the seven unidentified skeletons more interesting. Personally, I assume that they were the emperor's children. Some people find the fact that in the great pit there are two generals most interesting. I don't. I find it very Chinese. Grant neither full power. Make both go through the emperor. Balance the power between the two to keep each in check — very Chinese."

"In boxes," Fong thought.

"I have something else to show you."

The man headed toward the far door. Fong followed. This time they entered the night air only briefly before Dr. Roung opened the door of a late model Toyota

Santana and told Fong to climb in. They drove. The wind was full of desert sand. A cold scraping eternity. They had left the tourist's Xian behind and were racing along a dirt road.

Then they were in country.

Twenty minutes later Dr. Roung pulled the car to the side of the road and took a large flashlight from the glove compartment.

They began to walk. The night was getting colder. The wind abated and, overhead, Fong saw the brilliant desert night sky again. Fong was tiring. Late nights were no longer simple for him. He was about to request a stop when Dr. Roung crested a hill and pointed his flashlight at one of the oddest sights in China — a very large, empty plot of arable land.

Fong didn't need to be told what this was. He sensed the presence of the dead all around him. Huge numbers of them. Buried here. One atop another. Squashed side to side like eels on a cutting table. "The workers?" he asked, already knowing the answer to his question.

"Very good, Fong. There may be in excess of seven hundred thousand bodies buried here."

"Not nearly so lavish as the tomb of Qin Shi Huang!" Fong spat out.

"True, Fong, but are all lives really worthy of royal tombs — of immortality?"

That sense of falling came from the man at his side again. The sense of loss. Fong thought of Captain Chen's confusion about justice. Fong had been unmistakably moved by the achievement of the Qin emperor's tomb.

But was the emperor's life really worth that much more than the lives of all those who worked on the enterprise?

Again the archeologist put a hand on Fong's shoulder — so personal. So un-Chinese. "Two million visitors a year come to the terra-cotta warriors. The foreigners love it. We bake little replicas for them and they pay a fortune for the worthless things. That's a lot of money coming into the country. Some claim that the warriors are the number one tourist attraction in the world." Dr. Roung removed his hand and began to laugh, to cackle. "Personally, I'm interested in seeing Disneyland."

Fong turned toward the braying sound. The archeologist's face was dark; confusion and loss vied for prominence on his features.

"But our emperor did not meet an end any better than those seven hundred thousand souls buried out there, Fong. He died at forty-nine, after only eleven years of power." The man chuckled again, a hoarse, angry laugh. "Do you know how he died?"

"No, how?"

"Naked on a mountain top. Howling at the moon. He'd got it into his head that there was an elixir of life. A fountain of eternal youth." A truly ghastly laugh exploded from the man's face. A line of spittle crept from the corner of his mouth. "China's first emperor, perhaps the most powerful man the world had ever seen, sent his scholars out to find it. The whole of China was turned upside down in Qin Shi Huang's desperate effort to stop growing old, to defeat time itself. Thousands were executed when the substances they produced for the emperor had no effect. Finally, he was told of a mountain peak, a holy mountain. He climbed it with a single trusted serving man. Once they got to the top, the faithful retainer was sent down. They found the emperor the next morning, naked, clutching a stone to his groin — frozen to death."

Dr. Roung moved away, but Fong stayed where he was and drank it all in. A cold night. Seven hundred thousand buried souls to one side and the image of a mad emperor seeking the elixir of life on the other. Parallel patterns. His teeth clacked. They hadn't done that for a while. A surge of anger went through him and in his heart he knew what this was all about. What bound it all together — the elixir of life. Staying young. Fighting against the inevitable. That's what was in the islanders' DNA. That's why the foreigners want the patent. That's why Hesheng had been given a name that means "in this year of peace" despite the fact that he only looked to be in his twenties. Why there were so few graves in the island's cemetery, why Iman couldn't remember the words for the prayer to the dead, why the foreigners were so anxious to get accurate family histories from the islanders: from the farmers who were thought never to intermarry, but not from the fishermen who did. The islanders' DNA — the elixir of life.

From the missing piece he had deduced the whole.

He turned to the archeologist, "What's your given name, sir?"

"Chen. My science degree permits me to use the title doctor. So I am Dr. Roung Chen."

Fong laughed.

"What?"

"Chen is a common name, a very common name for one so unique."

CHAPTER EIGHTEEN

DREAM OF DREAMS

That night Fong wandered the deserted Xian streets alone. Visions of visions cascaded in his head. Seven hundred thousand bodies crammed in burial. Soldiers ready to attack, frozen in eternal stillness by the rising light. Seven unidentified corpses. Two generals kept apart from each other. Time itself standing still.

Then there was a shuffling of feet. Fong turned and somehow he was in pit #1 of the terra-cotta warriors. Before he could understand what was happening to him he sensed movement through the rank upon rank of clay soldiers in the pit. And colour. Then a shout. Someone shouting his name. Ordering him.

Fong moved past a kneeling archer and ran down a row of mounted cavalrymen.

And there he was.

Qin Shi Huang, dressed just as he was in the famous woodcut. On his head sat a rectangular, lacquered piece of hide from which hung silk strands — a dozen behind, a dozen in front. Each strand was strung with exquisite jade beads. His dark upper garment was of an almost blue-black silk. His voluminous sleeves were embroidered — light on the outside but dark as blood on the interior. The elaborate frontpiece was held in place by a white jade belt over an obi-like silk sash from which the jade handle of his sword protruded. Below the belt were silk skirts in several layers of light red that just exposed the tips of his wooden platform sandals. Fong vaguely remembered that the entirety of what the emperor wore was called Mian Fu. Both the name and the clothing style went back to the Xi Zhou people in the eleventh century BC.

"We've made it."

The man's gruff voice shocked Fong. The accent was unidentifiable.

"Help me off with this," he said indicating the broad obi-like sash around his waist.

Fong was frightened to touch the illusion lest it return to nothingness.

"Hurry, the light fades and I must be prepared."

Fong undid the white jade belt and put it on the ground. It was surprisingly heavy. Then he reached behind the emperor and untied the thin belt that kept the sash in place. The garment slid through his fingers with a silken whisper. The emperor bowed his head and Fong undid the straps and removed the headpiece, the Tong Tian, being careful not to snag the long ribbon attached to it that is supposed to connect the emperor to heaven.

A brisk wind picked up. Fong shivered. He looked around him. He was on the crest of a high rugged peak, timeless China down below.

The emperor stared into the distance. Fong knew that

Qin Shi Huang was actually his own age although he looked ancient as the rock.

With a huge sigh, the emperor sat heavily on the cold ground and lifted a foot. Fong found the delicate straps and snaps and freed the emperor's feet from the raised platform sandals. Then he slipped off the silk socks. The emperor's feet were severely arthritic; the joints were swollen or broken and his toes splayed in odd crushed patterns. His toenails were extremely thick and deeply yellowed from fungal growth.

The emperor lifted his upper garment over his shoulders revealing a sunken chest and sparse growth of greying hair, narrowing to a single line that ran from his navel downward.

Qin Shi Huang stood and turned to Fong. Clearly Fong was to undo the ribbons that held the emperor's lower skirts in place. He hesitated. His eyes were at the emperor's waist. He glanced up, aware of what this looked like. But the emperor was once again staring deep into the far-off.

Fong unlaced the ribbons. The emperor's skirts fell away. Before him, nestled in a bed of grey pubic hair, the man's penis looked at him like a one-eyed eel, frightened of the world.

"Cover him."

Fong whipped around. Dr. Roung was there holding a round flat stone, almost the size of a dinner plate.

"Cover him, Fong!"

The archeologist held out the stone. Fong took it. It was heavy and dropped to the ground with a thud.

"Pick it up."

This voice was different. Familiar but different. Fong looked up. Iman stood there, Jiajia at his side.

"Pick it up, Fong."

This voice was high, lisping. It came from his left. It was the politico.

Fong picked up the stone. It was suddenly light as the finest porcelain. He handed it to the emperor.

The old man took the stone and turned away — toward the east.

Fong turned back.

There was no one there. Nothing there. Then he looked to the emperor. He too was gone.

Of course.

At the end there is only ourselves — and what we know — and time which knows everything but tells us so very little.

CHAPTER NINETEEN

AT THE RECREATION

Fong's phone call to Lily in Ching was brief and to the point. She listened quietly — in shock — then began asking questions. Each one a better question than the one before. Then she, albeit shakily, agreed.

"How long do we have, Fong?" she asked.

"Say, four hours. I've got to get him and then haul him back. Does that give you enough time?"

"We'll make it enough." As she hung up the phone she was surprised to realize that she was excited. No. Thrilled.

Dr. Roung Chen didn't bother rising as Fong pushed his way past the secretary and into the archeologist's Xian office. The man looked awful.

Tough.

"Let's go."

"Where to?"

"Back."

"To what?"

"Not to Disneyland, Dr. Roung. To Lake Ching. You may recall there was a mass murder there — on a boat." The man was so flustered that he didn't notice Fo reach over and palm a small object from his desk.

They drove for three hours in absolute silence. "Maybe just as Captain Chen had on that frigid night over four months ago with the specialist," Fong thought. But Fong didn't linger on the thought. There was still something missing from the puzzle. A final link that connected the pieces he had to the rogue in Beijing — which in turn pointed his way back home to Shanghai. And Fong was aware that without the connection to the rogue in Beijing everything he knew was as useless as the bits of paper vomited from the shredding machine in the archeologist's office.

As he and Dr. Roung walked toward the abandoned factory in Ching, Fong sensed that he'd have only one chance to find that link. He threw open the iron door. They stepped in and Fong slammed the door shut. They stood in total darkness while the clang of metal echoed in the space.

Once the echo faded, Fong said, "It was a place of revenge . . ." he didn't wait for Dr. Roung to respond, " . . . and surprise. Wasn't it?"

Fong hit the wall switch that Chen had set up. All four death rooms snapped into being — floors, walls and ceilings.

Fong stared into the archeologist's pale eyes. They were retreating behind his army-issue metal-framed glasses. "Fine," Fong spat out and took three steps toward the projections. Then he stopped and turned back to Dr. Roung.

"It was a cold night. The whore, Sun Li Cha, waited

on the dock and greeted the foreigners. The other girls couldn't make it. Some god with a sense of humour, or maybe it was just Soviet drunkenness, produced a vehicle that broke down and kept them from getting to the boat." Fong looked back into the darkness. It was as if he was about to step onto a great stage and the archeologist was the only member of the audience. "But that wasn't the only unexpected event of the evening was it, Dr. Roung? Don't bother answering. We have lots of time."

"The foreigners went to the bar. The boat headed out on the lake. Once it was far enough out, the crew was ushered into a lifeboat and sent home. After all, one of the Taiwanese had a pilot's licence and what kind of trouble could seventeen foreigners get into on a calm lake? Right? Sorry, seventeen foreigners and a hooker — right, I'd almost forgotten — and Iman. Let's start in the bar."

On cue, the other rooms blacked out. Fong stepped into the projected bar room, the images playing across his face and body as he moved through the space. Dr. Roung followed Fong. The projections of the seven faceless bodies somehow stood out. The eldest, the one strung from the ceiling, even seemed to be swaying back and forth as if the boat were in motion on the lake. "Seven dead men. How?" The archeologist stared at Fong, the coloured lines of the projections playing across his face. "If you look about you, you'll see that there are no half-empty glasses. An odd bar that has liquor and clean glasses but no half-empty glasses, don't you think? Oh yes, there was the stain on the floor . . . right her
Fong was at the side of the room farthest from the

He opened the satchel he was carrying and pulled out a bottle of champagne. "Remember, Iman was there. You remember him, don't you, Dr. Roung? Sun Li Cha told me all about him being there. So as soon as the crew left and the boat was far enough out on the lake, Iman proposed a toast. After all, they had just completed a monumental business deal, hadn't they?" He held up his bottle. "Champagne. The foreigners were all there; hey, this was a big celebration. A deal done. A long march completed! Iman poured them each a glass and then held his aloft. He shouted a toast, 'To Blood!'" Fong shrieked. Then he paused and shrugged. "Perhaps it was more civilized: *To Life* or *To Money* or *To Hell*. Who knows? Well, of course you do, don't you Dr. Roung! Well, whatever Iman said, the seventeen men must have cheered and then drunk their champagne — like good little capitalists."

Fong opened the bottle and drank. It scorched his throat and made his stomach do a quick loop. "Don't worry, Dr. Roung, this is just alcohol. No sedative in this champagne." Then Fong turned the bottle over and the liquid splashed onto the projected image of the red carpet, beside the stain that was already there. "They didn't all drink though, did they, Dr. Roung? Iman allowed everyone else to swallow the poison while he tilted his onto the carpet behind him. Thus, the unidentified stain the specialist went to such trouble to photograph."

"It was the Triads . . ."

Fong didn't let him complete his sentence, "Right, the ˡs. I'd almost forgotten about them."

"That Triad medallion . . ."

"Found right here. Correct?" Fong pointed to a space two feet to his left. "I worried for a bit about the medallion. Well, not really about the medallion. About the chain. Actually, about the single broken link of the chain. Well now, that's not quite honest either, Dr. Roung. I was really worried about the four photographs the specialist supplied of the broken link. Four pictures, one link. Not very Chinese, don't you think? So I had an associate of mine buy some of those medallions in Xian. They're very popular with the tourists, don't you know."

Fong took one from his pocket and put it around his neck. He grabbed the medallion with his right hand and yanked downward. The chain broke. Fong held the broken thing up close to the archeologist's face. "How many broken links, Dr. Roung?"

"Two."

"Right. Two. Every time I've done it — two. But the medallion in the rug of the bar had only one broken link. Four photographs, one link — one attempt to blame the Triads for . . ." Fong spread his arms and turned, " . . . this."

Fong looked at the archeologist, but the man's face revealed nothing.

"During the toasts, and I assume there were several, Iman's people boarded the boat." He indicated a projected portal. When he turned back to Dr. Roung he said, "That's when he saw them, wasn't it?"

"Who?" snapped back the archeologist.

Fong grunted. "Fine." He began to walk and

Roung followed. Quickly he left the bar. It blinked out. The bedroom with the two beheaded Americans snapped on. Fong didn't bother to check if Dr. Roung was following him; he knew he was. "Sun Li Cha entertained the two Americans — briefly. She claimed they weren't up to the task. When she left the room the islanders slipped in and slit their throats. These were the first murders. Silent murders that wouldn't alarm the rest. After all, Westerners were so odd, who could tell what they were doing in their room? It gave the sedative more time to work on the Asians who just may not have drunk all their champagne — champagne is an acquired taste, isn't it?" Fong looked at the projection of the two dead Americans. "I put my money on Jiajia for this piece of work. The switching of the heads could have been done by any of them. A little *chi* let loose on the boat, huh Dr. Roung?" He paused for a moment, a new thought coalescing in his mind. "Or all of them," he muttered. He dismissed a vision of the room stuffed with islanders watching the heads being cut from the bodies.

"Next it was the Koreans' turn to face their makers." The bedroom disappeared and the video room came to light. Fong entered the projected room. Chen had set up the VCR and porno film as Fong had requested: a lurid image paused on the monitor. "The film was right here. Thirty-two minutes in. Thirty-two minutes since it had been turned on. At the point of the third copulation, if you'd care to check?" Dr. Roung stood like a man in an field during a lightning storm, unsure whether to run or stand still. "Well, don't check then. You'll just have to take my word for it. Be that as it may, thirty-two minutes was long enough for the poison to almost paralyze the Koreans." Then Fong turned to Dr. Roung. "These three men watched helplessly as they were hung by wire from that beam and then shot through the armpits and allowed to die. This one's actually the simplest. Someone had a score to settle. Foreigners always forget that we have long memories, don't they? Why do you figure that is, sir?"

The archeologist was about to speak then thought better of it.

"I figure it was sometime after they killed the Koreans that our intrepid hooker found her way to the deck and lo and behold, guess who's there? An old fisherman. Now why would he be there, do you think? Huh?"

The archeologist looked away. "It wouldn't have anything to do with you, would it, Dr. Roung? I mean this fisherman wouldn't, for example, be taking you to the boat, would he? Now why would he do that?"

"I don't know." The words sounded ancient in the man's mouth.

"Really! I thought you were the puzzle solver here, Dr. Roung."

"I don't know!" the archeologist said louder.

"Well, there were some things you didn't know. That I grant. Surprises. Oh, there were big surprises, weren't there? Follow me." After a moment of darkness, the bar room with the faceless Chinese men snapped on. For crossed to a wall and picked up the broad flat hewer that Lily had placed there. It was the kind the islanders used to build trenches and cleave paths. He held it up. The light glinted off its sharpened edge. "Very effective for removing faces, I'd think. Bloody though. I wouldn't have thought you'd be so bloody?"

The archeologist stood directly beneath where the swaying man would have been and turned to Fong. "Detective Zhong, I found something on that island — not something — someone. Someone and something of real value. Timeless value."

Fong stood and waited. He imagined the swaying man, a bizarre pendulum in a world where time stood still.

"The dead girl, Chu Shi, Jiajia's wife," Fong stated flatly.

"Not just her. The whole possibility of something that lasts. Something beyond time."

"And these mutilated men . . . ?"

"These Chinese men were willing to sell our very birthright. To sell something that is us — no, the *very* thing that is us — to make our entity into stupid little clay statues and sell them to foreigners."

Fong walked past the projections of the faceless men at the bar and the others by the mirror. Then he turned to Dr. Roung, a surprised look on his face. "This was your idea?" It wasn't an accusation. Just a simple question.

"Justice for what they were doing to us, don't you see?"

Fong allowed his head to nod slowly. "Traitors."

"'Traitors to the black-haired people — yes, Zhong Fong, traitors who met their just reward.'"

Fong nodded again then slowly walked out of the projected bar. Dr. Roung followed him like a beaten dog on a long leash.

Everything went dark. Then the runway room projection lit up. But this room was more than just a projection. The curtain was there. The runway was there. The six chairs were there — five occupied by dummies.

Fong entered the room. He pressed a wall switch and the runway lights came on. He pressed a second and the Counting Crows song "Angels of the Silences" began to play. He didn't look back. "The islanders didn't tell you about this, though, did they? Did they?" he snapped.

A harsh whispered, "No," came from the darkness.

"Justice is a hard thing, Dr. Roung. It's not a thing that can be pieced together from whole cloth. You never have all the pieces when you try to find justice. And your justice and the islanders' justice may not — no — are not the same. Are they?"

"No." The archeologist took off his army-issue glasses and rubbed his eyes. The last piece fell into place and Fong laughed.

"What?"

"Your glasses."

"What about them."

"Glasses are hard to get, aren't they? Especially designer glasses. Right from the start, your glasses bothered me. Thinsulate vest and old army-issue glasses Fong strode over to the dummy of the eviscerat

castrated Japanese man with the fancy Parisian eye-
glasses wobbly on his head. Fong pulled them off and
turned to Dr. Roung. "Want them back?"

The man went white and stiff.

Fong reached into his pants and took something from
his pocket. "Maybe you'd like this back." He opened his
fingers revealing the bronze statue of a horse's frontquarters that he had taken from the archeologist's
desk." Dr. Roung lunged at it, but Fong moved quickly
aside. "It's beautiful, isn't it?" Dr. Roung didn't answer,
then nodded. "The hindquarters are beautiful too."

"You've seen . . ."

He reached into his other pocket and brought out the
hindquarters. Fong continued quickly. "What an unusual girl she must have been. She died of the first recorded
case of typhoid on the island in — what — a hundred
years? Dug up so an autopsy could be performed. You
knew that, didn't you?"

Dr. Roung nodded slowly again.

"Then she was buried a second time." Fong paused
and waited for the archeologist to take a breath. When
he did, Fong added, "Then dug up again."

Fong moved to the light switch and dimmed the
lights. Then he plunged the room into darkness. "Did
you know the fisherman was her father? That's why her
immune system wasn't strong enough to protect her
from the typhoid." A long silence followed then another
Counting Crows song, "Daylight Fading," came up
·udly. Beside him in the dark, Fong could hear the
·heologist sobbing quietly.

Fong took a breath and pressed hard on the light switch. The stage blared into shocking light. And there, wrapped in filthy, night soil–sodden, crimson burial cloth, stood the partially naked body of Chu Shi, her back to them, held up by a pole.

A long tortured breath came from Dr. Roung.

The music increased in volume and Chu Shi seemed to move to the rhythm despite being dead and propped up on a stick.

"The Japanese were already dead when you arrived in the room. Weren't they? Sure they were. After the fun with the Americans, the islanders split up, didn't they? You and Iman led the revenge against the Taiwanese, but Jiajia had plans of his own in here, didn't he? He and his men killed them and cut them open. Their intestines in their hands facing the stage. When you finally arrived, all the islanders were here, waiting. This was the finale, after all! Sure it was. Absolutely. Except it wasn't the finale you thought. This wasn't for them. This was for you. For the one who dared to sleep with one of their women. This wasn't political. This was personal, wasn't it? This was to prove to you that Chu Shi was nothing more than a whore who'd take off her clothes for anyone who had money. Who'd fuck anyone, from anywhere — after all, she was just a whore — wasn't she?"

Dr. Roung fell to his knees and retched. His glasses fell off.

Fong knelt beside him. The vomit was surprisingly odourless. Fong whispered in his ear, "But what they did to her, to your precious Chu Shi, was not as bad as what you did to her. Was it?"

A torrent of bile spewed from the archeologist's mouth and slapped to the floor.

"How did the typhoid get to the island? It was man-made, cultured typhoid that killed her. How did it get there?" A moment of silence and then Fong screamed, "Tell me!" He grabbed Dr. Roung's arm and dragged him to his feet. Then he pushed him toward the empty chair at the head of the runway.

Throwing him into the seat Fong shouted, "This was your chair, wasn't it?" Then he tilted Dr. Roung's head up and toward the stage — toward the dead woman in the tattered, scarlet burial cloth on the runway — the tattered, scarlet burial cloth covered in night soil–laden earth.

Lily heard Fong yell. She had been holding her breath. Trying not to breathe in the filth. Trying not to imagine the horrible figures of the Japanese men watching her. Trying not to hear the music. Hoping this would be over before she shrieked or fainted or both. Then she stumbled forward.

Dr. Roung screamed and held his head in his hands.

Fong yanked the man's face up so it looked right into his. "Tell me how the typhoid got to the island!"

"From Beijing. They sent it in the ceremonial wine, from Beijing. The wine at the island banquet."

Fong stood and looked down at the man. "Did you know?"

Dr. Roung looked up at Fong and screamed, "No!"

The sound of the single word echoed off the walls of the old factory and repeated itself over and over and over again as it spiralled downward, like water from a dirty tub, into the nowhere beneath.

Fong knelt in close. "Where in Beijing, Dr. Roung? What box in that city of boxes sent you the typhoid?"

Dr. Roung Chen shook his head.

Fong got to his feet and turned up the music. "Dance for him, Chu Shi!"

Lily felt an odd relief to be able to move. Then a horror at what she was doing. She imagined men watching her coming to life. Their hands moving. Their mouths cheering her. The death shroud seemed to be falling off her of its own accord. As if seeking a way back to its mistress thrice buried on the island.

Fong turned the archeologist's face once again to the stage and using his fingers kept the man's eyes wide open. "Look, Dr. Roung. Look what they did to your Chu Shi."

The archeologist tried to pull his face away from the horror but Fong held him tight. Finally the man barked out, "The ministry."

"Which ministry, Dr. Roung?" snapped Fong.

"The Interior Ministry," the man cried out.

Fong found himself unable to breathe. The Interior Ministry! That was no small box of dissidents or hotheads. Not some solitary rogue. This was a full-fledged insurrection!

Dr. Roung fell to the floor on his knees. Tears streamed from his eyes. Saliva dripped from his mouth.

Then he shouted, a haunted cry to the ceiling. "My mother did this!"

Fong turned slowly, "Madame Minister Wu is your mother?"

*　　*　　*

Lily heard it but didn't hear it. Her own terror was rising. She was somehow or other back in the forensics lab all those years ago. The man on her. His hands ripping aside her skirt. Tearing her panties. Hurting her. Then Fong was there and somehow the man was gone and Fong was holding her, telling her, "It's okay, Lily. It's okay. You did great. We've got all we need."

But that's not what he'd said back then. He'd just held her. He'd hardly said anything. Then she felt his hard body holding her tighter. And she wrapped her arms around him and held him to her as if he were the last way out of a dawning nightmare.

CHAPTER TWENTY

THE DEAL

The door of the jail cell clunked as it opened. "You wanted to see me?" The politico looked as if he had been awakened from a deep sleep. "I said . . ."

Fong turned.

"I heard what you said," Fong snapped as he walked past the politico and slammed the door shut. "Okay!" Fong yelled.

Somewhere beyond their line of sight Captain Chen threw the switch to lock the door. The politico jumped when he heard the tumblers slam home.

Fong looked at the man. Something was missing. The thug, of course. Two generals. Always two generals. Parallel patterns. Fong knew that the politico reported to the Beijing government. That meant the thug wasn't here because . . . because . . . because he reported to the rogue — Madame Wu.

Fong laughed. The politico looked at him. Fong didn't explain. He was relishing a vision of the bull of a man on the run. China was a big country but it was impossible to hide in China. Fong knew that. Oh yes, he knew that.

"You have something for me, Traitor Zhong?"

Fong looked at the politico. The man looked ridiculous claiming to still have power.

"You need me. I don't need you," Fong barked. "This is a jail. I've lived in one of these cells. You haven't."

The politico paled. "What do you want . . ." his voice tailed off before he said the words "Traitor Zhong."

Fong pushed aside the surge of anger he felt and ordered his thoughts. "I know who murdered the foreigners on the boat in Lake Ching."

The politico pulled himself up to his full height, making as if somehow this dank cell were his office in some government building. "Yes — Fong. You have done your duty as all citizens of the People's . . ."

Fong spat. "This is a jail cell, not an office in Beijing." Fong spat again. This time the spittle landed close to the politico's feet.

The politico looked at the gob, then at Fong. Suddenly he seemed to see the jail cell. His eyes glazed over. He opened his mouth to speak but Fong spoke first. "And I know who in Beijing ordered the murders, which is what you're really after, isn't it?"

The politico was very still. As if his interior was reconstructing itself after a total collapse. Fong could almost hear the ticky-tack of the man's ribs reconnecting to his spine. "So do your duty and report your findings."

That floated in the thick air of the cell. Fong didn't move. Didn't speak. Didn't breathe.

"What do I get?"

"Excuse me . . ."

"You heard me, lackey. What do I get? I have information you want. No. You need. No. Your masters need. I have what they need and only I have it. Now, I want something too. Something in return."

The demand seemed to calm the politico. This he understood. "Of course it would," thought Fong, "I'm behaving like him." For a moment he considered telling the politico to wipe the sick smile off his face and fuck himself. Then he discarded the idea. "Let's deal."

The politico nodded, again in full control. "Tell me what you want, Traitor Zhong." He smiled.

Fong thought about justice. About the relativity of it. When he spoke, his words sounded like they came from faraway. "I want my job back — in Shanghai — head of Special Investigations."

The politico nodded as if it were nothing out of the ordinary to make such a request. He lit a Kent and blew out a line of smoke. "We assumed that would be part of the price — what else?"

Fong almost faltered then marshalled his forces again. "I want this damn thing taken off my ankle." He pulled up his pant leg and planted his foot on the wall beside the politico, who reached over and tapped in four numbers of the code. His eyes locked with Fong's. He was enjoying this. He tapped in the fifth number and the thing clattered to the cement floor. The sound it made somehow reminded Fong of the clinking his wedding ring had made when Fu Tsong hurled it against the wall of their small rooms in Shanghai.

Fong shook aside the memory and stepped away from the politico. The man was smiling broadly now. "You're no different than me, Traitor Zhong. There is nothing special about the great Zhong Fong."

Had he heard that or was it only his conscience speaking?

"What else do you want for the information that is rightfully mine, Traitor Zhong?"

"Tell me who the specialist was?" Fong knew he was on dangerous territory. Unscripted territory.

The politico laughed. A hearty, un-Chinese laugh. An are-you-kidding-me laugh.

"Madame Wu, Minister of the Interior is the rogue in your midst," Fong shouted.

The laughter stopped.

A tense silence followed. For the first time the politico looked wide-eyed at Fong.

"Are you . . .?"

"Sure? Yes. Positive. Madame Wu induced the deaths on board that boat. She might as well have given the order. She sent wine with the cultured typhoid that killed the girl on the island. Then she showed the islanders how to get their revenge. The farmers from the island committed the actual deeds. A man named Jiajia was the head butcher if that matters to you."

The politico was having trouble digesting the information. He couldn't care less who did the actual killing. He kept circling back to Madame Wu. Madame Minister Wu! Pieces began falling into place for him. His mouth opened then shut before a word could come out. He reached for a cigarette then realized he already had one in his lips. He removed it. "My partner . . ."

Fong nodded, "Madame Wu's man."

The politico took a wheezing breath and then removed the cigarette from his mouth.

Fong looked at the cigarettes. The Kents. "You were pretty lucky you didn't get on that boat yourself, weren't you?" The politico was about to protest but Fong cut him off. "You were the eighth Chinese man with a hotel room in Xian that night, weren't you?"

The politico started to deny it but decided against it. He nodded.

Fong smiled.

The politico held out his right hand. "Deal, done?"

Fong stared at him.

The politico pushed his hand out farther. "The deal is done. I said it, so it is so."

Fong reached out and grabbed the man by the collar.

The politico was remarkably calm. "Something else you wish to include in our bargain, Traitor Zhong?"

"Yes," Fong spat out. For a moment he couldn't make himself say the words. Then he vomited them out. "I want my fucking teeth fixed!"

The words came out loud. Too loud. And more embarrassing than Fong had anticipated. Too public. Too vain for a man about to be fifty.

CHAPTER TWENTY-ONE

RICKSHAWS, FATHERS, BABIES

"You're staring, Fong," Lily said. It was their first day back in Shanghai. They were on the Bund. A young man dressed in a shiny gold silk shirt, black pyjama pants and black cloth slippers was standing between the poles of a rickshaw on the other side of the six-lane road.

"What is that?" hissed Fong.

"You know very well what it is," Lily replied carefully.

Fong was staring at a vision from the past. A hideous vision of a time of shame. A rickshaw? Now?

"What has happened here?"

"You've been away five years, Fong."

"Human beings aren't animals. Is this legal now?"

Fong's father had read him Lao She's classic story, *Rickshaw Boy*. He had curled into his father's side and smelt his sour but pleasant odour. His father had beautiful hands. He read sweetly by the flickering candle-light. Fong had been only three or four but he already knew that his grandmother must have been out or his father wouldn't have dared to "fill the boy's head with a stack of nonsense."

When his father finished the story of the boy who was

little more than "a starving and crazy beast, who just wants to keep running," he'd taken out a pamphlet. "This is what foreigners think of us, Fong." He found a place in the pamphlet and read, "Rickshaw coolies live in dire poverty. Pay them liberally but not foolishly, for it is an idiosyncrasy of the coolie mind to mistake generosity for idiocy." He looked at his son. "Do you understand, Fong?"

Fong had nodded. It was then he saw the small satchel behind the door.

His father got up. He wasn't wearing his sleeping clothes. Fear began to take Fong. Something unnamed was in the room.

"Be brave, Fong," his father had said as he picked up the satchel. "This," he said pointing at the pamphlet about the rickshaws, "must stop. Don't you agree?"

Fong had nodded although all he'd wanted to say was, "Where are you going, Papa?"

His father slung the satchel across his back then knelt by Fong. "Be strong. Peace can only come with justice." His long tapered fingers touched Fong's face; Fong smelled him one last time, and then he was gone.

Gone.

He became the shame of the family. The Communist.

Two years later, when the Red Army marched into Shanghai victorious, Fong climbed to the rooftops to find his father. Row upon row of soldiers marched by. But no one with beautiful hands appeared. No one who smelled like his father. No one to tell him "to be strong." It was then, as the last of the soldiers passed, that Fong had discarded his childhood and decided to pursue justice; he joined the youth wing of the Party.

Lily tried to move Fong along the crowded sidewalk, but he pulled his arm from hers and darted across the busy street. Then he was screaming at the young rickshaw man while hundreds of dazed tourists gawked. Lily ran up to him and pulled him away.

"My father gave up his — my father . . ."

"Tell me, Fong."

But he couldn't. His past was his own. His shame. One fact would lead to another. Silence was a better alternative. Even Fu Tsong never knew his story. He had begun his life anew with Fu Tsong. He'd do it again with Lily.

Lily hung her head in disappointment and stared at the Pudong industrial region — all spanking new and proud across the Huangpo River. Then she looked at Fong. His new teeth helped a lot. She reached for his hand. "You don't have to go to work today. It's your first day back. They'll understand that you have to get acclimatized."

He allowed her to guide him by the hand.

He allowed her to lead him back to the rooms on the grounds of the Shanghai Theatre Academy, which had been returned to him.

He allowed her to undress him.

And they completed a dance that had begun long ago in the darkness of a forensic lab.

He sensed at the moment of his ejaculation that they had conceived a child.

His second — although no one except Fu Tsong and the butcher abortionist had ever seen the first.

As the sun rose the next morning Fong stared out the window. The courtyard still had the stupid statue. Drunken young actors still lounged on the tiny patch of grass.

Five years.

He looked at Lily. Her features were softer in sleep. Faraway.

They were having a baby together. Of that he was sure. What his relationship to her was he couldn't name. She deserved better. She deserved to be loved.

"Everyone deserves to be loved." He turned and Fu Tsong emerged from the washroom pinning up her hair. She was dressed for the final scene in *Measure for Measure*. One of her most famous performances. "I said, we all deserve to be loved," Fu Tsong repeated.

"Is that why Isabella marries the Duke at the end of the play?"

"It was the way I played it."

He nodded. The image of her taking the Duke's hand was still fresh in his memory all these years later.

"Was that the justice she earned?"

"Justice isn't earned Fong. It's understood." Then she was gone.

The raid on the Island of the Half-wits was carried out with military precision. The farmers were rounded up, Iman was publicly humbled, the population herded into boats to begin a long journey to disparate places west of the Wall. But not before each had been forced to give three large blood samples.

Jiajia was not accounted for. In a land of rocks it is hard to discern one from the next.

Once the islanders were safely on boats, the soldiers tore down the terrace walls, smashed the stone pathways and reduced to waste the entirety of what these people had laboured so hard for so long to build. They erased their history. Tore off the face of this place — and the fishermen on the coast watched and smiled at the possibilities that now presented themselves.

Madame Wu said nothing. The look on her face as the handcuffs snapped onto her wrists never varied. Only her hands betrayed her. They were red — angry like her mother's after hours of pulling silkworm cocoons from boiling water.

Lily was there before him. Naked and sweet. She curled up on his lap and looked into his eyes. "We can't live here, Fong."

"I can't live anywhere else, Lily."

She nodded sadly and touched her belly then looked up at him.

He smiled.

She smiled back. "I finally got that roll of film developed."

"What roll of film?"

"The one the specialist found in the Japanese guy's

camera."

"By the runway?"

"Yes, Fong, by the runway."

Lily waited and finally Fong asked, "So what's on the film?"

"Pictures." She opened a drawer and handed them to Fong.

They were all of a beautiful Asian newborn. A boy. A perfect new being. Fong gave her back the pictures and said, "It's almost dawn. I don't think they'd appreciate it if I miss two days in a row."

"As head of Special Investigations, Shanghai District, you have to set a good example." She laughed.

He took her hand. He tried to say that he was sorry, that he was unworthy of her, that he begged her forgiveness, but nothing came out. She put a finger to his mouth and said, "I know, Fong. I know. Now let's get dressed and go to work." Then in English she added, "Imagine, think what they did we." She stood up, stretched her strong back and smiled as she strutted, naked as the day was long, into the bathroom.

In English he replied, "You're something, Lily."

He heard the flame in the small water heater ignite.

"Yeah! What but?"

He was going to correct her then decided not to. The sound of the shower came from behind the ill-fitting door. Lily yelped as she stepped beneath the thin spray. She'd have to learn that about the place — the water heater worked fast. She began to sing softly. She was happy. Fong wondered if she felt the odd stirring within her. A life beginning. A baby. Lily would make a good mother. And he would never abandon his child. He had only one concern. He hoped their baby would learn English from him, not her.

Lily's singing continued as he stood up and moved to the closet. He opened it and reached for his padded Mao jacket with Fu Tsong's Shakespeare sewn into its lining. He allowed his hand to press against the pages. So much history. So many secrets. For an instant he wanted to wear it to work then just as quickly he had the intense desire to throw it in the trash. To start all over.

Lily's singing stopped.

He withdrew his hand from the coat and closed the closet. Then he stood very still and listened to Shanghai awaken. Listened to the slumbering, eighteen-million-headed thing shrug off its drowsiness and face the day to come.